Magic Bites

Tales of the Shadow Folk

Eris Marriott

ISBN Ebook: 978-1-7372711-5-4

ISBN Paperback: 978-1-7372711-6-1

Editor:

Stacy Sanford - stacysanf0rd@yahoo.com

Formatter:

Liz Steinworth - www.theartofliz.com

Cover Designer:

Jackie Zureich - www.etsy.com/shop/BestsellingBookCover

Chapter Artist:

Cyn D. Cornejo - www.etsy.com/shop/MerakiBookdesigns

This book is dedicated to my sister, Gabrielle.

Not a star in the sky holds a candle to the magic in your soul, beautiful girl.

Never stop dreaming.

Author Biography

Eris Marriott lives anything but a quiet life, residing with her 3 dogs, rabbit, 3 snakes, and 2 cats. Her dream is to make her property horse friendly so she can bring her beloved Andy home, too.

She adores writing fantasy novels for people of all ages and weaving her worlds together in ways that never cease. From unicorns to vampires to dragons, Eris can't quite pick a favorite and has resolved to write about them all, if she can.

CONTENTS

ERIS MARRIOTT

A NOVEL

MAGIC BITES

TALES OF THE SHADOW FOLK

ETERNAL FIRE

SADNESS ACHES IN MY THROAT, AND MY CHEST IS SHREDDED with grief. Staring into the abyss of shadows, I charge, gripping the hilt of my sword like a vengeful vice as I swing, justice my only remaining muse.

Having waded through grief my whole life, this pain is achingly new. I plunge my weapon into the throat of the first vampire and their head rolls off with little more than a sickening thud. The crunching of their bones is drowned out by the hundreds more that gather outside the gates of the kingdom I call home—Sunfall.

My shoulders slump with the weight of carrying the sins of my kingdom, where my people have been forced to prop up a tyrant for far too long. My father's iron fist and thirst for power led to this moment. With single-minded focus, I race through the onslaught of shadows, their piercing fangs bared and ready to consume all that I am.

Over the din of anguished screams, I hear my brother, Maverick, calling out for me. He fears for my life more than I've ever cared for my own existence; my breath is more a burden than a help. The wretched sunlight, no matter how much I've called it, fails to pool within my palms as it so easily does for him and our father, Alaric.

Maverick is barren of an heir, and I am barren of any power that could save us. Our father, wandering somewhere drunkenly in the castle, will wake to find his head being served on a platter to the Shadow King.

But I will not die without a fight.

Bringing my blade up, I prepare for the next onslaught, my skin numb to the pain as vampire after vampire and shadow after shadow take their hits at me, their speed incomparable and their magics deadly. It is a miracle from Siralto herself that I still stand, though she does not lend me the power I need to defeat our foes as more and more of them arrive before our gates.

Our luxuries and ignorance have cost us. The Kingdom of Sunfall will soon be eaten alive after spoiling away for too long, ignorant to true fear and hardship. The soldiers from many decades ago laid down their lives for nothing, as the inevitable power and rage of the Shadow King was far more eternal than anyone could have fathomed.

But still, I keep slashing and moving forward. The vampires' dark, inky blood spills upon the ground, staining my chain mail and leathers to a far darker hue than any craftsman could dream. Behind me, I hear Maverick taking aim, blasting them with bolts of light that, despite their power, are too weak to hold off the vampires' attack.

Revelry from the day leading up to this keeps our remaining soldiers in a foolish stupor that our victors will laugh at not too far in the future, our spot in the history books both a comedy and a tragedy. We will be a warning to all about the dangers of complacency—of wanton pride and spoilage. Still, I broaden my stance and breathe deeply, letting the stench of death propel me onward.

I will not hand my soul over for little more than a squabble.

A part of me laughs at my own delusion. This battle is far from a squabble. This is a targeted attack inflicted during a moment of weakness. A day of celebration has turned into a holiday for the dead—a shopping spree. And the blood of me and my fellow mortals are at too great a discount for these leeches to pass up.

Somewhere above, a deep, rumbling laugh sends shivers down my spine, cutting me to the bone with fear. Peering up into the sky, I spot him at once. It's hard not to, for the massive, black dragon taking flight above our kingdom can be none other than the Shadow King himself...

Mars.

And the vampire king has taken on the form of the beast of shadow and damnation flying above us.

Swallowing my dread, I thrust my sword at another of the Shadow Folk as he looms treacherously close to me, his fangs mere inches from my neck. If I keep letting fear consume me as it does now, the next one will have a full meal. Truthfully, I would scarcely notice it save for the fear and pain shooting through my arms and legs.

"Sunfall, bear witness to the first days of darkness, for they shall last *forever*!" Mars booms. The terrifyingly deep voice is seared into thousands of memories of the citizens of Sunfall who watch behind the false safety of walls as he spits flames that cascade like rain.

I cover my face to shield myself from the flaming embers skyrocketing toward me, and pray Maverick has shielded himself from this vampire god's unfathomable rage and prowess.

To Mars, I look like nothing more than a meal with a pre-equipped toothpick. Without the Siraltona, the deadly light of the first Goddess and the only real weapon against them, I am little more than a nuisance. If anyone here is in danger of a fate worse than death, it is my brother, Maverick. His head bears a heavy price as a carrier of the Siraltona. I wonder if by announcing his impotence, the Shadow Folk will spare him a life as their slave and mascot in favor of the embrace of the Reaper, whose presence I never wished to summon until this day.

"Adelaide!" my brother shouts.

I turn to see him swarmed by the Shadow Folk and my mouth stretches into a silent scream. My thoughts of death subside in favor of only one thing. *I have to save my brother.*

As I scream my rage and race through the horde of vampires that stand between me and my brother, I am shocked they have not come for me, stunned my veins are not currently being dined upon by one of these foul creatures. I know it is because they are drawn to my brother's light and his life is in the most danger. To them, I am little more than an irritant they must bat away.

I have no doubt that some of those very same shadows I've slain will regain their limbs and heads before long. The Siraltona is the only thing that can truly *end* them forever.

"Maverick!" My yell is so loud, I wonder if my ribs might crack and cave in beneath the strain of the dragon's smoking fires that engulf the outer barriers of Sunfall. I look up and make eye contact with Mars, and his great, flaming eyes seem to peer down into the depths of my very soul. But then those eyes take note of Maverick and any chances of distracting the foul beast king crumble.

"There you are, you shining whelp. Your Death has come to claim you!" Mars hisses, his deep voice rumbling throughout the kingdom.

By now, I know my father will have awakened, but he will be too drunk to help us. On any other day, I would let the resentment and rage for my father consume me. I am horrified at how he let his power and greed become so great that he couldn't see the growing weaknesses clamoring at our walls.

His light cannot shine forever.

I reach out, standing mere feet from Maverick, and prepare for the worst, as I can only catch glimpses of his armor through the shadows. His power sporadically surges through them and cuts down several of the Shadow Folk, sending them to the eternal graves where they belong. I envy my brother in moments like these. He can ban the shadows for good. He can do what I wished I could on the night my mother was murdered in front of me. The night I stood by helplessly as the vampires consumed her.

Rage burns through my body, giving me strength to hack through the vampires who nip on the edges of my brother's battle. My blade is keen and fatal—to mortals, at least. I reach out and Maverick grabs my hand, pulling me to him.

He shoots an arc of light into the air to keep Mars at bay, but we both know it's not enough. The dragon king is darkness incarnate. I fear his darkness might be enough to cut through even the Siraltona.

I hug my brother tightly, prepared to do what I must to give him enough time to escape. He can't afford to protect me this time. Sunfall can't afford to lose its future king. He's our only chance of a revival.

"Maverick," I gasp, "you have to get back inside! If Mars takes you, all hope is lost."

Maverick glares down at me and pushes me away, but I know it's only a show. The way his icy eyes have paled betrays his terror. He knows this is the end.

"Father can send a search party for me," Maverick says sternly, his jaw tensed.

I huff, irritated at how stubborn he's being. *Doesn't he realize what's at stake? Our father be damned—he cannot save us if he does not learn to be a real king!*

The sky fills with fire again and I know our time is running out. I must convince him to run.

"Maverick, I—" I start to argue, but my words are cut off by a bloodcurdling roar from overhead. With a sinking feeling in my gut, I realize my brother's light is not enough. By the time our father gets here, it will be too late.

Above, I watch in terror as Mars dives. His massive maw stretches wide, ready to slash through our flesh and swallow us whole. Without hesitation, I push Maverick behind me and fling myself over his body to shield him. I know it's pointless, but I pray to Siralto it will be enough to spare him even a moment to get away. I plead for Mars' massive jaws to miss him and take only me.

I will die to save Maverick. Siralto, please, spare my brother's life and welcome mine into Tyrladan.

I cross my arms in front of my face and take one last look at the razor sharp, flaming teeth bearing down on me and close my eyes, accepting the darkness. The dragon can swallow me whole, for all I care.

Just spare my brother.

From my arms and hands, searing heat erupts and the backs of my eyelids light up. I never feel the kiss of sharp teeth or the destructive embrace of dragon flame.

Instead, I open my eyes. Everywhere, there is light.

DAWN

KING'S PAWN

About 1 month earlier

AN UNCOMFORTABLE SILENCE DESCENDS OVER THE GRAND hall. I close my eyes and take a deep breath, fighting the irritation that creeps along my spine at the sound of my father's fingers thudding a steady rhythm on the thick mahogany table like a horse thundering through the night. Not a soul dares speak, not even me, though I wish I had the courage to walk down to his end of the table and slap his hand to make him quit fidgeting.

Just beyond the doors to the grand hall, my brother and his wife, Beatrice, are in the medical wing. They wait, hope, and pray that she has taken with child. It's been two years since their marriage and there has been no success in securing Sunfall's next heir. My father, whose beard and hair grow grayer by the day, has grown impatient. I know if my brother does not succeed, my future is at risk of being forced into an arranged marriage, though it is doubtful I can even produce the type of heir Sunfall wants—the heir it *needs*.

Even so, my father has grown desperate. Across the table, his silvery-gray eyes, a mirror of my own, lock with mine. A pained silence strains between us. Were it not for my dark auburn hair, I would be the spitting image of him with no trace of my mother to be found. It's rare that he ever gives me notice anymore. Since my mother's death, which I failed to prevent, our relationship has been terse and distant. Still, in a moment like this, I believe he is looking to me for comfort.

Unfortunately, I have nothing left to give.

Lowering my gaze, I realize I am gripping the table with white knuckles, my breath coming in slow and almost ragged gulps. I close my eyes to focus and center myself. While I am not a magic user like my father, Alaric, or my brother, Maverick, the principles of wielding magic —the motions, how to stay grounded, and how to channel emotions— have been taught to me since I was a small child in the hopes I might someday prove the doctors wrong and show some promising talent.

It is my twenty-sixth year of failing them.

On a whim, I clench my fists and hope to call the very same light— the Siraltona—that has marked my father and brother with greatness. Cracking open my eyelids, I look down and find them empty. They are just as dull and devoid of hope as what resides in my heart and soul. The future lies with Maverick and Beatrice. With me, there lies only a set of hands capable of wielding a sword or dagger. In a normal kingdom, these skills would suffice. In a kingdom under the threat of a vampiric takeover, I might as well be a peasant.

The sound of the doors to the grand hall opening snaps me to attention. I jerk my gaze over to the doorway and find my poor brother with his head hung low, walking with the weight of another failure on his shoulders. My heart aches for him. He is the sun in our family, shining greatness, while I am the moon; when the sun fizzles, I plunge into darkness, too. Dark days lie ahead, from the way his face is pulled into a determined frown.

He does not evade my father's pained gaze. Maverick is unafraid to stand before our father. King Alaric has prided himself in raising a son with mettle. Maverick never disappoints or appears unpoised; he is a trained politician as much as he is a warrior. He can fit in among even the most powerful nobles and wildest courtiers, and is favored by women even more than men.

Of course, his loyalties lie with his beautiful wife, Beatrice, who strides in behind him. Her eyes are full to the brim with unshed tears. I want to rush to her, hold her in my arms and reassure her. She is just as much a sister to me as Maverick is my brother, even if we do not share blood. It pains me to see her suffer, with much of her personal life on display for all to see. There is no privacy for her. The walls of her bed chambers might well be made of crystal.

"Father," Maverick starts, but Alaric holds up his hand. A few more seconds of silence pool in the grand hall and I wonder if we might all drown in the discomfort. At times, I would find such a fate favorable.

"Am I to understand this is another failure?" Alaric's burning gaze settles on Beatrice, who shrinks behind Maverick and seems to cloak herself in his shadow.

"Yes, Father, but it is not my wife's fault," Maverick defends. "The consequences of my injuries have gone bone-deep. Not only did the Shadow Folk leave me with a limp, but they robbed me of the ability to produce heirs."

At this, several gasps sound in the grand hall. The nobles in attendance were unprepared for such a scandalous announcement. I can't help but stare at the way my brother stands as he always does—slouched to the left, his leg in a permanent twist from a battle that happened long ago between him and the Shadow Folk. At the time, my father was separated from him and he was new to bearing the Siraltona. One of Mars' favored sons took a swing at him, blinding Maverick long enough to damage his leg beyond full repair.

"How does a leg injury lead to infertility, son?"

Maverick's cheeks redden. The subject in question has grown far more personal than anyone in attendance could have imagined.

"I was poisoned with the shadows. Just as they are dead yet alive, their touch deadened the part of me that would be, ah... needed... to produce an heir. Though not fully impotent, I... I struggle. And what I do manage to give is, unfortunately, not enough. The doctor has suggested I undergo therapy with the power of the Siraltona, but the results are yet to be seen and the process is experimental."

Only I hear Maverick's voice crack. Behind my brother, Beatrice grabs his shoulders to lend him feeble support as she continues to sob, her soft blonde hair shielding her from the judgmental stares of the nobility.

I turn to our father. "Father, I think this conversation would be better held in private. Maverick has provided the nobles with enough information." My voice is hard, and I send a warning glare to everyone else in attendance. "You all may leave now. This is a troubling time for my family, and we would like to finish this discussion in private. As promised, he has provided the most recent medical update. My father and I will devise an announcement to send to the citizenry once we have further updates from the doctor about the experimental medical process."

A few jaws drop in shock at my brazen dismissal of them. Few of the nobles have ever seen me, let alone interacted with me. To them, I am the rebel princess who stalks in the woods, borrowing jars of my father's light with which to imbue my weapons to cut down Shadow Folk for fun. I am a hunter. I am far worse than a shadow. I am a killer. I have not been trained for politics. I have been trained for war.

But in a time like this, the pampered nobles are the enemy to my brother's privacy. I don't care what they want to hear from him. Above, I notice the lights flicker in the chandeliers, and I know my brother and father agree. The lights have a way of giving out in the presence of great power, which Maverick and Alaric both possess. Whenever they are angry or sad or experience intense emotions, it's always a gamble as to whether the castle's torches and lamps will remain lit.

"My daughter's decree is to be taken in the same light as mine or Maverick's."

When Alaric agrees from where he stands behind me, I am shocked. My father has never openly supported my orders, but in desperate times, I suppose anything is possible. I turn to him, finding something like pride in his eyes, but I won't let my heart be fooled. It tries to kick up with hope and I can't let it do that. It will only lead to pain if I do.

To my relief, the nobles start to exit the grand hall. As they leave, the pressure in the room lightens and the sun's rays glisten brighter on the long mahogany table that stretches across the room. Its grand length is empty of food, mirth, or celebration—things we all hoped would happen today. Though the news is not what we wanted to hear, I am content with the peace that settles in the dust forming where said merriment would be.

Once the last noble walks out of the room, the four of us stand and absorb the quiet for a moment, enjoying the bliss that royals often miss out on when their lives are on constant display. I am spared the most from these burdens, but it does not make the trouble any less real when

I find myself under the scrutiny of those who would seek to prop themselves up by my coat tails.

I am no spoiled royal, though I can't quite say the same for my father, whose midsection has widened considerably in the last few years. One might liken this change to the grief he experienced from losing my mother, but his general lack of self-care and fitness have become a source of talk in the kingdom. Paired with my brother's inability to provide an heir—which now has a medical basis—I fear the peasants will grow restless.

There is no one to replace the Sunfall royals. Only we possess the Siraltona.

My heart grows weak at the thought of the word *we*, because it is a constant reminder of where I fall short. I wish my mother was still here. She possessed little light, and even it left her in the end. What little she did possess wore through her and departed early in her life. As such, she knew what it meant to be *normal* as I am.

I still hear the sound—the sickening thud of her head against the floor of our shared chambers when I was merely ten years old. Now, sixteen years later, I am bereft of friends, lovers, or power. I am naught but the king's pawn—a symbol of rebellion and death to the Shadow Folk. They don't know my face because of the mask I wear in battle, but I am still a nightmare that haunts their children's stories.

If my skills with borrowed power were not so strong, they would have my head within a fortnight.

Shuddering, I try to ignore thoughts of my life being cut short the same way my mother's was. Instead, I focus on the conversation that's been carrying on while my thoughts wandered.

"Father, you know this blame does not fall on Beatrice!" Maverick hisses. "The doctors made it clear—there is something wrong with *me*."

"Nonsense, boy! We all heard the rumors when we chose her. Witchcraft is practiced regularly in Underland. Who's to say she hasn't cursed you? Childbirth is painful—maybe she fears pain," Alaric charges, his rage directed at my sister-in-law, who is still crying.

I step in and attempt to brush away his worries. "Father, someone could accuse our family of the same. Possessing power is not a crime. Beatrice does not turn the shadows to her whim, nor does she take the form of a familiar. She is simply gifted in the same way our family is."

On any other day, I wouldn't dare challenge him so directly. I never sought to entangle myself in his grand schemes. The only time I speak to him with authority is when I help him draw battle plans and devise the next attack to volley against our enemies. Politics, though? Those discussions have been off the table since I failed my first magical assessment. My bones sing no ancient songs, and no light fills my veins. Instead, rage and spite supplement them.

"What do *you* know of witchcraft?" Alaric sneers.

The venom in his voice takes hold in my heart, though I won't let him see it take root. I will purge it later through tears and angry swings of my sword. Right now, my brother needs me.

"I have been raised around it, Father," I argue. "I borrow your powers all the time. I have been trained how to wield it and know how it works, even if I do not have magical abilities myself. Beatrice and Maverick cannot be held accountable for things beyond their control." I send a sheepish look toward my brother. "Even so, the nobles will talk, with or without an answer. Now they know the doctors are working to find a cure, but it will take time. I believe it's time to start looking at other solutions."

At this, Maverick and Alaric raise a brow at me.

I've been thinking about this for some time, hatching back-up plans in my mind in the event we couldn't secure an heir through Maverick and Beatrice. At night, the thought of the Shadow Folk overtaking our kingdom and eating every precious citizen alive has haunted me.

I already know what the response will be, but I say it anyway. "I think we need to infuse weapons with the Siraltona and give them to our soldiers as standard issue."

"No!" my father and brother say at the same time.

With a dramatic eye roll, I cross my arms. "I'm tired of this, you two! I know the risks." I tick them off on my fingers. "Weapons falling into the wrong hands. The potential of one or both of you losing a fraction of your power or being weakened when we need protection. I get it. But the Shadow Folk have not attacked as much as of late and, even if they were, we are running out of options. We know they're lying in wait and if we don't get a head start, they'll come for us when we're at our weakest. We can either keep pointing fingers and prodding Maverick like he's a test subject, or we can start facing the reality that we might never get an heir from him.”

This last statement coats the room in ice. Their stares threaten to pierce me where I stand. Beatrice’s bright blue eyes have begun to dry, and I’m relieved to see they are the warmest.

“I think this might be wise,” Beatrice says haltingly. “We cannot let the kingdom fall because of our personal failures.” Her voice threatens to crack, but I respect my sister-in-law’s guts. She is not one to let setbacks stop her from seeing the logic of things. It’s one of the aspects of her personality I admire most.

“Adelaide,” my father growls, “just because you have had success with imbued weaponry does not mean it will work as a long-term solu-tion! The light eventually wears out of your swords and daggers. I’ve heard even the arrows become snuffed and you are forced to strike our enemies several times before there is enough light to make them collapse. Between using my light to keep the storms at bay and ensuring the kingdom has enough light and warmth to produce crops... I’m spent.” Throwing his hands up, my father looks every bit as exhausted as he claims to be.

True to his argument, he has been propping our kingdom’s ecosystem up with his magic. The Shadow King, Mars, has grown more and more powerful with each passing day, his dark magics threatening to swallow Sunfall whole. While our kingdom has grown complacent, the reality is that the threat to our kind has become more potent since the vampires were first driven back from our borders. My mother’s death did not mark the end of our worries. It was only the beginning, despite what the history books would say.

The nobles, as worried as they are for an heir, are under the delusion that there is no real threat to Sunfall anymore. Only my family knows the truth. I pray to Siralto that our lies will not catch up with us, though I know our deceit cannot carry on forever.

“But Father,” I argue, “Maverick can step in for this. We do not need to tax you any further. We can lace our blades with light and attempt to assassinate the Shadow King!”

It’s a bold ask and I know I sound no better than a loon, but I don’t care. Desperate times call for desperate measures. The other part of my plot has always centered around eliminating our biggest threat—Mars,

King of the Shadow Folk. If nothing else, we could take out his sons and daughters, as many as he has. A man cannot stand alone forever.

Yet he is no man.

I shuffle this doubtful thought aside because I can't give it the weight it deserves. It will be the death of me. I cannot stay awake with that ache in my chest any longer. Actions must be taken. Something must be done for Sunfall.

"Adelaide, this is a foolish errand," Maverick starts. "You know I abide by most of your strategies—they are normally sound. But here? You're reaching. You know as well as I do that the Siraltona, as powerful as it is, is not strong enough to kill him. We have taken several shots at him and while it burns him, it does not consume him as it does the others. In a time where we need to concentrate our powers and grow our line, we cannot be expected to shatter our powers into pieces any more than we already have. I will make you more swords if that is your request, but our only hope is for Beatrice and me to produce an heir."

"And subjecting yourself to tests where you lend your power to doctors to prod around on you is somehow better?" I lock my jaw and meet the challenge in my brother's eyes with my own. "At least hear me out and agree that we need to take more offensive measures."

Before my brother and I fall into one of our rare squabbles, my father holds up his hands. "Enough. That is enough. I have a better solution, Adelaide, and while it's one you won't like, you and I both know it's a necessity at this point." He sighs heavily. "There is a prince leagues away who has shown some promise with power—maybe not the Siraltona, but at the very least, he is a carrier, just as you are. I will dispatch a letter to his father and see if he will entertain the thought of a betrothal."

My father might as well have struck me down with a blade with his words. My cheeks grow hot. "You want *me* to bear children? To be laid up for *years* as little more than a factory of children who might have a *chance* of bearing power?"

The steely gaze in my father's eyes grows colder and I know I don't have a leg to stand on. When his face sets like this, I know there is little room to argue and, unfortunately, he still carries the most power in the room. I am helpless to stop him if he chooses to strike me down, sell me, or keep me prisoner. Such is the reality of living under Alaric's rule. A thin veil of kindness covers a grim truth—he is as much a bloodthirsty tyrant as any other ruler.

"Adelaide, I've settled my mind on the matter. Your brother will undergo the treatments and we will find you a suitor who can help us produce an heir, even if Maverick cannot. Until then, you will continue training and hunting, but you are *forbidden* to hunt down the Shadow King, understood?"

My mind is already hatching plans that veer otherwise, but I don't say them out loud. My face is a blank slate; I wish my father silent luck to ever be able to read it. I dip my head in assent, choosing to let the argument die.

Maverick catches the sudden change in my resolve but, even when we argue, he is my partner in crime first and a prince second. He will never betray me to my father. On that account, I can be sure.

"Yes, Father," I say dutifully. "If everything is settled, may I be excused to go train?"

Once again, I am little more than a shadow—a pawn. My father waves his hand at me, dismissing me from the duty of being in his presence. With a small bow, I turn and stride from the room, refusing to let anyone see the tears running down my cheeks.

Kiss From a Blade

I TAKE A SWING, THE SWORD MY VESSEL FOR THE RAGE STILL pouring from my body.

How could he just decide something like that without consulting me?

Another *thwack* from my sword downs the next straw dummy propped up in the courtyard. A silent blanket of snow has begun to pile up around my feet. My hands are raw with cold, but I'm numb to the nipping pain. It doesn't matter if my fingers snap off like icicles. Before long, I will be married off like chattel and expected to bear children at the whim of another, anyway.

Mothering is better suited to my sister-in-law, whose kindness and patience know no bounds. I snort at the thought of being a mother, let alone an obedient wife. I know nothing of housekeeping, acting appropriate for court, or wearing fashionable pieces to capture the awe and respect of nobility.

What I do know, however, is the art of taking down foes. My blades are my paint brushes and the blood of my enemies my paint. Were there real enemies now, the snow would bleed like a white canvas streaked with red slashes of fury. Just the thought pulls a smirk across my resolute face. Once upon a time, I would have found this type of violence repulsive. I remember more than others know, the comfort of sitting in my mother's lap to watch her crochet or embroider tapestries. A few of my mother's works still hang around the castle. The last one she made before she was murdered proudly hangs above my headboard.

That life died with Amelia. Even the thought of my mother's name makes me wince. Instead of becoming mired down in grief again, I grip the hilt of my sword and swing it back, ready to hack into the next dummy. Its seconds are numbered as I pour all my strength and rage onto it, cleaving it in two.

Years ago, I managed to out-train even the most skilled of Sunfall's knights. I eagerly sought fighters of all skills...all except magic wielders, who are not useful to my progression as a fighter. They are the very people I yearn to learn from the most, but breathing exercises and grounding go but so far. Without some sort of sign of a divine gift, I'm limited to the harsh mortality of steel and sharp edges.

Nothing is more potent than the sweet kiss of a blade.

I step back and assess my handiwork. Not a single practice dummy still stands in the practice yard. I smile. The anger stirring within me hasn't quieted, but its voice is softer. I don't feel as though it screams in my ear with a bullhorn any longer. If my father were to come out and spar with me, he might become another dummy.

If it weren't for his magic.

Part of me misses sparring sessions with my father. He taught me how to be a skilled fighter, even with my magical limitations. He taught me to seek out traces of magic—to taste where it's been and identify its signature. His lessons made me an adept hunter. I can even find where the Shadow Folk have breathed because I can hear the very magic I was denied at birth. Not so much as a flicker of light or dark may leave my hands, but I know where it has been and how to find it in others. I've become a veritable nightmare to the Shadow Folk, and I seek them out wherever they are and squash them. At times, Alaric made it seem like he might be proud of me. *Might.* I'm not holding my breath on a hunch, however. All I can do is continue to train hard and keep myself in peak physical shape, which is more than what my father can claim.

Sweat pools on my brow as it tries to crystallize in the bitter air. It's not cold enough to succeed at freezing, but the air conspires and tries to trap me in the testaments to my labors. I peer up at the castle, which towers against the gray sky as it darkens, the winter sun more absent than its summer counterpart. I yearn for longer days and warmer weather. Looking down, I realize I have not bundled up like I should. I can hear Maverick lecturing me about falling ill. I don't heal like him and Alaric do.

Another drawback of being a boring mortal.

With a heavy sigh, I begin the arduous process of trudging back inside. It's not so much the journey, but the thought of my destination that makes me think twice about wading through the snow, which piled up higher and faster as I trained. I don't know how many hours I've spent out here, but I'm certain I have not been missed. As long as I show up for meals, no one questions where I scurry off to. My father has learned over the years that if I'm not training, I am nose deep in a book on strategy or sealed in my room, contemplating what life might have been like if my mother had not been murdered.

I've developed a reputation for being a closed-off hermit. Outside the battlefield, some might say I am unapproachable. I keep my countenance stiff and cold, not unlike the weather now pelting me from the heavens as a grim reminder that my time here is more limited than I would otherwise like.

But why would I want to live longer? And who is to say my father or brother will outlast me?

The Siraltona, in many ways, is a mystery. Through the years, not many have possessed it. Siralto does not grant it to just anyone; she is not even alive to do so. The magic is an echo of who the goddess was before Tryta murdered her in a heated argument about the creation of mortals and life as we know it—at least that's what the texts imply. But I'm not a religious scholar and her being dead does not stop me from praying. I have found the dead listen far better than the living.

Snow drifts onto the hard cobblestones that lead inside the castle. Now that I am not held captive by the winter wind and snowflakes intent on freezing me, I realize just how cold I am. My teeth chatter and I scurry faster into the bowels of the castle. I contemplate grabbing a torch from one of the sconces to warm myself, but I doubt the medical ward will appreciate treating me for both frostbite and burns.

Hunching over, I curse my error in judgment for not bringing a cloak or even a simple wrap while I trained. When I first stormed from the grand hall in a fit of rage, any thoughts other than *kill* and *fight* were foreign to me. To remember a coat? Preposterous.

My feet carry me to the spiral staircase that winds up to the towers where the royal bedchambers are situated. While spread out, the family all shares the west wing of the castle. Even so, I have a whole section partitioned off just for me. My father seemed intent on allowing me privacy, for which I am grateful. Though I already know how many steps there are—two-hundred-fifty-six—before I reach my floor, I make the dutiful effort to count them all as I make my way to my bedchambers, my mind consumed by thoughts of a hot bath.

If I slip into thoughts of betrothal and Shadow Folk, I'll go mad. The cold would be a kinder fate to fall victim to, as far as I'm concerned. When I reach the top of the stairs, I push the door to my hall open and shut it behind me. The clatter of my boots echo in the otherwise quiet corridor. The nobles are not allowed in the west wing without explicit invitation, and I've opted to pass on guards. I *am* my own guard.

Given the lack of importance in my blood, my father never saw fit to argue. My very soul hopes he does not change his mind about this as he did with the betrothal. A quick glance around betrays no changes to my wish for no guards and I breathe a sigh of relief. If my privacy can remain intact I will remain grateful, though I know it's a smokescreen hiding the truth that someday soon, I will never know what it is like to be alone again.

I almost choke on this thought, and hurry to push the door to my bedchamber open. I swear as tears prick my eyes again, blurring the soft, warm light from my chandelier, already lit by the servants, and rush into my private bath. Our plumbing system is advanced enough that I can call up water, and my father's magic means it is blissfully heated.

I turn on the faucet and plug the drain. As water pours into the deep basin, I allow the thoughts from the day to swim to the surface, as treacherous as they may be. I wish to Siralto my father would hear me out about imbued weapons. Perhaps a plot to overthrow the Shadow King with them is a bit much—I'll grant him that. But to rely on a gamble of an heir who may or may not have power, let alone the kind we need?

I shake my head, dissatisfied with my father's complacency. It worries me how reckless he has become. I've heard rumors of taxes being raised and more provisions being dispatched without regard to who truly needs them. Things are somehow cheaper-made and more expensive to purchase than they have ever been in Sunfall.

Our people have enjoyed the false luxury of safety, many of them having never known what it means to fight. My father, so sure of the Siraltona's power and the gifts he and Maverick share, was unprepared for this outcome. Now our safety is at stake, to the point where they're willing to gamble on my womb to produce a backup. I clench my fists and fury boils within me again.

I was not raised for this! I was raised to fight.

I swallow my heated breath, the wrath within me almost enough to drive away the winter until next year. The fire in my belly would put Mars' dragon fire to shame.

I could burn the Shadow King several times over should he cross my path today.

It's a stupid thought—one that is far from the truth, but it gives me the push I need to shake off my bitter thoughts and take a bath. On days like this, the simple act of removing and putting clothing back on becomes difficult. My skirts might as well weigh a thousand pounds.

"What are you doing with your life, Adelaide?" I mutter. When the water level rises, I sink beneath the surface and wet my hair. Reaching over to a small table near the tub, I pluck a few bottles of my favorite scented bath oils. I drop a bit of each into the water before stoppering them and leaning back against the cool marble, lulled by the sound of running water as it continues to fill the tub. I close my eyes, take a deep breath, and let the relaxing scents soothe my frazzled nerves.

I'm surprised that neither my brother nor Beatrice have come to speak to me yet, but I'm glad to be left alone. I decide to pass on dinner; I don't care if it arouses suspicion. My father must know I am angry, even if he does not care to fix it. His foolishness will cost me my life and I resent him for it. I resent Sunfall for it.

Then, an unsettling thought. How could they be so foolish to believe the vampires would just stay idle? That, perhaps, they'll never be a threat again?

These are the thoughts that scare me the most—the ones that make me doubt not just my father, but the integrity of my kingdom and its people. Killing vampires is a personal vocation—one I willingly took on to avenge my mother. But as far as Sunfall is concerned? At times, I find myself indifferent to it. It pains me to admit this, even if it's only within the confines of my darkest thoughts.

I am a princess. I have a duty to our people... a duty that has deemed me a failure because I lack powers. A duty that has doomed me to a life married to someone I don't know, forced to bear a child who may or may not be able to save them.

And if I fail?

I know what happens to royals when kingdoms are overtaken, and I shudder to think how bad it will be when the conquerors have fangs and an unquenchable thirst for blood. I hope that exsanguination is as swift as they say.

By now, the water reaches up to my nose and I turn the faucet off with my foot. If I don't rouse, I will drift off and fall asleep in the water and wake up to wrinkled skin and water pouring from the sides of the tub. I can't do that to the maidservants again, so I shake myself awake. I steeple my fingers together, a habit I have acquired from my father, and think.

No matter how many times I try to hack this problem, my lack of magic is always the barrier. Even if I go against my father's wishes and hunt the Shadow King, who is to say I will succeed? I have nothing to slay him with and my father is right—no amount of Siraltona in its present existence has proven enough to slay him, and not for lack of trying. Mars is an annoyance that refuses to pass. An immortal irritation is the worst kind, and I've yet to meet the bastard.

As many times as I have been out on the battlefield, I have never seen the vampire king as anything more than a distant, dragon-like speck on the horizon. He has no reason to keep his distance from me. I am anything but a threat to him and would be a juicy steak if nothing else, but he still refuses to come near me. I doubt I even warrant a visit in the first place, but I've always wondered why he hasn't tried to take me out, if for no other reason than I slay his citizens with borrowed light. Of course, he does not know I am a royal. My eyes wander over to my mask, which sits on my bed in the other room.

If the snow lets up in the morning, I ponder whether the cover of winter would prove fruitful in finding more vampires to slay. I know a hunt is foolish at a time like this, but I can't be bothered to care. I need something to take the edge off, and making them pay for their sins is a release that cannot be compared to anything else.

My eyes flutter shut and my thoughts drift to my mother again. Her gruesome death has a way of sneaking up on me, playing over and over in my mind like some wretched ghost doomed to roam the worlds of mortal minds forever.

What a terrible punishment.

I wonder how things might have been different if I had been able to save her. I was the tender age of ten, nothing more than a child, really. My hair had recently been cut short and flounced along with the little bows she had tied in my hair that day. We spent the morning serving tea to each other and talking about what pretty dresses I would soon have for upcoming dinners. By nightfall, she was being wrapped in a mourning shroud for her casket and I, rather than wearing pink and sparkles, wore grieving black.

Grief aches in my chest now as freshly as it did nearly two decades ago. At twenty-six, I still relive that night like it happened yesterday. As I soap my arms and cut away at the grime caking my skin, I hear the ping of rocks and pebbles being launched at the window of my bedchamber.

I freeze, hoping the pinging belongs to birds whose beaks sound like stones. A pervert hurling pebbles at my window is the last thing I need on a day like today. A homicidal, naked princess hurling through the window with a sword is hardly the way to keep nobles from sniffing around. They would have me sent away, and *fast.*

Instead, I gather my senses and reach out for the towel placed nearby. I pull it around my torso and grab my sword, the hilt glinting in the dying light of the day. Before long, the moon will swim in the skies overhead and the cover of night will conceal whatever bastard has decided to be a little too brave.

As I near the windowpane, my breath fogs up the glass. Under the cover of frost, I peer down to the grounds below, hoping to catch a glimpse of the criminal I will soon behead if they come any closer. Instead, my eyes land on the last person I expect to see...

Finch.

My brother-in-law stands in the courtyard, waving up at me. A dark fur cloak is pulled around his shoulders and a stark grin is painted on his face. My heart lightens, but my eyes refuse to see the truth.

Can it be?

I'm not sure whether to run, scream, or cry. My heart is alarmed, and panic sends it careening through my chest like a runaway horse, its rider long since thrown off into the underbrush.

I wave to him, careful not to drop my towel and evoke further scandal than what might already be derived from this innocent interaction. As attractive as he may be, Finch is not my type and is nothing more than a brother to me.

The problem? Finch was presumed dead months ago, killed by the Shadow Folk.

"I'll be right down, Finch!" I call.

I run from the window and, this time, am careful to draw the curtains closed so no real perverts can easily peer inside my window. While Finch is not one to climb, I realize there might be some who are daring enough. But my thoughts abandon these considerations in favor of the most pressing matter.

My brother-in-law is alive?

By the time I hurriedly dress and stuff my boots on, my brother is pounding on my door.

"Adelaide!" Maverick's voice booms from the other side. "Are you seeing this?"

"Yes!" My voice catches, and my hopes are dashed with fresh realities of suspicion. "Did you see him?"

"I did. Hurry, Adelaide. We need to get down there and see what trickery this is."

From the bottom of the door, I see a surge of light and know Maverick has the Siraltona at the ready. I picture my brother's fists clenched, his knuckles whitened and screaming for the prospect of a fight.

The part of me that is still in denial of Finch's death is reeling. I haven't even bothered to think of losing him because my mind won't let me live in a reality where he is not there. I know Beatrice and Maverick feel the same, so even the sight of him standing in our courtyard will take a lot of convincing that this is not some enemy ploy. And if it is? I fear the consequences the deceiver will face.

I wipe away the open merriment stamped on my face and replace it with stern suspicion. I cannot let anyone think I am easy to dupe—

because I'm not. But when I think of how Finch playfully tossed those stones and smiled up at me, and the way his presence puts to rest the prospect of having to say goodbye forever, my heart longs to leap into the lie—even if it leads to my doom.

At the very least, if I die, I won't have to go through with a betrothal.

I quiet these traitorous thoughts. Maverick greets me in the hall and we march downstairs to meet Finch.

"Where's Beatrice?" I whisper.

"She's sleeping," Maverick answers. "I wanted her to rest after today's events."

I nod. I can't blame my sister-in-law for needing a break. I also envy her. If this ends up being a farce, she will have dodged the very real emotions evoked by it. Her slumber keeps her safe from the clutches of a hope worn false.

"How is it that he's just... standing out there?" I ponder. "One minute, I'm bathing in peace, and in the next, he's tossing rocks at my window. And why not go to your window first?"

Maverick shakes his head. "He left from the direction of your window and started towards mine. I happened to be looking out the window and spotted him. I raised the alarm—he will have been intercepted by now. We must confront him under strict and safe conditions."

The hard lines of his jaw are set with determination that reminds me why he will be king someday. Were it anyone else, I might feel robbed or cheated. But I love and trust my brother. I know he makes good choices. I'm proud of who he might become someday.

"Have you warned Father?"

The question lingers and the pregnant silence answers my question. He is undoubtedly in a drunken stupor again. Our father uses liquor to ease his pain and anxiety, and after today's turmoil, I have no doubt we will find him passed out in his chambers with at least one empty barrel of ale and a few glasses stained with the fiery remnants of Sunfall's finest whiskey.

"Up to us, then," I sigh. "I believe in what we can do." I can't stop the grin that spreads across my face and see Maverick struggling not to break into laughter. The exhaustion wears on both of us, forced to cover for our father's shortcomings. Siraltona or no, we are equal in our efforts to keep Sunfall alive and well, despite its inebriated crown.

We turn the corner, our feet leading us back to the grand hall. It's where all our most pressing, public business is conducted. I wonder if it might have been wiser to direct Finch—or the not-Finch—to the dungeons.

If things go awry, everyone is about to know...

I try not to think on this as the massive, gilded oak doors swing open and mahogany and gold are replaced with the dotted presence of nobles, knights, and, most importantly, Finch, as they all stand in front of the long dining tables.

"Brother!" Finch calls. "It is so good to see you!"

At once, I am struck by how well this trickery is being put on. If this is not Finch, the Shadow Folk have mastered his voice and mannerisms. I shiver at the thought of being so easily mocked.

"Maverick!" Finch calls out, his arms spread wide. As much as I want to believe the joyous occasion, suspicion creeps along my spine and through my stomach, tying it in coiled knots.

Before Maverick or I can respond, Beatrice comes rushing into the great hall. My heart crashes at the anguished look on her face. Maverick intercepts her, cradling her in his arms as she collapses into them, her loud sobs echoing along the walls.

"Brother?" she calls, her cries muffled by the fabric of Maverick's silken black shirt. "Where have you been? We thought you were dead!" When she pulls away, her face is a torturous sight. Pain is etched onto her mascara-stained eyes and cheeks. The day has not been kind to Beatrice.

Finch looks surprised. "I escaped them, Sister! I was never struck down—the reports you heard were false!"

At this, I take a step back and put my arm out to protect Beatrice. There is no way Finch escaped. While I was not on the battlefield that day, Sunfall's scouts would not have lied about a murder so gruesome. Drake, Beatrice and Finch's father, put on a funeral for his son over the reports alone. They were too detailed to be falsified.

"Finch... how can you say that?" I whisper. "How can you claim you escaped when so many saw you fall?"

Finch blinks. "But... I didn't fall."

His smile doesn't reach his eyes, and at once I am struck by the darkness swirling in his blue irises.

"Finch... how did you get here?" My voice is calm but resolute. Beside me, Maverick stiffens. Siraltona crackles to life in his palms and I am assuaged that he, too, has caught on to the sudden shift in my brother-in-law. He's a Shadow Folk. He has been turned. But... does he know that?

He shakes his head. "I woke up? I was left out in the snow. It felt like eons had passed." Finch's eyes widen and his throat catches. Realization dawns on him and he begins to shake. "No..." he gasps in horror.

The damage has already been done, though. Guards swarm him and Maverick takes a hesitant step forward, the light burning in his hands even brighter than it did beneath the door frame to my room.

"Wait, Maverick," I say, unsure where I have gathered the gall. "He doesn't appear to be here on behalf of the Shadow King. Can we at least lock him up instead of killing him? Maybe talk to him and learn more about how vampires are turned?"

Maverick turns to me, stunned, but Beatrice's shrieking sob pierces through us before we can begin arguing.

"Don't kill him, Mav, *please*!" she begs. "Not yet. At least let me talk to him, even stuck in this form. If he must live as a shadow, let him live as a good one. He was loyal to us for so long—he came home rather than join their ranks as so many do. Can't that count for something?"

Her voice is hysterical and her shoulders shake. Maverick is back at her side in an instant and the light gathered within his palms dims.

"Brother, I think it's best to lock him up for now. We can decide what to do with him later. We can send down a flagon of blood to keep him satiated, so long as we get answers and allow Beatrice to have peace."

Maverick nods at me, his eyes full of pain and worry. I am glad our father did not come to this meeting. A drunken fit would have reduced Finch to a pile of ash and further injured Beatrice.

"I'll escort him down," I offer. "He's not here to harm us, and the guards can accompany me as a precaution."

Finch, whose eyes are full to the brim with tears, falls to his knees. "I promise I would never hurt anyone here." The sincerity in his voice tugs at my heartstrings, but I have no choice but to take him as a prisoner.

The Shadow Folk are adept at deception and manipulation. They also live far longer than mortals, so just because a mortal thinks enough time has passed to trust them does not mean that's the case. Shadow Folk can play the long con better than anyone. The only thing that stops them from succeeding is their insatiable lust for power and blood.

"Finch, if that's the case, you will follow me down to the dungeons and go peacefully. I'll ask the guards to get you something to nourish your... changed appetite." I'm not sure why I am so willing to gamble, even knowing the danger. Granted, my lease on life has been cut short today, which probably accounts for my recklessness. Any fate seems better than being subjected to a marriage I don't agree to and bearing a child that may or may not succeed at saving our kingdom.

Still, a small part of me refuses to register that Finch was killed, let alone that he came back as the very thing I have grown to abhor.

"You have my word that you will be unharmed." Finch holds his hands up, ensuring that no one can think his fingers are crossed.

My thoughts swim through the treacherous seas of doubt and curiosity, which threaten to drown me. I extend my hand. "This way, Finch." No one says a word as he steps forward and takes it. At once, I am struck by how cool his skin is. I know this means he must be hungry. Shadow Folk only run cold when they have not fed. The field guides and biographies I read about their greatest have served me well in hunting them with cruel expertise.

Know thy enemy.

My brother looks murderous as I step out of the grand hall with my hand still laced with Finch's. I know he will be after me in a heartbeat to ensure my safety, but I need to take this leap of faith with Finch. I need to know if *all* Shadow Folk are doomed to mindless evil from the moment they are turned. If they are, then why would he come here first, right into the arms of those who would kill him? And how is it that he only realizes now what he is? Did his sire abandon him out in the woods of Leyun?

All these questions and more threaten to break the surface and tumble from my lips, but I have to maintain neutrality. If he's here to harm us, he can't have the upper hand. My questions must wait until he is behind bars.

We pass through the halls and down the stairwell in silence, not a guard in sight. Though I know Maverick is not far, he hasn't caught up. Whether Finch is cooperating because he knows he would lose his head faster than he could say "vampire" or out of respect and love for his family, I still don't know.

My hands want to break out into sweat and I know my forehead is clammy with terror. This does not compare to the look etched on Finch's face as he comes to terms with his own reality.

The hunter has become the hunted.

Finch was an adept vampire slayer for many years. To be turned into the very thing he wanted to etch from existence is a fate worse than death.

"How are you feeling?" My voice is muffled in the darkness as we reach the hall that leads to the dungeons.

"I... I don't know, Adelaide. I truly did not realize... I did not know... I remember a fight. I remember falling. And then I don't remember anything until I woke up."

His voice cracks and I turn away, giving him the privacy to cry. Finch always prided himself on his stoicism; I won't rob him of that image he has made for himself, even if he has become something dreadful.

We stride toward the biggest cell I can find. Not many are kept as prisoners and, as of right now, there is no one else down here. Alaric is not keen to take prisoners in the first place. Mercy is extended by the embrace of a blade or the Siraltona, not from the padding of metal bars.

Finch eyes me with hurt and agony as I let the door to his cell slam shut. It occurs to me that what I have just done is both reckless and unheard of. To walk alone in the dark with one of the Shadow Folk and emerge unscathed? Everything I know about them threatens to crumble, but I refuse to release it without a fight.

"Finch, I'm sorry," I offer, but my voice is firm. "We must make sure you are safe before we let you roam the castle. We need to figure out how this happened to you and learn more. It's for your safety too, you know. When my father hears that you returned in this state...."

Finch holds up his hand. "I know, Sister. I know. I appreciate what you're doing for me. If I knew what I had become... had I realized..." He shakes his head, his eyes still wide with disbelief.

A low grumble echoes between us and I realize how hungry he must be. Before I can call out, three guards come striding after me with urgency, holding three canteens of blood filled to the brim. They open the gate and pass them into Finch, who does not move to escape. Instead, he takes the first container and downs it. He doesn't pause. There is no hesitation. He does exactly what he was created to do. He *feeds.*

Maverick sidles up beside me and watches in awestruck horror as his brother-in-law consumes gallon after gallon of blood. I can only hope it's animal blood and not human. We have no reason to possess the latter, but the thought makes my stomach churn.

Maverick swirls his hands and forges runes of light that float from him and disappear within the metal lock that holds the bars to Finch's cage shut. I know he's placing a hex upon it—Finch cannot escape if the bars are charged with the Siraltona.

But Finch doesn't look up. Instead, he focuses on his last course, which is gone in mere moments. When he looks up, his cheeks are flushed with the warmth he lacked only moments ago.

It has become too much for me. I cannot bear to see him like this. Without a word to Maverick, I flee the dungeon. The tears fall like rain by the time I reach my room and, for the second time today, I give in. I slump to the ground and sob.

A Gift From the Shadows

I DON'T REMEMBER THE DAY ARRIVING SO MUCH AS I DO THE sun assaulting me from above, its light threatening to burn my eyelids off if I don't pry them open myself. The winter sun is fickle. It disappears long before its summer counterpart, but it seems to burn brighter through the gray haze that settles with the ice and snow.

Shivering, I bundle up beneath my furs to try and chase out the winter chill. No one has come to disturb me, so I remain locked in my bedchambers. I open the window so the winter wind can remind me I am alive as it whips at my raw skin. I wear the furs as a half measure against it. I cannot appreciate the effect if I go numb.

Propped up on my desk sit numerous books on Shadow Folk that I've pilfered from the library over the years. I scan paragraph after paragraph, hoping one of them will allow me to glean some information on what happened to Finch. The night before plays on a steady loop in my mind. I wonder at what point I decided to be downright foolish and escort Finch, alone, to the dungeons. If I could slap myself for my actions, I would. Still, my gamble paid off. I'm sure the nobles will be informed that their princess is a crazed lunatic by sundown today, but the risk yielded a reward no one saw coming.

One of the Shadow Folk has been captured—a neutral Shadow Folk. Some might even dare to call him an ally.

I muse at the thought of having one of the Shadow Folk at court, Finch dressed just as he was before being carted off to the battlefield to protect Sunfall and our neighbors from the immortal threat of the shadows. Perhaps he could be used to lure other Shadow Folk within our gates and turn them to our side. *Would it be possible to establish peace by destroying our enemy from within?*

I know these thoughts are grandiose and would take years to implement, but my mind wanders with the dream anyway, prepared to dance away with it.

A soft knock at my door disturbs my daydreaming and I stand, careful to mark my spot in the open book before answering. Standing in the doorway is my sister-in-law, whose face looks far more refreshed than it did the day prior. Some of the light has returned to her eyes and she wears bright blue silks atop her gray winter gown.

"Beatrice," I say, my voice cordial. "It's good to see you. How are you feeling?"

"Better," Beatrice admits. "Yesterday was... not great. But I'm feeling well now. Where have you been? Maverick has been looking for you."

Chuckling, I know this is not the case, or else he would have found me by now. But I humor Beatrice. "I've been here in my room, studying. I want to know more about how the Shadow Folk are turned to try and understand..." My voice drops off. I fear what might happen if I accidentally unearth some of Beatrice's traumas from yesterday. I don't want her to cry again or cause any hurt. She has endured far too much for someone so kind and soft.

"Oh? What have you found?" Beatrice, to my humble surprise, jumps right into action, her eyes tracking the book lying open on my desk.

I motion for her to come over and I point to the page where I left off. "Not much. I only know there is more than one way to become one of the Shadow Folk, but the most common method is via exsanguination. Their magic poisons your empty veins, which causes new life to sprout from within. You get just enough blood to be up and running, but your body cannot produce it alone. You must feed to build your strength..." My train of thought gets carried away and I ponder the sketched images of a corpse coming to life that accompany the various entries by scholars who have observed the change over the years.

Such research, of course, is now banned, and many of our accounts are grossly outdated. My father refuses to budge on re-opening any research, given the risks. While I understand his reticence, part of me resents the lack of updated knowledge. Many of the books in our library are older than even Alaric, leaving much of our field notes to the messy realities of war, which blur the truth of what we are fighting and taint our pages with bias—a bias I hold and know well. It impedes our ability to truly grasp how our enemy evolves and adapts.

My notes are scribbled in sheafs of paper I have amassed over my years of encountering them, but the battlefield presents different results than, perhaps, a marketplace or a classroom. The thought of buying wares from a vampire makes me giggle. Beatrice shoots me a curious glance, but I don't offer an explanation.

Instead, I motion for her to give the book back to me. I leaf through a few more pages and land on the next entry, which I think she might find interesting.

Behaviors of the Newly Turned

"Based on this entry," I say and point to the page, "it seems that Finch is truly an anomaly. A new vampire is protected, typically, by the one that turns them. Whether it be a mate, a father or mother, or just a friend, the actions of a new vampire are learned from their 'sire,' which is the term given to the originating vampire. Shadow Folk learn their powers this way, along with their cultures and religions. So I don't know why Finch came here..." Dread pools in my soul. "Unless his sire... followed him here." A hollow cold gusts through the room and I'm on my feet, the book clattering to the floor.

Beatrice's eyes widen with alarm. "What's wrong? Are you saying another Shadow Folk is nearby?"

I spot Maverick hovering in the doorway and run to him, then turn and retrieve the book, carrying it to him in a flurry of panic. "Maverick!" My voice is rushed. "There must be another Shadow Folk nearby. I think it let Finch come here... I think it used Finch to find a way inside. Only Finch would know the entry points... I think we've been breached!"

As Maverick reads over the pages and the notes I inscribed in the margins, his eyes widen. "We must bar the gates, Adelaide. We must bar the entry points and let Father know."

Deep down, I already know it is too late. I know that the way in has been found.

"If we can intercept the sire, perhaps we can prevent the word of our entry points from getting back to the Shadow King. We cannot let them know where our protections are weakest. How did Finch even remember..." I shake my head, frustrated. "Why haven't we strengthened those points?"

But I already know the answer. We carry the bodies of Shadow Folk through those entry points to dispose of them inside these walls—to ensure that nothing is left and they are incinerated by the Siraltona. This is to make sure they don't come back to life, but the wards are weakest there to allow us to bring them in for execution.

Except now those points have become our own execution.

The irony stabs me in the gut as I race with Maverick to Alaric's private chambers. I don't care that my father is probably drunk again— he needs to be informed immediately. Maverick shouts orders at every guard we pass, but I don't hear them. My mind is lost in a tunnel of grief and terror.

The world is falling apart.

We crash through Alaric's doorway and find him sitting up in bed with several empty canisters of ale beneath his covers, the bedsheets stained with the vile beverages.

"Father," Maverick pants, "we've been breached! Finch... came back last night, as one of the Shadow Folk. We secured him in the dungeon, but we have reason to believe he was led back here by his sire so our entry points could be identified. We need to switch up the wards and close off the entry points. At least for now. We can hunt the Shadow Folk again once we have thrown them off our scent. And we need to try and find this bastard, wherever he is, inside our walls."

Our father blinks at us; it is clear his sleep and ale-muddled mind has not registered what Maverick said. Before I can add anything, my brother throws his hands up in exasperation.

"Father, we've been over this! You cannot afford to be drunk on your ass all the time when we have a kingdom to run and protect! You have no problems lecturing me and Beatrice about securing an heir or marrying Adelaide off to some magical stranger, but you cannot be bothered to stay sober?"

Alaric reels back as though he's been slapped, and I wait for our father to blow up. Anger is evident in the hard, etched lines of his withered face. But I have no interest in waiting for the explosion.

"Father, regardless of your current state, I need you to infuse my sword with light and let me go down to the dungeons to interrogate Finch. Do you understand? I need to know what he knows and get answers."

To my surprise, Father doesn't even blink. He holds out his hand and I give him my sword. He slurs a few muttered spells and, at once, my blade is charged with light that crackles just beneath the steel surface. Without waiting for him and Maverick to continue their argument, I sheathe my weapon and dart from the room, racing toward the dungeons.

I am enraged by my own foolish complacency. I am furious at how easily the guards let this man slip past our gates without so much as a *question*. Does Sunfall not possess the bravery it once had to stand against the darkness? Is this how we fall—by being lenient with just about everything?

And the worst part is that I am just as guilty. I led Finch down to the dungeons.

What if vampires can link minds like the legends say? Did I give them an internal map of the castle through Finch's eyes? What if Finch is no longer down there? What if they have already released him?

I know the Siraltona is relatively foolproof, but there are legends of those who can withstand its force longer—Shadow Folk with a tolerance to the raw light of Siralto. While vampires have never been able to wield it, there are some that might be able to survive its wrath. Tryta's darkness delivers the worst of them, I'm sure.

It would be just my luck if those rumors are true.

As I turn the corner, relief floods my lungs when I spot Finch sitting within his cell, his head between his knees. It takes a few moments before he looks up at me, his face stained with tears. I know his world has been rocked way more than mine in the last few hours, but the urgency of a potential intruder thrusts this concern for him aside. We can talk about his feelings later. Right now, the entire kingdom could be at stake and he's the only person who might have a clue how to stop its downfall.

"Finch," I gasp, "you said you woke up alone. Do you remember anyone being with you when you woke up?"

Blinking, Finch does not respond right away. He doesn't register anything other than the sudden urgency in my voice. Even though I know it's a lot to ask of him to pop up ready with answers, I want to slap him for being too slow.

Now is not the time for shock and awe, Finch! I need steady, level-headed answers.

Finch shakes his head. "I don't remember anyone being with me."

"Impossible!" I blurt. "Every available source of information we have on Shadow Folk tells us that there must be a *sire* of some kind. You must have been drained and then turned."

Finch furrows his brow. "I... I don't remember being attacked that way, Adelaide," he argues. "I remember a glancing blow to the neck. I thought for sure I would be missing my head, but here we are."

A shout erupts from behind me and I turn to see Maverick rushing towards the cell. "Adelaide, we have bigger problems than an intruder!" he gasps. "The guards know which way Finch entered. We received word that he entered alone."

At this, a weight unfurls from my chest, though my suspicion lingers. "How can that be? We just read my books—all vampires must have a sire. They must have missed the sire or perhaps they snuck in under the cover of magic. It's not unheard of for Shadow Folk to hide in plain sight."

To my horror, Maverick shakes his head. "Adelaide... I managed to get ahold of the party that was with Finch."

"That fast?" My voice pitches high with incredulity and I swear my brother flinches. But he recovers quickly.

"Yes, Adelaide, I knew where to find them. If anyone would know what the person looked like, why not the people who were with Finch when he died?"

I want to slap myself for being so slow. My brother is light years ahead of me with logical thought today, and I am supposed to be this kingdom's most fearsome planner. I always proceed with logic and reason. I take level-headed action. I don't let myself become swayed by fear. How is my brother beating me at my own game today? Perhaps it's the way I'm crumbling at the thought of being married off or the idea of Shadow Folk—the creatures that killed my mother—running amok in my kingdom and not knowing where they are.

I don't know how I will sleep tonight if I know something is lurking about. But the weight of Maverick's claim starts to settle in my gut until it threatens to make me heave. I'm still not convinced, as much as I want to believe we have not been infiltrated.

"So... if no one was with him... how is he back? Why is he here and drinking blood?" I point to Finch, who cuts us a weak grin—a hallmark of his dashing personality.

Maverick scratches his head, a sign that indicates our mystery just got more convoluted than the thought of an intruder.

"Are you telling me he just... woke up? As one of the Shadow Folk?"

Maverick nods. "I believe something strange is happening at the border. For someone to turn like this and become a Shadow Folk with no apparent sire? Something has to be up. If *any* dead soul is at risk of becoming turned, then we need to know it so we can adjust how we bury our dead."

"And you're sure no one turned him... *after* he was dead? I know there's no record of true necromancy among them, but if we are batting around the potential for strange magic, then we must consider all options." I cross my arms, my mind running away with a myriad of terrible possibilities.

Finch pipes up. "I'm right here, you know. You could ask me. Have I lied to you thus far? Have I harmed you? Would I harm the family of my sister or try to lead them astray? If I was with Mars, I would have gone back to him with as much intel as I could."

I turn to him, my gaze meeting his with sharp suspicion. If not for the bars separating us, I might have slapped him. "Why didn't you come straight here, then? How do we know you didn't tell Mars all you knew? That you didn't go straight there so you could lead them back through the entrance?" My heart lurches at the thought, though the way Finch recoils makes it hurt even more.

"Adelaide... I was confused. Disoriented. It took me a while to figure out how to even get back. I could not remember where I was. Hunger gnawed at me the whole way here and I didn't understand why... So yes, it took me *months* to get here. The first of the autumn leaves were just turning when I first woke. If I had a sire, don't you think they would have given me sustenance to keep going? Wouldn't they tell me what I was?"

Finch's earnest points are not lost on me. As much as I want to believe him, we must err on the side of caution before releasing him or giving weight to his input.

Maverick looks just as conflicted as I do, his mouth stretched into an uncertain frown. I try again. "Brother, are you saying we should call off the efforts to look for his sire?"

Maverick shakes his head. "No, what I am saying is that we need to expand our efforts. We should look for evidence of a sire, but we should also launch an investigation along the borders. We must figure out why or how a Shadow Folk would rise without a sire. If this is a real threat, then we need to start burning our dead and scorching our cemeteries."

Maverick's voice is heavy with the grim implications of this sort of order. The people will panic. There will be uncertainty. Sunfall's lack of a royal heir will send everyone into a flurry of outrage and threats of revolution.

We cannot afford to let the people of Sunfall know. But we also cannot afford to not *let them know.*

I am ever more grateful that I don't wear the crown, nor will I be expected to at any point in my life. As Alaric's rightful heir, I can't imagine the thoughts racing through Maverick's mind. What will he tell his people? How will he rise above this if there is a chance we will all be eaten by the shadows when we die?

I look down and see that I've been wringing my hands, rubbing my skin raw with worry. I break them apart and set them at my sides, unwilling to descend into the terror nipping at my heels. Instead, I look at Maverick.

"So, which one of us will go to the border and which one will search for the sire? You already know which path I want to take. We cannot divulge our fears to many people, and we cannot raise the alarm without giving the search an honest try."

Maverick grunts. He knows I'm right, but he's far more cautious than I am. He plans on the side of skepticism, and I plan on the side of action. But right now, we don't have time to be hesitant.

"Brother, I know this is hard, and there is a lot going on. We have been thrust into a sea of sadness and insecurity, but we have to act and act *now*. We need to know if the people of Sunfall should be burning their dead or if our walls have been breached. Either of those realities is cause for chaos. If we are wrong on both counts, then we have happy news to share with the people. If our fears are confirmed, we can show them that we took swift and purposeful action."

"I know, Adelaide," Maverick grunts. "That also begs the question: What do we do about Finch?"

"Again, right here." Finch waves. "You all may think me a villain, but I promise you, I am here to help. Why not let me go with one of you? You can shackle me if need be, but let me prove my worth. Let me prove I am still Finch as you knew him... even if my dietary needs have changed."

I raise my eyebrow at him. I wish I could laugh at his dark humor, but at the thought of how much blood we would have to secure for him on our journey, I suppress a shudder. Then again, it would be a boon to have one of the Shadow Folk's *own* with me while searching for their magic. I would prefer to go out on the hunt. Maverick is better suited to spotting a fake—a planted spy in plain sight. He is the political master. I am better situated to find flaws in the fragments of the battlefield.

"Maverick, if you must, imbue my weapons to give yourself peace of mind, but you know it's important that I bring Finch to the place of his creation. You might drive the shadow magic away with your light, but I can call it forth and bring one of its own with me," I say aloud, shocked at my own conclusion. I'm even more surprised when Maverick nods.

"Adelaide, I think you're right. But before we go down this path, we must take careful measures and inform our father."

I hold up my hand. "I respectfully disagree. You saw him earlier. Distract him if you must. Tell him I left for a week or two of sport to get it out of my system before entertaining potential suitors. He will buy that excuse, and he's never had a problem with my hunts. But you know he is not fit to weigh in on this."

A dull sadness settles in Maverick's eyes. His shoulders slump, already heavy with the weight that only a king carries. He dips his head.

"Yes, you're right. I'm lucky to have you as a sister, Adelaide. Siralto knows this kingdom would have fallen ages ago without your leadership."

Stunned at this admission, I engulf him in a hug without hesitation. "Maverick, we're going to be okay. I promise. We will figure this out. And if Finch is a friend as he claims, I won't be alone."

Maverick casts a worried glare at our brother-in-law, who remains quiet but enraptured by our conversation.

"You have my word that I will defend her to the death." Finch crosses his heart with his fingers. "I would never let our sister die. Not without a brutal fight."

Warmth trickles into my heart, but I cannot let it spread as I wish to. I cannot allow myself to be swayed by Finch's words. They could be pretty promises, but full of poison all the same.

"Then it's settled," Maverick declares. "We can take tonight to procure weapons and get your munitions and supplies. We will see about finding a way to supply you with enough... *blood*... to support Finch for a week or two. But if you don't find answers, you must turn straight back and we will regroup. And if Finch so much as *sniffs* at you as a meal, he is deemed a sworn traitor against Sunfall and you are to destroy and burn him at all costs."

"Ouch, brother. But fair. I expect nothing less," Finch teases, his voice lighter. "I look forward to proving myself as your stalwart ally."

Maverick shoos him away. "We will discuss this in more detail later. Right now, we need to plan. Adelaide?"

When Maverick motions for me to follow, I take his hand and we leave the dungeon. After tomorrow, we will be lucky to see each other in one piece again.

Maverick's limp thumps steadily up the stairs, masking the hurtling thuds of my heart.

Saddles and Scouts

At first, it takes me a moment to register where I am. My body aches and I feel like I have been smashed into wine like grapes that have begun to rot. I look down, half expecting to see bruises all up and down my flesh. Instead, I realize I am buried beneath my covers and I have fallen asleep.

The night before was a blur. Maverick and I sat together and planned out our course of action. He came up with several events to attract nobles to the castle—dances, dinners, and salons—to try and lure a sire out of hiding. Once they arrived, he would require each one to pass through a ward made of the Siraltona before entering our walls, but he wouldn't tell them such a ward was in place. Light can hide in plain sight just as shadows can. Only he and I know of the plan, to avoid the chances of this information spreading. It is risky, but until the plot is discovered, he can use it to his advantage to try and spot anyone unable to step through the ward.

I hope he only finds one Shadow Folk.

My stomach churns at the thought of finding several unwanted guests. I wonder why we have not thought to use this ploy before, but then again, the word would eventually get out and the Shadow Folk would get craftier. If we do find an intruder using this method, we won't be able to use it again. If we have spies or turncoats, the Shadow King will know before dusk tomorrow that we have upped our security.

It is time to peel back my covers and slip into the chilly winter air, but my body revolts. We agreed I would take Finch with me in Siraltona-infused shackles on my journey to the border, where I will scout for where he was turned. In addition, I'll take the party that was with him when he died to ensure he won't lead me astray. They will serve as backup if I find myself engaged in combat. Maverick imbued my sword with enough power to last for weeks and made sure the guards were readily equipped as well. To my surprise, Maverick did not weaken as much as I expected from using so much power.

Granted, he takes better care of himself than Alaric. I'm grateful my brother knows how important it is to keep in top shape as a ruler. Our father deserves grace, sure, but he cannot stay drunk and asleep when tens of thousands of people rely on him to be a solid ruler and protector.

I finally gather the strength to toss back my sheets and hiss when cold air hits my skin. Most days, the winter winds and chill don't bother me. Today, I am already nervous, and my body is weakened from the night terrors that threatened to keep me awake all night. I'm sure the last few hours were the best and only real sleep I got.

Wasting time is not a luxury in which I dwell, though, so I go about the business of dressing in tough leather armor and cover it with a thick fur cloak to fight the cold. I loop my best scabbard onto my sword belt and sheathe my trusty blade. Though I have never named it, it is my fiercest defender in times of trouble. The hum of the Siraltona through its steel brings me peace. Its power will allow me to cut through countless enemies and return home safely should things go awry on my trip to the border.

I don't bother taking makeups or perfumes, though I dread the stench I'll carry if we don't find anywhere suitable to bathe. I pride myself on staying clean, but war seldom leaves time or resources for such pleasantries.

Down at the stables, our saddlebags are being packed to the brim with provisions. I opted to skip wagons and take bows and arrows for hunting instead of carrying additional meals. We're already traveling too high-profile for my liking, but the situation calls for it. A wagon would make us an easier target.

I fear what might happen if we are intercepted unawares or if Finch's turning was a smokescreen to get us to leave the castle and search for his sire. I worry this is a trap, but I have no choice but to go see if it truly is possible for a vampire to rise from the dead without a maker. If that's the case, then we have bigger troubles on our hands in Sunfall.

There have been no reports of citizens turning or showing up after burials, but that does not mean things cannot change with little more than a whisper of a breeze. Life is consistent about few things, but among them, one can always count on change. Existence is dynamic, as is our perception.

I don't bother to stop and look at my room one last time. It's plain—not even my bedsheets are embroidered. My private bath is the most elegant part of my quarters. I do not stop to enjoy rest like others do. It's simply not a priority for me. My priority has always been avenging my mother, supporting my brother, and trying to be a good princess. I see it as a way of atoning for failing my mother. If I had just been born with the right power, I might have been able to slay the beasts that took her head. Deep down, I know my father thinks the same of me. He blames me for what happened, even if he doesn't speak it aloud. It's in the way he stares at me.

As much as I know Maverick appreciates me, I cannot relate to him without having the powers he does. He and my father are bonded over something I will never know. Instead, I work to prove that I am a valuable killer and strategist.

I will not let them down.

I make my way to the stables, where I hope Finch is already shackled and ready to go. The sun has not finished rising and the pinkish tinge of dawn stains my cheeks with frost as I step out into the open. Now that I'm bundled up, I don't mind the frigid sting so much. By the time I reach the row of saddles and horses being tacked, a few errant snowflakes have settled on my eyelashes. I blink and assess the horses that have been chosen.

My eyes brighten at the sight of my boy, Challenger. His coppery red coat is fluffier than its usual silken finish, but I don't mind. We won't be able to push hard, though. If he sweats too much in his furry coat, it could be bad for his health. I curse whatever stable boy forgot to shear him for the winter and make a note to come down and do it myself when we return. Carrying an extra blanket would be far less troublesome than sacrificing speed.

I notice the other horses haven't been shorn for winter and wonder if the stable hands are on strike again. My father has not been fair with taxes and provisions lately, which is disappointing. I've lobbied with him time and time again to stop cutting so deeply into our people's pockets, but he insists we need to store up and fund our soldiers.

The weakened armor my squad wears makes me wonder if that is actually where the tax money goes. While I am a skilled warrior, I am not typically allowed to know the kingdom's finances. It irks me. I hear enough through the rabbit trails of nobles whispering in the halls while I pass, but it's not sufficient to make the changes we need.

Maverick can only do so much until he ascends to the throne. He and I are always scheming to find ways to convince Alaric to grant him more power, but since Maverick cannot provide an heir, he maintains little leverage to sway our father's mind.

Ronald, one of the lead scouts, approaches me. His close-cropped dark hair and wild beard make him look more bear than man, but I know better. I reach out and grab his hand and he pulls me into a rough hug. Ronald has trained and hunted with me often. He was close to Finch, too, which is why they went out together on the wretched hunt that was my brother-in-law's downfall.

"How is the little princess?" Ronald raises an eyebrow and lets out a hearty laugh, knowing full-well that I *hate* being compared to anything that might be thought of as dainty or weak.

"I'm faring well enough. The winter's bite is rougher than normal today, I think, but nothing I cannot bear. Has Finch been brought up yet?" I don't bother to spare feelings or mince words, and Ronald doesn't expect it. Ten years my senior, he is more of a warrior than I am. He knows death is a part of life. What neither of us expected was for death to return one of our own to us in such a cruel way.

"I think they were finishing up the fancy shackles you and your brother dreamed up. If he so much as sneezes out of line, I will lop his head off myself. It's what he would have wanted before he died. The fact that the bastard had the nerve to come back..." Ronald shakes his head.

The laugh that I let slip is harsh and barking, betraying my discomfort with the situation. Challenger nickers at me in response, sensing my unease. I center myself, realizing this journey will be much more difficult if my boy sends me flying into a ravine in a fit of bucking terror. I cannot let them know I am scared.

Ronald claps me on the back. "We've got this, princess. Don't you worry. If he turns out to be an ally as he claims, then we've got a real ace up our sleeve. And if not? Hey, he's one more head to mount on my wall and use as a prop when I tell my kids stories."

This gets a real laugh from me this time. Ever since Ronald became a father, he's become lighter and more jovial. He loves telling them stories from his battles. Watching their little eyes light up while he mimics chasing down a vampire or charging alongside his fellow soldiers is always a delight.

"How are Rose and Sean?"

"They're good. Brenda takes good care of them. Rose is three now and Sean is two. Their little gums are full of teeth and opinions now," Ronald chuffs.

I smile and nod. I'm glad to hear of their good health. I make a note to send them gifts when I return. While I don't want children for myself, I do love spoiling them and letting my friends' children know they are cared for.

"So which direction are we heading? I believe Maverick mentioned the north," I start, my voice hesitant.

Before Ronald can answer, Devon and Jack come out into the courtyard with Finch shackled between them. I don't know these two soldiers well, but they both have honorable reputations. I'm grateful for their company and happy there are four of us armed with formidable weapons should Finch decide to breach our trust.

"Hey, Sister!" Finch calls, his face bright and his eyes merry. I know he's reveling in being out of the dungeon. Ours are drab and dreary—pretty lonely, too. It could drive someone to madness if they were locked in there for any length of time.

"Finch," I greet, though my voice is not as cold as I wish it would be. My heart wants so badly to know it's still *him,* even if he has to drink blood now rather than dine on bread and meat. I could live with such a change if he was still my brother-in-law.

Ronald steps between us before Finch can approach me. Ronald towers over Finch but doesn't say a word. A glare is enough to get Finch to step back with his hands raised, though still shackled. "Alright, I got it, tough guy. I'm still your friend too, you know," Finch jokes, though his voice is fresh with grief.

"I hope for your sake that you're right," Ronald says, his voice stern. He doesn't wait for Finch to answer. He turns and strides back over to a horse named Blade and finishes the job of tacking him.

I make a point to finish tacking Challenger myself, leaving Finch with Devon, who's been charged with saddling up one of the braver horses to carry Finch. Ironically, Finch's mount is a black horse named Shadow. *How appropriate.*

Jack rides a gray horse named Phantom—a mare with a little attitude and a lot of stamina. We are well-suited for the elements. I don't wait for the others as I swing up into the saddle. I glance down at my saddlebags and note the provisions are enough, though wanting. Again, I wonder where our funds are going if not to our soldiers and scouts. These missions are critical to the survival of Sunfall.

Are we wasting our coin on mead and dances? I wonder.

I tend to remain removed from those events, but I do know we've had more than usual as of late. A lot of fanfare has been necessary to distract the nobles from Maverick's lack of an heir. I set these worries aside in favor of focusing on the task at hand.

We've got shadows to hunt.

Turning to one of the soldiers, I note that Finch looks worried about not being able to hold Shadow's reins. I ride over to him and, without a word, tie his horse to mine.

"What are you doing, Adelaide?" Devon's brown eyes are alive with worry. "Your Highness, I thought Jack and I were to escort him."

I wave off his concern. "You are. I'm just making sure he's secure in his saddle and has someone to steer. Challenger is less afraid of him than Phantom and Honey are." Devon's horse, Honey, is a small palomino who looks mismatched with her strong, burly rider. Only their manes are close to matching, with Devon's hair almost stark white. He's a rider from the north with a reputation as a superior scout.

"Honey will be alright if I tell her to be," Devon argues. "She knows —we have encountered much stranger things."

His horse snorts in response, the whites of her eyes showing and betraying her wary nature. I laugh. "I think we'll let her take a break on this round."

Finch smiles at me and I decide to smile back. The moment dissolves quickly as Ronald rides up alongside me on Blade, whose pale white coat gleams in the winter light, the sun now full over the horizon.

"We're losing daylight," I say, my voice stern. "If you're going to lecture me about being safe, leave it. Instead, ride with me. You and I knew him best. We'll know his tells before the others."

Ronald doesn't argue. Instead, he spins around and takes up Finch's other flank. Shadow never stirs or spooks; his dark eyes stare out at the horizon in wait. He knows the real adventure is outside our walls. If I was in need of another horse, I'd surely take him. But Challenger is more than enough for me.

I click my tongue and urge Challenger with my feet at his sides, though I don't ask him to go fast. A soft trot is all we need to reach the border by dusk. The real challenge will be tomorrow and the next day, when we must figure out how and where Finch fell and rose again. Tyrladan does not return souls without reason, and aside from communing with the gods, our only hope of figuring out the truth lies shackled between us.

Finch and I share a glance as we begin, our path ahead already darker than any Shadow Folk could fathom.

THE BORDER

I'M GRATEFUL FOR THE THICK LEATHER OF MY BREECHES. Without it, my legs would be chafed and bleeding. The ride to the border is rougher than I remember, though the thick blanket of snow and nervous sweat I've built up aren't helping.

Finch hasn't shown signs of betrayal yet, but the journey is still too early to make a call about his true nature. No one has spoken since we left the safety of the castle walls. Hunts are known for their fun jokes and stories, but this is a much more somber situation.

Even Finch remains silent, which worries me. I clutch Challenger's reins, careful not to tug on his bit, and focus on the way my knuckles whiten as we near the wall. The wards will be lowered so we can pass through without Finch getting injured; I'm grateful security has been upped. Alaric will want to know why so much of his and Maverick's powers are being diverted to the outer walls, and I hope my brother has devised a decent enough story to keep our father from realizing the true threat at hand.

Several guards salute us as we approach. I curse the shorter days of winter, as the sun has already begun its descent for the day. A few hours are all it takes for the light we need to burn out. I doubt we'll make it far from the border walls that tower up into the sky, their dark brick stained with the golden hue of dusk.

"State your business!" a guard calls.

As I draw closer, the guard takes a step back. "Your Majesty, my apologies. I didn't realize it was you. Is everyone here well and accounted for?"

"Yes, thank you. We are operating on business for Maverick and Alaric. You are to tell no one that we've passed through here unless Maverick himself asks."

The guard salutes without another word as the wards are raised just enough for us to pass through. How they are able to channel the Siraltona this way remains a mystery to me. It's a facet of the magic that Maverick and Alaric either haven't been able to explain to me or have chosen not to since I don't wield it myself. All I can see is the light peeling down much like a drawbridge might.

When we pass through the exit, the light raises back up behind us and I breathe a sigh of relief. I watched closely for signs of Shadow Folk seeking a chance to break in but find none. If anything slipped through, I hope it's nothing more than a church mouse.

I look back at Devon and Jack, who remain stoic. Ronald looks over me across Shadow's neck and smiles. "How far do we want to press on, Princess?" The sound of Ronald's voice makes everyone in the party jolt a bit. To my relief none of the horses spook, though I curse myself for being so easily frightened.

"A few miles and nothing more. We'll have to set up camp and strategize for the day ahead. I don't want us fumbling about in the dark without a fire. We'll have to trade shifts, as well."

Everyone murmurs their assent, and we continue into the dreadful quiet. A few birds call out ahead. Crows. Their caws carry an omen of death and loss. I shudder and this time, Challenger shakes with me. It doesn't faze me, though a newer rider might have been jostled from their seat.

Up ahead I see the narrow, twisting path that everyone described when they set off on the hunt that killed Finch. He had been visiting Sunfall and this was the way they'd chosen. The Shadow Folk that lurk in the areas north of us are notorious for being swifter and more challenging to kill. Finch always loved challenges.

I wonder if he still would've gone on that hunt, knowing what he does now.

I glance over at him and the dullness in his eyes gives me all the answer I need. I pity him. I wonder what he might be thinking.

"Your Majesty?" Jack calls out. "Would it be wise for one of us to ride ahead to warn the others if something strange is spotted? I can take up the front and Devon the rear."

His reasoning is wise, but the idea of splitting up makes my heart flutter. We'll be easier to pick apart if we spread ourselves too thin. "Not by more than a half mile. Any farther than that, and the enemy might see us as easy pickings. Ronald and I will stay flanked against Finch."

Jack doesn't wait for me to finish speaking before Phantom takes off with him at an easy pace. Within a few minutes, I can see very little of them on the horizon. Before long, the night will swallow them and I won't see them again until we are standing around the fire this evening.

If I see them again.

Thinking this way is poison to the mind and I scold myself for giving into my woes. It won't help if I'm a quivering mess. I slay Shadow Folk all the time. So why does this feel different?

I can't help the urge to glance at Finch again. I know why the stakes are different for this hunt. It's easier to stay ahead of your fears when you can leave the monsters outside your walls. Once they break in, however, things are different. Then anyone and anything could be a threat. Living under the constant pressure of who may or may not be a predator is the last thing Sunfall needs. The enemy wouldn't have to take us down with anything more than the fear crawling in our own minds.

I press on, eager to cover as many miles as possible before we stop for the night. The trees, barren of leaves save for the evergreens, seem to etch out warnings as the dusk creeps up on us, their ragged branches spelling doom with every step we take.

I wish all trees were as unaware as evergreens. They remain cheery and abundant while the rest of the Earth's living beings have taken the hint to curl up and hide. The cold is no place for the living to thrive. My skin is raw from the wind which continues to whip at us, angry that we've trespassed against it.

As much as my cloak helps, being outdoors presents unique threats and dangers. We could fall asleep and never wake tonight, our bodies frozen in time to serve as a warning for all future travelers. We need a fire soon if we are to survive until morning. We'll have to huddle near each other for warmth. I wonder if Finch will need the fire to sustain him in his altered state.

I note that he seems largely unaffected by the cold, his layers lighter than the rest of ours. The Shadow Folk are seldom bothered by weather. It's a perk of being dead, I suppose. I resent Finch for this, wishing for once that I, too, possessed such a power.

I decide to break the silence, my mind numb from the lack of engagement. If I don't speak now, I'll descend into my worries and they will consume me. "Do you remember anything else from the day you died?"

"No, not much," Finch confesses, the relief in his voice evident.

The silence appears to have affected him most. He's been picking at his nails almost the whole trip. I wonder how fast they'll grow back, given his new state of being.

"I know I was taken by what I felt was a blade, though I wonder now if it was fangs I felt at my neck. I don't remember much from the attack. I remember being left behind—though I think I was mostly dead when everyone else rode off. By the time I woke, I was... different."

Ronald looks at him with hurt in his eyes. "We didn't ride off until we were certain you were dead. And it was a blade that took you. Some sapling Shadow Folk took a swing at you. I remember thinking it was odd that they carried a blade..."

Uneasiness pools in my gut. *If they're carrying weapons, what does that mean? Most Shadow Folk attack with their teeth and their powers.*

I gnaw on this thought, unable to set it aside.

"Was there anything strange about the blade?"

Finch is the one to ask this and I wonder if he's on the same trail I am—if he's thinking the same possibilities I've already allowed to sow themselves into my mind.

"If you're thinking they had some strange shadow blade similar to the ones we carry with Siraltona, then no," Ronald answers.

So he thought it, too.

I glance down at my sword and blanch at the thought of a shadowy counterpart. *Would that shadow be able to infect its victim? Is that what happened to Finch?*

I shake away those dark thoughts. We must focus on pressing on and searching for clues at the scene of Finch's death. If such a thing as infecting others with shadow is possible, we'll have to think about it when we return.

When we return, not *if*. I don't let myself think of alternatives.

"Finch, do you have any other ideas about what happened when you woke? You're certain there were no signs of anyone else around?" I don't dull the sharp suspicion in my voice. I let it jab at him, though he doesn't flinch as much this time. He's grown used to the accusations with each passing moment. I'll have to think of new tactics to catch him off guard.

"No, Adelaide," Finch groans. "I've been thinking of that day over and over again. When I woke, my first and only thought was that I had to get home. At first, I didn't even remember the blade. I didn't remember falling. I thought maybe I'd been struck and presumed dead, but it never occurred to me that I *actually* died."

His voice is thick with grief and I hurt with him—for him. I can't imagine how I'd feel if I woke up the same way.

"Is there anything else about the day you rose that stands out?" Ronald doesn't wait for me to continue asking questions. I know he is just as saddened by Finch's death as I am.

"Nothing," Finch mutters. "No matter what I do to try and remember... I'm useless." He throws up his shackled hands.

"Don't start throwing a pity party now," Ronald growls. "You're still of use to us even if you can't remember. But you won't be any use to us if you become a blubbering mess."

Finch laughs at this. His humor remains alive, even if the rest of him isn't. "You're right, Ronald," Finch concedes. "I just wish I knew how to prove myself to everyone—to let them know I'm just as horrified by my change as they are. You think I relish drinking blood? Or that I'm proud of the fact that blood tastes good to me and doesn't make me retch?"

Ronald and I both cringe at the thought but say nothing. For a moment, the conversation lapses and we return to silence.

"I do remember that the blade that hit me felt... strange. It's not how I imagined having my head chopped off would feel."

The mention of his method of death makes Ronald and me stop in our tracks, pulling Finch and Shadow to a halt.

"You remember losing your head?" Ronald looks more fascinated than horrified. I can't say the same for myself.

"Yes," Finch answered. "But I do have to ask...why didn't you all collect my body? Why leave it for the Shadow Folk?"

Ronald crosses his arms. "We had no choice. We were being pursued. We saw your head roll and it was too dangerous to tread back. We assumed you would've been buzzard food by the time we got back, and bringing back a headless prince didn't seem to be a smart way of securing good fortune of any sort."

As sensible as it sounds, part of me resents that they didn't collect Finch's body and bring him back to the castle. If there is errant shadow magic on the loose, Finch was left as the perfect victim to it. If he'd been brought back, he could have been laid to rest with the proper rites and avoided coming back as one of the undead.

I wonder if it's right to feel that way—that I'd rather have Finch dead than half-alive. As disgusted and scarred as he is, he doesn't seem to be suffering how I thought he would. And he's not a mindless young Shadow Folk who can only think of feeding and slaking his thirst. Bringing him along with us like this would've seemed a greater risk if he acted like so many of the newly turned I'd seen and read about. Some of them became blinded by hunger. So far, Finch has taken only one sip from his first canister. Several are packed in our bags and at the time we worried if it would be enough. Now I wonder if it might be too much.

I turned to him. "Finch, you say you only woke up recently?"

Finch shrugs. "That I remember."

"So your body just stayed in the same place for months?" This is the part of his story that doesn't add up. His body shows no signs of rot or decay. Like Ronald said, the buzzards surely would have made a meal of him by then.

"See, I don't know. Part of my memory is a hungry blur. I wonder if... I wonder if I've been feeding for months and wasn't aware what I was doing. I don't know how else I would've had the strength to get home."

This is a more plausible explanation, but the thought of Finch as a mindless bloodsucker on the loose makes me clench my fists. It also brings back the real possibility that there is a sire involved that we haven't met yet.

"And you're certain in those memories you don't remember another vampire?" I know by pressing him for answers I'm probably annoying him, but I don't care.

The sun gradually dims and darkness starts to coat the valley. As much as I hate it, I whistle ahead to Jack. I need him to regroup with us so we can get under the cover of trees, even if they look more like ill omens than good. Within them, there could be hundreds of Shadow Folk lying in wait. I hope we've carried enough Siraltona with us to keep them at bay, but I fear we may have doomed ourselves more than anything else.

I see a dot on the horizon that had begun to fade start to get larger and know Jack is pushing hard to get back to us.

"I don't remember anyone else," Finch sighs. "I'll keep trying to search my memories, but if there was someone, they haven't left any notable mark on my mind. I remember having to learn quite a bit by myself, but the memory is hazy—almost like it was a dream."

I wonder if Finch merely lay asleep the whole time and imagined having his head cut off. Maybe this is a strange ailment caused by a living nightmare. Maybe Ronald and Devon and Jack saw him die because it was an illusion and Finch was duped into thinking he's something he's not.

It's a terrible thought—crazy. But the pieces don't add up and I've got little more to go on than outright conspiracy.

When Jack catches up to us, I motion toward the trees. "We need to start a fire and hunt something to eat before it's too dark. A few rabbits should be enough," I say, my voice blunt. "I can go about gathering firewood and looking out for potential threats."

"No, you'll hunt the rabbits and *we'll* scout," Devon says sternly. "I won't have our princess out in the woods looking for Shadow Folk alone. You and Finch can sit by our camp and level arrows at woodland creatures instead."

I roll my eyes, but I'm in no mood to argue. I motion for Finch and Ronald to follow me, focused now on finding a decent place to camp. My goal is to maximize our sight of the surrounding area while taking advantage of the landscape to shroud us from outside view. The sun won't give me much time to accomplish this, but there's nothing to be done for it now.

A copse of trees calls to me for the way their branches lattice themselves against the horizon. They curve inward, which will cage us in while diminishing the view from the outside. I plunge within their embrace, Challenger's ears alert but not pinned; he hasn't sensed a threat yet and he's my first tell. A Shadow Folk has yet to get past him and his finely tuned senses.

Sure enough, I find no enemies waiting and a perfect nest among the tall birch trees. Their white, slashed bark is a fixture of the barren winter that rages on, indifferent to our struggles.

I slide from my saddle and lead Challenger over to a thick group of trees. I drop his reins. He knows to stand tied and I'd rather him be free to take off should there be danger. He has a better chance of survival out here than we do, which is okay with me. I untack him, careful to set the canisters of blood in my saddlebags upright. The last thing I need is freshly spilled blood in the presence of a newly turned Shadow Folk, no matter how controlled he seems.

Content that Challenger is comfortable enough, I motion for Ronald and Finch to help me gather bows and arrows from the assorted saddlebags to hunt our dinner. Finch is useless in this regard, but I'm not about to let him stand by himself, even if he's within arm's reach. All it takes is a moment with your back turned for one of the Shadow Folk to make you their lunch. I'd rather live with the false hope that Finch might still be normal in at least *some* capacity.

I grab a quiver of arrows stuffed in Devon's pack and watch as he and Jack stalk off into the wilderness to gather wood and scout for any enemies we haven't seen yet. As much as I want to go with them, part of me is grateful they stepped in for me. It's not often that I can take a step back and let others lead or face danger first—not that I'm out of the woods yet. Not by a long shot.

Ronald hands me a small, supple bow that he took off the pack strapped to Blade's back. With any luck, if we stay quiet, we might bag a rabbit or squirrel that scampers out at the wrong place and right time. Their misfortune will be our bounty.

Finch huffs and I turn to him. "Something wrong?"

"I could catch something easier than your bow could, you know. I feel it in my veins—I'm built to hunt. You sure you don't want to unshackle me and let me do the honors?" He shoots me a wide grin and I scoff at him.

"And let you go off on your own and accidentally kill Jack and Devon and leave it to just me and Ronald? Not a chance. Besides, you know I'm a good shot." I wink, trying to lighten my grim observation.

He isn't insulted, though, choosing to laugh along with me. "Suit yourself, Sister. I can't wait to see how well this goes for you. I'll be right here if you change your mind." He dangles his wrists, letting the chain between them jingle for effect.

I turn my back on him only when I'm confident that Ronald is behind me and ready to defend me the moment Finch turns. Together, we trudge through the trees, careful not to let twigs snap beneath our feet and betray our position. My eyes dart through the inky shadows that have begun to disperse into broader puddles of pure night, the sun now almost gone from view. We don't have much time to catch something and I'm not keen on letting Finch have his way and go out on a hunt. I'd sooner starve.

Ahead, I hear a rustling noise and motion for everyone to be quiet. I don't wait for them to get the message and neither does the hare that's dashing away from us. Its unlucky choice to flee has granted me a boon. I pull back my arrow and level it, knowing it won't miss. It doesn't.

I hear the wind whistle from another arrow and a sickening thud behind me; Ronald caught something at the same time I did. Our forests outside the kingdom are more abundant than those in it. This helps because Shadow Folk are more likely to hunt bigger prey, and there aren't many humans daring enough to come out this way. Since the animals are too unfamiliar with the patterns of their two-legged predators, they are easy to take down.

Of course, deer are scarcer, as are elk and bear. Those are the Shadow Folks' first choice, and without humans in the woods, they make for a fine supplement.

Not enough to convince the Shadow Folk not to try for better meals, though.

With a grimace, I walk up to the rabbit I felled and scoop it up once I'm certain it's dead. If it wasn't, I'd quickly snap its neck and ease its suffering. I don't like to let my dinner suffer for its sacrifice. I'm not a fan of hunting like this, either, but it must be done.

Ronald and I bag a few more hares. Once we're satisfied we have enough for tonight and possibly the next, we head back to the clearing where Devon and Jack are already waiting for us with a fire lit.

Finch stays quiet, which makes me uneasy. That man has always had more to say than most, so when he stays like this, I know his thoughts are either taking him prisoner or he's scheming—or both.

"Cat got your tongue?" I tease, nudging him with my elbow once I pass the rabbits to Jack to clean. Jack has the best knife skills of anyone in the group. At least that's what he boasted to me. I watch him struggle a bit and wonder if it's more rumor than truth, but he quickly gets the hang of what he's cutting and does a clean job of it.

"It's just... a lot, you know? One minute I'm alive and hunting and fighting... the next I'm back as the very thing I was tracking down. I can't prove to anyone that I'm okay to be around and I get it—I do. But living only to be shackled? Only to become the very monster you hate most?"

Finch's voice catches and I reach out to hug him from the side, a motion that gathers wary glances from the group, but I don't care. Monster or no, everyone deserves comfort. He can't hurt me now anyway, so what good does it do not to try and ease his mind?

I meet his gaze unflinchingly. "Finch, once we get back, if you continue as you have, I'll be the first to vouch that you're not like the others. You are well aware that you'll be killed the moment you step out of line, so this is more for your safety than anything. You're newly turned, and you remember how they can be... and think about it. What mad creature comes back to the lair of the very thing that hunts him most? That creature clearly must not know what it's supposed to be about." It's a lie I tell myself to ease the discomfort I feel watching him suffer, but it does little to reduce the sting.

"You're too kind, Sister," Finch says.

There's a tinge of bitterness in his voice, but I can't do anything to remove it or magically change the situation. All I can do is shrug and return my attention to the three rabbits we've put over the spit.

"Ronald, what do we plan to use for shelter and warmth for the night? Just coverings, or will we use tents?" I haven't thought to ask anything until now—an uncharacteristically lax notion for me. I always know things well in advance. I don't like surprises.

"We've got some coverings and blankets, but no tents. We'll be taking shifts anyhow, and we don't want to be caught unawares. I don't want to take our eyes off the horses, either. Bigger animals like them might be too good a snack to pass up."

I nod, and worry etches my face at the thought of losing my precious steed to some horrid creature's midnight snack run.

Before long, we're all sitting around the fire eating a dinner of roasted rabbit. Without seasoning, the meal is more a necessity than a pleasure. The meat is dull and offers little more than distraction.

Looking over at Finch, I see that he's struggling to kick back his canteen of blood with his hands shackled. I sit and debate for a few moments as I finish picking the last of my rabbit's bones clean, which I toss off into the woods so they can feed the earth. Standing, I walk over to him. Without asking the others their thoughts, I unlock his shackles and set him loose.

"Your Majesty, what the hell are you *doing*?" Devon is on his feet in an instant and Jack soon follows, but I hold out a fist in their direction, drawing them to a halt.

"He can prove himself while we're all settled here and someone is watching at all times. We will re-shackle him in the morning. The power is still in our weapons and the metal of his restraints, but he needs to feed uninhibited. If he manages to get loose by other means, having him out and about *and* hungry is worse than if he's full."

Ronald grunts in agreement. "She's right. The man deserves to eat. He won't escape like this, anyway. Not when we're all settled together with weapons pointed at him from all directions. Unless he's suicidal, of course."

Finch shakes his head. "No, just famished." He doesn't say anything else before grabbing his canister and tilting it back all the way, the sunken lines of his face betraying just how hungry he must be—how hungry he must've been with all the wandering in the woods and not remembering what he was.

Yet he remembers hunting? Was he not... fully sentient? Conscious? Or did his sire remove his memories when he finally 'came to'?

"Then I'm glad we let you eat, so we don't end up the main course!" I quip. "Should you choose to make a break for it, I hope you'll remember our kindness."

Finch pulls the flagon away from his face to sneer at me before returning to it, blood dribbling down his chin. Now I'm convinced we either packed just enough blood or not nearly enough. He must've been feigning contentment the whole ride here, or else his bindings made it impossible for him to take a drink as deeply as he needed.

I'm growing too complacent.

Once he finishes, he holds up his hands to be re-shackled. I shake my head. "I told you, not until we take off again. This is so we can get a sense of what you're about. Enjoy the freedom of dining and relaxing this evening and know that you will not have a shift alone. You're not free and clear just yet."

"Darn, just when I thought you were slacking," Finch teases, though the sparkle in his eye is brighter now that he can clasp his hands together in front of the fire.

I snort. "Never. Speaking of shifts, who wants to take them and in what order? I want to make sure everyone is well-rested."

Ronald pipes up. "I'll take first shift. Finch can stay up with me and the rest of you can sleep."

The wary glance from Finch isn't missed by me, and I know he's still nervous about gaining his friend's approval. It seems the part of us that wants to belong does not die, even when we become monsters.

"I'll take the next shift," Devon offers. "I'm thinking between four of us, there should be plenty of time to get at least a good five to six hours."

"I'll take the early morning shift." I throw my hat in the ring, leaving Jack the last shift in between. I prefer to be up before the sun when I'm out on a hunt. Still, a curling nausea waves in my stomach and I worry about the consequences of resting my eyes. If there are Shadow Folk rising from the dead without sires, who's to say we won't be overrun? Who's to say Finch won't attract others of his kind to our camp and we become swarmed anyway?

I walk away from the fire and lay my furs near Challenger, who grazes peacefully on tender blades of grass he found huddled beneath the snow. I gave him a healthy scoop of grain earlier and wish we could have brought more hay with us. His weight will drop some while we're out, but I hope we brought enough to keep most of the wasting at bay until he returns to the warm stables he calls home.

Once my space is situated, I decide to skip the evening's pleasantry and get a head start on sleep. The rest know not to bother me. I'm quiet when I'm tired and prefer to keep it that way. They know I'm the best sort of company in the early morning.

As I sit and listen to Challenger graze and my friends laughing and chattering by the fire, I can't help but wonder what it will mean if we find what we're looking for. What will become of Sunfall if there really are monsters within all of us when we die? I roll over to one side and let the thudding of my heart lull me into a restless sleep.

An Abandoned Grave

THE MORNING SUN BEGINS TO PEEK THROUGH THE TREES.

In my hands, I hold a mug of hot tea I steeped over the fire I rekindled at the start of my shift. Devon and Jack remain asleep, holding precious to their last few hours of rest. Ronald is awake, though only in body. His spirit is still stuck in dreamland somewhere.

Finch sits propped up on a log with his eyes leveled on the distant horizon, his thoughts still plaguing him into a silent watch. It bothers me that he's still not as talkative as he once was. Did the second life steal his voice and merriment that much, or is it the thought of heavy shackles and persecution that keeps his lips sealed?

I take a sip of my drink, letting the warmth soothe my throat. I did not sleep well. My dreams were full of fitful nightmares and at one point, I startled everyone awake with a shout. I don't remember what I was supposed to be shouting at, but no one commented on it and I'm grateful for their attempts to act as though I'm normal and not plagued by sleep demons.

Stretching, I pour the last of the dregs out into the snow and use the rest of the water to douse the fire. Ronald takes this as his cue and rousts Devon and Jack, who both rise without complaint.

I walk over to Finch. He stretches out his wrists, but I wave him off.

"If you run, I'll use the light arrows to shoot you down myself, understand?"

Finch nods, but his first grin of the day cracks his grim brooding and I'm grateful. I don't know what he's going through, but I know we are good enough to take him down if he tries anything stupid. His horse, Shadow, seems relieved that his rider has the reins and they can adjust their pace. Shadow is more methodical and slow-paced than Challenger. Truthfully, it's hard for most horses to keep up with my steed. If we were to take off at a gallop, Shadow might fall behind.

Once everyone is mounted, we set off, our pace unyielding. I'm determined to find where Finch was slain and get answers as soon as we can. Maverick is counting on me, and I can't let him down.

The days stretch on much the same.

With each sunset, I am more impressed by Finch's self-control. He doesn't drink as much as the days progress, and his hunger seems to ease. I wonder if his unyielding thirst was the product of so many weeks without feeding and less-so an indication of his being newly turned.

If he continues like this, I really will make the argument to Alaric and Maverick to let him live with fewer restrictions. I'm a woman of many things, chief among them my word.

I hate seeing Challenger grow thinner as the days pass. There is not enough grass or grain to keep the weight on him, and our chances of finding what we seek diminish with each day. Had he been clipped, we would have arrived already. I really would like to meet the stable hands who failed him at this simple task, but their necks will have to be wrung later.

When Ronald calls out to me on the sixth day, I know we've reached the place of Finch's demise. Finch's eyes widen, confirming that Ronald is not the only one who found this place familiar.

We ride up and, at once, I am relieved. Shadow magic has a way of leaving a trace wherever it goes. It hums and hovers in the air, especially where newborns are prevalent. The magic it takes to bring someone back to life leaves a mark. If it entered him any way other than fangs or a blade, it would still permeate the air and cause a reaction with our weapons. I can't taste it the way my father does—my teeth and veins don't tingle with the anticipation that dark magic often ushers in with it.

I know we look like fools, all of us walking about waving our swords and waiting to catch some arc of light that might react as an instinct to the strength of the darkness, but nothing comes.

Turning, I look at Finch. "There's no evidence here to suggest you don't have a sire, Finch. Are you still claiming you were reborn thanks to the embrace of a shadow blade?"

Finch shrugs. "You can ask anyone here. That's how I was killed, was I not? And, try as I might, I can't find any fang marks. You can look yourself if you wish, though I recommend that Ronald or Devon or Jack peek in the places that might make you blush."

The joke brings heat to my cheeks and I swat his arm. "Now is not the time to make lewd jokes, Finch. This is serious! If you're telling me they've learned to imbue their blades with shadows, that's a serious threat, even if it's not as terrible as the alternative." Even so, hope rises in my chest with flames like a phoenix soaring from its ashes.

Our dead don't have to be burned. We do not have monsters in us when we die.

I realize that by now, any signs of a sire would be long gone. The magic and its mark went into Finch when he was raised from the dead. Our only hope is to find the blade used to kill him, and that's somewhere on the hip of some Shadow Folk that rides free, unpunished for their crime against my brother-in-law. My fists clench, ready to strangle whoever had the audacity to do such a thing. Choking them would only give me the satisfaction of killing them once, while the blade that came after would give it to me twice. I grit my teeth, swallowing the rage that pools in my throat.

"We need to get home and tell Maverick," I say. "He needs to know about the shadow blade, unless, of course, he's already found your sire."

"I think we can set a more aggressive pace going home," Ronald offers. "The air is a bit warmer, which means the horses won't freeze in their own sweat."

"They'll still overheat in these coats," I counter. "We can speed up some, but not too much. We can afford to cut our journey home by a day or two, though I agree time is of the essence."

Among us, only Finch looks unbothered and unchanged by our journey. The rest of us are tired. It's a testament to our mortality and, once again, I find myself in the odd position of envying Finch.

Imagine never getting tired as long as you feed!

"And we're certain this is the place?"

The group nods in unison. Finch smiles brighter than ever and sidles up alongside me on Shadow, who has grown more impatient with the journey. I'm glad Finch has been able to ride with reins or we might've had a few spills along the way.

"So, do I take this to mean you can start trusting me now?" He raises an eyebrow and nudges me with his shoulder. Challenger doesn't react at being shoved, but I could kill Finch for being so reckless.

"Maybe, if you don't do stupid shit like that to try and get me killed!" I snap.

Finch raises a hand to his open mouth, mocking me with false shock. "Such language from a princess, Sister! What would Beatrice say?"

I roll my eyes, but I can't help but laugh. Beatrice is always fussing at me for not acting more proper in the courts. She's only trying to help me, but everyone knows I'm a lost cause.

It's a good thing I've proven myself a better asset at battle.

"She would leave me alone," I retort. "Now, I say we have done our due diligence. Along the way, we saw no evidence of bodies rising without sires, and there is no magic loose here. We know where it went now, though how it was dealt is still an open question. We won't be solving that mystery here, though."

"I agree. We should head back." Ronald's voice is hard, but weary.

He hasn't begun to trust Finch as much as I do, but I have little reason to suspect him at this point. There have been several instances where he could've snuck up and killed us or slipped away—things I'd never admit to the others. But it's hard to stay alert when you're dog tired and six days into a journey through the wintry forests beyond Sunfall's borders. It was a risk I had to take for Finch and me.

I don't wait for the others to reach this conclusion before setting off with Challenger, letting him break into a swift canter and praying that slicking the sweat off him at the end of the ride will be enough to spare him any consequences. I add in time to let him walk and cool off at the end and hope it will be enough, but I can't be too careful with all of us in such haggard condition.

To my surprise, Finch keeps pace with me. Worry flutters in my chest and, unconsciously, I grip the hilt of my sword, still waiting for him to try and take me by surprise and lash out. I would be much more easily taken in my current condition, but he maintains his steady pace and only looks over at me to smile.

We ride hard for several miles, covering much more distance than we did the day prior. By the time we stop for the night, I have the feeling we might have shaved as many as three days off our journey. To my relief, Challenger and the rest of the horses seem unfazed. If anything, they're less restless and I'm happy to feed them more grain, knowing we're close enough now that they could make it home themselves even if we are intercepted. Food and shelter are much closer at hand for them than us, should something happen.

Tonight, I let Finch do the hunting like he offered before. It's something I settled on yesterday—a chance to see him in action and give him the opportunity to test out his predatorial reflexes. In a matter of minutes, he returns to camp with a deer, which everyone heartily shouts over.

The men get to cleaning it and refuse to let me help. I protest, saying chivalry has no place in the woods, but they won't listen. I hate when they do that, as though I'm some fragile thing.

While they're busy preparing dinner, I decide to go and search the wood line to check for threats. I'm uneasy, my arms and legs twitchy. Spending the ride worried about Finch and the possibility of shadow blades leaves my adrenaline piqued and unruly. I ponder the idea of hunting before something catches my eye.

In the distance, it calls to me. A tall, wiry tree stands out from the rest. The bark has an almost golden hue in the dying light and golden fruits hang from its branches. Every part of my body screams not to go investigate—to leave the fruit where it dangles and go back to tell the hunting party what I found. But my mind and heart are wrapped up in the smell I can almost *imagine* wafting from the soft skin of it.

I'm lulled forward as though tied by invisible strings, little more than a helpless marionette. As I approach the tree, I am aware of how quiet my surroundings have become. Looking around, I don't see any of the Shadow Folk lurking, though that means very little. They can disguise themselves as all manner of creatures. The more powerful they are, typically the larger the creature. In this case, though, it's the small ones that terrify me. While they can do plenty of damage, their primary job is to alert the muscle for where to strike.

The branches hang just low enough for someone to reach their hand up and grab the small, golden globes hanging from them. They look almost like pears—a fruit I've only gotten to try a few times in my life. They're not abundant in Sunfall and fetch a handsome price. It's not something I can justify buying all the time, especially not in winter.

I reach up, still transfixed by the thing. For a moment, I could swear it sings to me. My heart hammers with alarm and my muscles tense, but I can't stop myself. Whatever strange spell has come over me has a chokehold that refuses to let go until I've tried this fruit for myself.

Before I know it, my teeth kiss the skin and leave their mark. The juice touches my tongue, the flavor sweet and crisp. I take a bite. My body does not catch fire. I don't fall apart. The world does not explode. Somehow, though, I know I've done something irreparable. I have changed the world and myself forever. Shrugging, I take another bite. A few moments pass, and I consume the whole thing. Suddenly, the trance leaves me.

Only now do my eyes open. I realize I've dozed off at camp. I'm relieved, knowing I never left.

"Did I imagine walking away from camp?" My voice is hesitant, strangled.

"Walking away?" Finch looks up from the fire where the deer is roasting over a makeshift spit. He chuckles. "I've been keeping an eye on you. I know you're exhausted... but no. You've been here the whole time."

I look down at my legs and find that the snow around them is untrod. Turning around, I see no footprints heading off in the direction of where that strange tree grew.

"Tired much, Adelaide?" Ronald laughs at me, but his gaze drops to my hand and his eyes glower. "Where did you get that?"

The change in his tone freezes everyone in their tracks. Finch looks at me with alarm as his eyes reach the place where Ronald is staring. I look down to see what the fuss is about. To my horror, in the grasp of my palm, I find the fruit. It's been eaten down to the core.

"See? I told you I left camp!" I say. "I found this fruit hanging from a tree just along the tree line."

"You *WHAT*?" Ronald thunders.

Everyone is on their feet, but I'm too enamored with the strange fruit to react on equal footing. My eyelids are heavy with sleep.

"Where did you get it?" Finch is in my face first. He places a hand on my forehead and clucks his tongue. "No fever. She's disoriented, though. Sister, what are you doing going off in the woods and eating strange fruits? Has no one told you not to eat things you don't recognize?"

I slowly reach out, offering him the core. "I'll show you where it came from." My voice slurs. I try to stand, but my legs don't follow.

Finch's eyes widen. "Can you point? Ronald, get her some water from the stream north of here. Past the evergreens we just left behind us. Now!"

Ronald doesn't have to be told twice.

I manage to turn my head with great effort, looking in the direction where I thought I had walked. I barely raise my hand and point. In a blink, Finch is gone. Part of me worries he's taken this as his cue to exit. I wonder if he's the one who gave me the fruit. Maybe it's true that Shadow Folk can haunt dreams and possess people. I've fought many and never seen it, but maybe Finch is among the few who can and I'm learning the hard way.

I breathe a sigh of relief when he returns to me. His hands are empty and he shakes his head. "I don't see anything out there, Adelaide. Are you sure this wasn't in our pack? Did someone slip you a poisoned pear for the road?"

My heart lurches. *Who would leave poisoned fruit in our provisions? Was it Finch from the beginning? His sire? Some other nefarious noble trying to hijack the throne?*

But the dream still rings real in my mind and I know—although I don't know how—that I got this fruit by some other means.

"I'll hold onto this. We need to get you to a medic," Finch says, his voice stern. "I won't be told no. We're taking Challenger and we're going *now*. I can see my way in the dark."

Devon and Jack say nothing, standing planted where they are. Ronald returns with a bucket of water and cups his hands in it, offering me a sip to drink. I manage a few mouthfuls before Finch pulls me away.

"Shadow will follow us. I'm taking her back. *Now*. If you want to lock me back up when we get there, fine, but I'm not letting her die out here!" Finch growls.

Ronald doesn't even flinch. Instead, he salutes him. "I'll fight the first person who tries to lock you away after this, Finch. But if you hurt her on the way—"

"I'll offer you my neck myself," Finch finishes, then picks me up with little effort.

In my delirious state, I am aware of him mounting Challenger without his tack so he won't be burdened and hear the thundering of Shadow's hooves behind us.

"I'm sorry I doubted you," I whisper, unsure if he can make sense of my words.

Finch looks down at me, tears staining his eyes. "I doubted me, too, Adelaide. It's okay. But we're going to get you help."

"Do you still have the fruit?"

He nods, but his face is focused on the road and nothing else. We thunder onward in the night for what seems like a blink before we pull into the stables.

I don't know how he convinces the guards to let him in, but the sight of their princess in distress probably helps. I look up to see several guards following, and Finch is being assisted in his efforts to carry me to the medic.

"Bathe and clip the horses," I call out, my voice weak. One of the guards salutes me and runs off to do what I know the stable hands won't, but it's enough to fill me with relief.

Finch looks down at me with a grimace worthy of a funeral and I wonder how terrible I must look. The thudding of hurried footsteps approach and, somehow, I know Maverick has joined us.

"What happened to her?" Maverick's voice quakes with rage and worry, both ingredients for disaster if Finch doesn't quickly come up with a suitable answer. In some ways, I pity him for being the one to bring me back like this. If I wasn't tucked in his arms, I know Maverick would've lopped his head off without a second thought.

"She had some strange fruit in her hand, which we only realized after she ingested it. She can't remember where it came from, but I believe someone packed poison in our packs and she made the unfortunate move of consuming it. I looked everywhere for signs of a tree that would bear such a strange object... but no dice," Finch says, his voice clipped with concern and determination. "I have to get her to the medical ward. Either come with me or get out of my way. Our sister needs medical attention."

Maverick steps back, stunned, and I know he's wondering how Finch arrived without his shackles or why I haven't fought back against the clutches of a Shadow Folk who, only weeks ago, was a prime suspect in what we thought was a plot to infiltrate the castle.

"Maverick," I manage to whisper, "he's helping me. I promise. He's proven himself. He... hunted for us. Protected me." My words are lost to my slurring confusion, but I'm glad to have gotten my point across.

"Where is everyone else?" Maverick matches Finch's determined strides and I hear the suspicion dripping in his voice.

My eyes trail the billowing cloak my brother has donned for the day, its unyielding black a tempting thing in which to get lost. Darker than the night sky, it's a soothing object to focus on.

"They're en route. I rushed her here, given the urgency," Finch answers. We swing to the right and the increased number of torches and hovering lights in the hall tell me we're near the medical ward, if not already in it.

Before I can interject or ask any questions, I'm thrust into the soft embrace of a bed. Finch steps aside while a team of medics swarms me with wide eyes filled with concern and terror as they realize their princess has arrived for an emergency healing session.

Cold hands touch me on all sides and blood is taken. A glass cylinder is placed beneath my tongue and a nurse clucks her tongue when she pulls it back out to read it.

"Her temperature is elevated," she says. "She's got a fever. We'll need to make sure she stays hydrated and receives proper nutritional input, though we can't afford to make her vomit. When did she last have water?"

"I'd say about four hours," Finch guesses. "I pushed hard to get here as soon as possible from the camp."

When they realize who's speaking, many of the nurses and medics take a healthy step away from Finch. Having one of the Shadow Folk in their midst is cause for concern for everyone involved. But I know Finch won't hurt me or put me in harm's way. He worked so hard to save me from destruction, why kill me now in broad daylight? Why attack now when he knows I will most likely die anyway? He could have offed me at any point in our journey and chose not to.

I want to say something to defend him, but my mouth is robbed of words yet again. Whatever strength I had to speak a few minutes ago is gone, drowned out by the blood rushing in my ears and the drying of my tongue.

A short brunette woman struts over with a large glass of water. She places it up to my mouth and I take a few greedy sips. It hits my stomach and nausea curls throughout my body. But the nurse won't budge and motions for me to take more. I bear it for her, the authority radiating from her tiny frame intimidating. I may not know her name, but I believe she runs the place.

"What's your name, my lady?" Maverick fixes the small nurse with a curious stare.

"Rose," she says. "I'm the head nurse. I'll summon Doctor Richards to come see her as soon as he can. He's coming back from a trip to gather herbs. He'll be back in a few hours, based on our last communication. In the meantime, I'll be tracking Adelaide's vital signs for any major signs of change. May I see the fruit that was ingested?"

Without a word of protest, Finch procures the remaining core of the fruit from his pocket and hands it to the nurse. I raise an eyebrow as I realize she put a glove on the hand she uses to grab it. *She was smarter than I was.*

I want to kick myself for being so trusting, even in my dreams. The whole incident is a blur and I can't quite convince myself it was even real. Maybe Finch was right. Maybe I grabbed a snack from our saddlebags and ate it. Maybe the fruit made me hallucinate my experience with the tree.

Rose stalks away with the fruit, saying no more to me or my brothers. My head lolls to the side to look at them, my voice anxious to be loosed by whatever invisible muzzle has been placed over me. I want to scream, but the sound won't come.

As much as I hate it, the dreadful pull of sleep starts to wash over me. *Will I wake again, or is this the end?* Part of me wants to stay awake and fight; the other wants the blissful darkness of the night to slip up and swallow me whole. I'm not sure which is the right choice.

Rose comes back and looks at me, her lips pressed into a thin line of worry. "I think it's safe for you to sleep. Your eyelids are fluttering. I'll send the princes away, if that's what you're worried about. We'll keep an eye on you and wake you if we think you're in any danger by sleeping."

Relief floods me and I nod. Rose snaps her fingers and points to the door. "Out. I'll summon you both when she's better."

Before they leave, I motion to Maverick. I jerk my eyes between him and Finch and move my hands together in a mock handshake. I can tell Maverick gets the message when a smile flits across his face.

"Yes, Sister, I will treat him as a friend. A friend who needs a *lot* of supervision and inquiry. But I'm not going to shackle him again, if that's your concern. He'll just have guards posted at his door while we continue to figure out what happened to him. What's *really* going on with him, anyway."

I smile and slide back onto the bed as Rose ushers them out of the ward. I don't wait for her to come back before I crash into a deep, dreamless sleep.

LASIRA

WHEN I WAKE UP, ROSE IS GONE AND NO ONE IS WITH ME. The window behind me spills bright moonlight through the window-panes and I groan. The sound isn't suppressed now, for which I am grateful.

"Can I talk now?" I whisper to myself, almost giggling at how stupid I probably sound to any other patients nearby. But my worries subside. I am vocal again.

A thin sheen of sweat has broken out along my forehead, which I hope is a sign that my fever has broken. My skin feels cooler to the touch when I press the back of my hand to my cheek, though I know it's better to have someone else check. The body has a way of playing tricks on itself because it doesn't want to admit its weaknesses.

A trait I understand deeply.

Looking around, I notice there are a few lit torches down the hall, which show I am alone in the medical ward. I wonder how much trouble I'd be in if I slipped out of here and went to my own chambers. I can't imagine Maverick would be happy.

I suddenly hear scuffling boots out in the hall, followed by Finch, who looks calmer and less stressed. We make eye contact and he grins. His pale eyes glitter in the wan light from the moon.

"I see you're finally awake, Princess."

"Yes," I answer, my voice still hoarse. "I just woke up. I think my fever broke."

Finch pulls up a chair and sits next to my bed, then reaches out to grab my hand. I take his fingers and lace them with mine. It's good to have my brother back, even if he's not the same anymore.

"Is Maverick treating you well?" The question sounds as hesitant as it feels when it leaves my lips. I worry that Maverick might have gone back on his word and locked Finch away out of concern for the kingdom's safety.

Finch laughs. "I am a free man. Unless you count the four guards posted outside my bed chamber door or the four guards out in the hall waiting to pounce on me should you make a sound of distress."

I laugh. His humor has perked up a lot since we first left on our journey together. It warms me to see him responding so well to the recent changes in his life... well, afterlife. Even so, part of me feels evil for entertaining him. He's one of the *Shadow Folk*, our sworn enemy. But he brought me here and risked his life to save mine. He's just like the brother I knew. My mind trembles beneath the weight of so much confusion. There's no instruction manual or grimoire out there to provide helpful advice on how to come to grips with your newly-turned vampire brother.

I swallow, ignoring the rising trepidation creeping along my spine. I could counter any attacks he would wage against me and hold him off long enough for Maverick to come down here, but something still feels wrong. The world feels... *off*.

I am sensitive to every move and shift in the atmosphere. Little sounds are suddenly thunderous, and I am aware for the first time just how *ravenous* I am.

"Hungry, Sister? Your stomach is growling so loud..."

I glare at Finch. He's oblivious to the strange feelings holding me hostage, but it doesn't make the urge to slap him any less real. "Yes," I say instead. "I... I don't think I've eaten since the fruit. I missed out on some good venison."

Finch offers a wry smile. "What shall I steal for the princess from the kitchens?"

My stomach growls louder, pulling a laugh out of both of us. "Anything, apparently," I say.

"Got it. I'll get you some pickled beets and fermented toad eggs," he teases.

"If you do, I'll kill you," I hiss. "Get me some bread or soup or something. Nothing too fancy."

At this, Finch salutes and strides from the room. I wonder how long he would've sat here if he'd come to find me still asleep. I wonder if he would've slit my throat while my eyes were still closed or if he would've held my hand instead. I refuse to consider the former option any longer than I already have.

He returns with a half loaf of bread and some dried meat. I devour it all in a matter of minutes, relief pouring over me with such a rush that I fight back grateful tears. "Thanks," I manage to mutter.

I hear another set of footsteps approaching from the hall and brace myself. If it's Maverick, I'm certain he'll be angry that Finch is down here with me. Maverick is protective to a fault. It's one of his many redeeming qualities. He doesn't ever stop thinking about how to look out for others. I wished I could say the same for myself.

I shoo Finch from the room, ordering him to stay out of sight.

Instead of Maverick, a man with white hair steps into the room. *Doctor Richards, I presume.*

Without stopping for introductions, the man strides over to me, his gray eyes fixed with the lethal precision of poisoned daggers. They are dulled by a kindness, though, that puts me at ease regardless of the severity of his angled features.

"Your Majesty." HIs voice is a soft blanket of snow.

I wonder how fast that voice could turn to ice when enraged. Something about him unnerves me, even though I know he's here to help me. This man has seen things—done things. I have a way of reading energy from people and I've rarely been wrong. Still, I know he wants to help. That part of his intentions is clear in the way he pulls out a satchel, from which he procures several vials of what I assume are healing potions.

"Are you Doctor Richards?" I ask, my voice quieter than I remember.

"I am." He smiles. "Am I to understand that you've eaten a strange fruit?"

I nod, though my response is dull and slowed by my suspicion, which I try not to put so squarely on display. It's hard to appear neutral when you're under such intense scrutiny. Maverick was always better suited to politics for a reason. I shoot straight and true without fail, even to my detriment.

"Rose gave me the core a few moments ago. Tell me, Adelaide, are you familiar with a Lasira fruit?"

I pause. I've heard the term *sira* in countless contexts. The language of the gods is used frequently in texts on magic since that's where it comes from. But I haven't heard *la* quite so much.

"It translates loosely to 'fire fruit' or 'light fruit', depending on the way you read the texts. When Rose first brought it to me, I was struck by the similarity of it to what I've read in my ancient texts on maladies and cures from Tyrladan."

At this, my right eyebrow rises and I have to weld my jaw together. *The fruit is from Tyrladan? The gods sent me a piece of fruit?*

"Are you telling me that I've been cursed by some divine figure?" I brace my nerves, waiting to hear that my days are numbered because I somehow angered some god from beyond the mortal veil.

Doctor Richards shakes his head. "Adelaide, as much as this fruit made you sick, you're not exhibiting any signs of a divine curse. Instead, I believe this was a gift, though I'm not sure for what purpose. The Lasira fruit is known for its cleansing properties. It is often used to create elixirs of fortune or brew courage draughts. Most notably, though, it is used to cure poisoning—the opposite of what your Shadow friend thought." The doctor peered around the clinic. "Speaking of whom, where is the Shadow Folk? I'm operating under the assumption that he's allowed to move freely within the castle?"

To my surprise, Doctor Richards seems... *pleased* by this. I make a mental note to have Maverick investigate him for any sympathetic ties to our enemies, but for once, my face doesn't betray these thoughts.

"He is under constant supervision, but he is no longer a shackled prisoner, if that's what you're asking." The doctor nods and he wipes a flicker of disappointment from his face so quickly, I almost think I imagine it. "Could you tell if I was poisoned before? How does the fruit work when it hasn't been brewed into some magical concoction?"

Doctor Richards smiles. "You'd make an excellent medic if you put that mind to the test for healing and not warfare. When unbrewed, the fruit is almost solely used to reverse poisoning. Deep, magical poisoning, anyway. Tracing what was undone, though? That would be impossible now because you've already ingested the fruit. Whatever was *in* you that the divine sought to cleanse is no longer present. There will be nothing left for me to observe. I can only ask—did you *feel* poisoned in any way? Were you ill on your trip for any length of time?"

I shake my head, unable to hide my utter confusion and worry. *How long had I been poisoned? Why did the gods intervene?*

Just when I think my lungs might shut down, Finch comes waltzing back into the medical ward. I glare at him, but he waves me off. He pauses and warily eyes Dr. Richards.

"Who is this, Adelaide?"

I note the way Finch's left hand drops to his waist, seeking the hilt of a sword he no longer carries. I almost chuckle at how ready he is to fight and how little he relies upon his newfound fangs to engage in combat. The one edge he has is the one he hasn't settled into. It's an important thing for me to track and I make a note of it. The more experienced he gets, the less likely he'll be to reach for a sword. Instead, he will embrace the shadows curling in his veins that arm him with sharp fangs.

"I'm Doctor Richards." The physician stands with his hand outstretched.

Finch carefully takes the offered handshake.

The doctor's eyes gleam with inquisitiveness. "I don't suppose you'd be interested in letting me draw some of your blood, would you, Finch? I hate to start our conversation out so boldly, but you're a curiosity and your participation in our research would help us better understand our enemies."

I don't like the eager edge in Doctor Richards' voice. I clear my throat. "Let's let Finch get acclimated before we start asking him to be a test subject," I say, letting a hint of authority creep into my tone. It's not often I pull the princess card, but today, I will for Finch.

He's not a science experiment.

Finch grits his teeth and stretches his lips into a pained smile. "I'll think about it," he says, his voice cool.

"I didn't mean to offend you," Doctor Richards hastily says, his voice cracking. "I merely have never had the opportunity to meet one of the Shadow Folk, outside of executions."

"That makes me feel just peachy," Finch growls, rolling his eyes.

Doctor Richards turns back to me and I shrug. "He's not going to be executed any time soon." I smile at Finch and wink, but he still seems tense. "So, if I'm not poisoned anymore, does that mean I'm free to go?" I can't contain my urge to get up and walk out of here. Sitting idle isn't something I do well, and for good reason.

"I believe so," Doctor Richards muses, his eyes once again full of curiosity and a spark for learning.

I know that if given the chance and if I was of a different status, he would likely run tests on me before letting me go.

"Make sure you stop by here once a day for the next week or so," the doctor adds. "I'd like to track the progression of your behaviors and health now that you've consumed the Lasira. If we notice any tangible changes in your person, we might be able to deduce a general understanding of what happened based on physiological changes. It won't be a controlled experiment by any means, but I think it might be enlightening, regardless."

With a hurried nod, I push back the covers of my bed and rush over to where Finch left the rest of my food and grab a loaf of bread. I don't wait to devour it before I step out of the medical ward. Before I leave, I have a sudden thought and turn back around to Dr. Richards.

"Could I have what's left of the fruit?" I know it's a long shot. That thing is probably tucked away in his laboratory somewhere for testing. To my surprise, he pulls it from his pocket.

"I've looked it over, though I'm not sure there's any magic left. Testing didn't reveal a signature," he says, a grimace forming.

Ah. It made it through the lab. I'm lucky he didn't pitch it out the window in a fit of rage once he realized it was a dud. I take it from him and tuck it into the pocket of my tattered dress.

"Thank you, Doctor Richards. Tell Rose I said thank you as well. I'll be back soon for a check-up." I don't wait for anyone to respond before Finch and I are out the door.

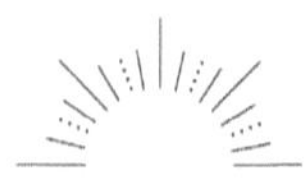

I FIND MAVERICK IN THE GREAT HALL AND HIS FACE FLOODS
with relief at the sight of me. He rushes over and gives me a once-over,
not believing what he sees.

"Maverick, I'm okay." My belly, now full with bread and soup, no
longer churns with nausea and I can breathe for the first time since
leaving the ward. Whatever was killing me from the inside is gone now,
thanks to the gods themselves. I'm giddy at the realization that I've been
given a gift, though still terrified at what I might have been poisoned
with and for how long.

*My death would have been slow and painful, if it was progressing at
that rate.*

I try not to shudder. Doing so would alert Maverick that there is
something wrong, though I know he'll need to hear about the Lasira
sooner rather than later. I decide to go ahead and broach the topic. Just
as I start to tell him what happened, Finch slips up behind me and grabs
my shoulders.

I shriek and turn on him. Smacking his chest with all my might, I
fight to control the flush of embarrassment emblazoned across my
cheeks. "What do you think you're *doing*?"

"Having a go at scaring my sister," Finch teases. "You should have
seen your face!"

Even Maverick joins in laughing at my expense. As they chuckle, I
think of several ways I might murder them in their sleep.

"No, in all seriousness, I was going to see if I could sit in and hear
more about the fruit. I believe the doctor called it a La... Las..." Finch
scratches his head.

"Oh, what, you want my help now?" I tease. "Maybe I should make
you grovel first."

He turns and starts to stalk from the room.

"Where are you going, brother?" Maverick calls.

"To go ask the doctor what that fruit was called before your sister's
head gets any bigger."

All of us burst into laughter, unable to keep it contained any longer.
When I'm certain I might drown in my tears, I do my best to regain my
control. Laughter and mirth are all fun and games until they get in the
way of real work, and my brother needs to know what happened to me.

"Maverick," I say, my breath coming in broken gasps, "I wanted to tell you about the Lasira."

"There it is. Didn't have to make me grovel," Finch quips.

I can tell it's taking more from him to keep the laughter under wraps than the rest of us. "Yes, the Lasira. It means Fire or Light Fruit, *depending on the context,*" I say, inadvertently mimicking Doctor Richards.

"I didn't take you to be the mocking type," Finch says, feigning shock and throwing his hand over his forehead.

"Finch," I say, my tone more serious, "now is not the time for theatrics."

Finch sticks out his lower lip and pouts, but he quickly pulls himself back to attention and runs long fingers through his pale blond hair, which has begun to grow out since he returned from the woods.

Since he returned from Death himself.

I wonder when I'll ever stop fixating on that part. I doubt I ever will.

"The Lasira is a fruit from Tyrladan," I add.

Maverick holds up his hands and shock flashes across his face. "Are you telling me the gods gave you a curse?"

I shake my head. "Not a curse, a gift. The Lasira is a fruit they give to reverse poisoning caused by dark magics. It can be brewed to make other things, but the fruit by itself is some sort of magical antidote. Apparently, I was poisoned by something that the gods saw fit to rescue me from."

I give silent thanks to Siralto, for whom the fruit is named. Dead or not, her essence lives on in everything and I like to think that at some level, part of her exists enough to know when she is being worshipped and praised. The irony is not lost on me that the goddess of life itself is dead while the god of the dark and dead lives on, the victor over her in the end. But I don't trouble myself with these stories for long. Right now, I've got a serious job of scooping Maverick's jaw from the marble floors.

"If you don't close your trap, you're going to drool all over the floor and Father will *not* be happy about having to clean up the newly polished marble," I say.

Maverick glares at me but collects himself with great effort. "You're telling me that you were poisoned before, and the *fruit* is what saved you? When exactly did you ingest the fruit again?"

"Shortly after we visited where I died," Finch answered. "To answer the questions I can already hear coming, no, there was no sign of any loose Shadow magic near where I died. We were going to report to you that we think the Shadow Folk have started infusing their blades the same way the Siraltona is infused in Sunfall's most powerful weapons. And while we believe I had a sire, they've erased any memory I have of them. If I must submit to weird tests by that quack of a doctor you have downstairs, I will, but not without Adelaide or someone with sense to chaperone. No offense, Maverick," Finch teases, though the barb in his words is not hidden well.

I suddenly notice how tense they seem with each other and wonder why Finch is no longer tense with me in the same way. *Did I not also recommend he be put in a cage?* This fact doesn't seem to bother Finch, whose eyes drift to mine again.

"My sister-in-law was poisoned at some point, but not at that part of our journey. I believe she carried something in her for far longer, though who knows how long and what sort of poison. I will say, she seems... brighter now. More alive?" Finch scratches his head, his head cocked to the side with pure curiosity.

"I feel better," I agree. "I don't know when I was poisoned, but I felt normal throughout my journey. I was tired at the end, but nothing more."

Maverick's face was grim. "It sounds to me that you suffered a more long-term affliction, which means we could have been compromised a while ago. Someone in our walls wanted you dead and the gods decided it was not your time yet."

Maverick strokes his chin which, I notice, has started to develop stubble. *Let's see if he can grow it into a proper beard this time.* If I was standing with our soldiers or if Finch wasn't one of the Shadow Folk, I'd be taking bets, regardless of the seriousness of everything going on. Poking fun at the future king is fantastic when it's your brother. Luckily for me, the rules don't work the same way for younger sisters.

"I wonder who would've been trying to harm me?" My thoughts return to my apparent brush with Death. "Why not try to poison you or

Father? I'm not in line for the throne, I don't possess magic, and I don't have any heirs."

"Does anyone in the castle have a personal vendetta against you?" Finch looks at me with squinted eyes.

He, too, finds it all puzzling, and I'm grateful for his input more than ever. *Just like old times.*

I shrugged one shoulder. "I haven't enraged anyone—at least not to my knowledge, if that's your question. I haven't overpowered anyone in the practice arena of late. I train by myself now. Alaric ordered that I seek most of my training out beyond the border or in more contained environments since my blades are almost always laced with Siraltona."

I add this last bit to remind Finch that, trust or not, any violation of this trust will send him hurtling back to Tyrladan before he even realizes a second blade has plunged through his neck.

"Well, I think someone should go about gathering intel and see if anyone has said anything untoward about you lately—if anyone's mentioned holding a grudge." Finch glances at Maverick, who nods.

"We can tell our father about it. It's time he gets looped in, anyway," Maverick remarks.

My stomach flips. *Tell Alaric?* Just the thought of my father getting his grubby hands on the hint of a potential traitor in our midst makes my insides want to explode. He may be a drunk, but our father is cruel and delights in finding even the slightest reason to hunt potential traitors for sport. He'll put on fanfare and balls and all sorts of royal processions to commemorate the death of whatever fool got in his way, guilty or not.

"Can we leave Father out of it?" My voice sounds smaller than usual and Maverick blinks. "You know how he'll react to something like this, and the last thing we need is the traitor to know they've been outed. If he gets it wrong... we'll never see the traitor again."

"I think she's right," Finch offers. "Alaric isn't known for having... decorum. He thinks long after he acts and gives little regard to consequences."

"Are you worried that we might look into *you* as a potential perpetrator?" Maverick snaps. "The uncomfortable reality we're dancing around is that you've been alive far longer than you've been back with us. How do we know you didn't sneak into the kingdom before you made yourself known and poison Adelaide?"

Maverick's voice is laced with venom and Finch and I take a step back, unsure how to read this sudden outburst.

"Maverick... if it happened as you say, then why wouldn't he have just killed me instead of waiting for the poison to take hold? Why risk being apprehended by guards and rushing me back to the kingdom to be healed?" I almost blanch when I realize I'm defending one of the Shadow Folk, even if he is my brother-in-law.

Maverick stammers. "I—I mean..." He sighs. "I suppose you're right. Sorry, Finch. I just don't know who to trust. Someone who is supposed to be on our side tried to kill Adelaide. Brutally, no less. A slow death is anything but merciful."

To my surprise, Finch doesn't look the least bit fazed. Instead, he nods.

"I know, Brother. You and I want the same thing for Adelaide— safety. Listen, I think we should devise a plan that allows us to investigate this poison angle in secret. There will be answers, but your father will get in the way of them. We need to operate in such a way that doesn't rouse suspicion. I think you should install more tasters in the kitchens, though. None of you should eat anything without prior oversight."

I glance down at the bread in my hand and Finch shrugs. "I tasted that myself and inspected it for odd smells, Adelaide. Don't panic. I'm on top of very little, but keeping you safe is a priority."

My cheeks warm, but I don't respond. "We should tell Father our theory about Shadow blades and that we haven't found Finch's sire."

"Will your father have me killed?" Finch blurts.

Maverick and I turn to him and I'm crestfallen at the beads of sweat pooling on Finch's brow. The nerves have been left to settle within him for too long. I know just how terrifying it is to be on the receiving end of Alaric's sharpened swords and explosive personality. Despite being my father, he's given me quite a few scares over the years, especially following our mother's death.

Queen Amelia was the last string of sanity my father had.

Before any of us can think to say something, the doors to the grand hall swing wide and my father storms in.

A Monumental Celebration

I DON'T THINK BEFORE SIDLING IN FRONT OF FINCH TO protect him from whatever violent outburst my father might be plotting. His silver eyes peel through my soul and seek answers for why I'm harboring a Shadow Folk, but I tip my chin up and meet his glare with a defiant gaze. *You don't scare me* is the image I'm trying to convey, even if he actually does.

"Step away from the Shadow Folk." Alaric's voice is cool and lethal.

"Father, he saved my life!" I declare. "I was poisoned on my trip."

The lie slips from me before I can stop it. I only pray my father doesn't visit the medical ward anytime soon to corroborate the story I'm about to tell. I note a small nod from Maverick and know I made the right choice to weave a tale of deception.

I turn pleading eyes to my father and infuse all the sincerity I can muster within my words. "When Finch came back, Maverick and I wanted to search for signs of his sire and, if there was no sire, we wanted to know how a Shadow Folk might rise from the dead with no maker. Along the way, I plucked a piece of fruit from a tree I thought I recognized. It ended up being a deadly thing that almost killed me. Had he not rushed me here and given me the antidote—a Lasira fruit he found along the way—I would have died.

"He traveled with me, Ronald, Devon, and Jack for weeks, Father, and never once gave us cause for concern. He carried me back with no shackles. A risk, yes, but a necessary one, given that I was incapacitated and he could ride the fastest." Even I am shocked at my ability to keep the shaky disbelief from tainting my tale.

My father steps back. "*That's* where you've been off to? I thought you tried to escape your betrothal." The growl in my father's voice makes the hairs on the back of my neck stand on end. While I can't smell alcohol on him, it doesn't mean it's not lurking beneath the surface, waiting for me to say the wrong thing and put a bounty on my head. Maverick and I never let each other deal with our father alone for this very reason.

"No, Father. Maverick and I were attempting to keep the kingdom secure. We knew you had your hands full dealing with the nobles and matters of betrothal. It was no more than a routine border check—"

"In the middle of the worst of our winter months, Adelaide? Really? Terrysa is the coldest month of the year. You could have caught your death out there!" my father scolds.

For a moment, he goes soft and I almost see a glimmer of the man who once proudly carried me on his shoulders through the halls of the castle when I could scarcely walk. But when his eyes harden, that man is crushed by the shadow of the monster that remains. I don't bother to keep looking for the glimmer of hope I almost deluded myself into believing still existed.

"Father, we thought we had no choice. Maverick needed to look for an intruder within our walls, and he is better suited politically. I am better with weapons and strategy. We did things just as you would have once ordered them," I defend. "I know I have to be more careful to assure that we have proper dowry arrangements and such."

Just saying these things aloud makes my stomach turn. It still doesn't feel real—my father's proclamation from weeks ago is more a nightmare than reality until this moment, when my ultimate value feels more tangible. I don't dwell on this more than I have to. I can't bear it right now.

"I won't make that move again, but at least we can rest knowing that Finch's sire is not within our walls and Shadow Folk cannot rise from the dead without a maker. Would you rather us live with that uncertainty?" I cross my arms and do my best to look intimidating, pretending my worth is in more than the sort of ring and power I can secure through a husband.

"Father, if I may," Maverick smoothly interjects. "In hosting several parties and dances, I was able to vet the nobles more closely and assure ourselves that there are no Shadow Folk in our midst. The wards and spells were strengthened at the border walls and our guards know to be on the lookout for individuals who look to be influenced by shadows. In the meantime, Finch saved our princess. Your daughter is alive thanks to his quick thinking and action."

Alaric steps back and his clenched fists fall open at his sides. I take a breath, knowing that the storm has passed for now.

"Father, I promise, he's under close supervision and we're not trusting him lightly," Maverick says, his voice stern. He casts a wary glance at Finch, who shuffles closer to me.

"He hasn't fed on anyone. We've been giving him blood from the farm animals we routinely slaughter," I say. "He's handled his appetite rather well and has used no shadow magic. I had a blade to his throat for most of the journey, but when he was finally loosed, he took no revenge on me and my party, choosing to save me instead."

Alaric strokes his graying beard, deep in thought. "If he is to stay, I want above average surveillance of him. This man isn't to piss in a pot without me knowing, are we clear?"

Finch squints and I can tell he manages to swallow several insults, but all three of us nod. It's best to give Alaric the semblance that he still controls the kingdom. If Maverick was not as powerful as our father, he might've had him beheaded years ago for challenging him for the throne "too soon". Our father is mercurial, but we've learned to predict his outbursts and violence when he gives in to his rage.

Now Alaric's gaze is on me and I freeze. The last thing I want is further interrogation.

"Are you okay?" His voice cracks a bit, which gives me further pause. Sometimes, my father is afflicted by something that could pass as a paternal instinct and it's uncomfortable for everyone involved. I can't rely on it, so I give it little weight.

"Yes. I can't tell you how I was poisoned as I don't remember, but the fruit and Finch's quick thinking got me home unscathed. The

Shadow Folk were nowhere to be seen." I cast a glance at Finch. He offers a wan smile but says nothing more.

A smug, manipulative smile appears on Alaric's rugged face. "So, our princess has been blessed by the gods and saved from death?"

My stomach flips and I can already tell he will use this for political gain. *Not a paternal instinct, after all. A ploy. A boon of favor with the nobles.*

"I... I guess so, Father," I quietly agree.

"Then it would be fair to say this is a miracle—a miracle that you stand here before us today, your very life blessed by the hands of the gods!" he muses.

The sparkle in his eyes makes the temperature drop. I shiver, knowing my life is nothing more than an incentive for him to grasp for more power.

"I think this testimony is deserving of celebration, don't you, Maverick?" Alaric casts a glance back at his son, daring him to argue.

"Father, I will not question your judgment in these matters," Maverick concedes.

I wish for once that he'd stand up to him. My brother knows whose side I'd take should he decide to commit patricide, though I'm certain the nobles would throw a fit.

Then there's the matter of losing a wielder of the Siraltona.

My hand slides to the hilt of my sword, whose weight suddenly seems much heavier. I bite my lip and dart my eyes between the two of them. I notice that Finch has edged away from the other men, his feet pointing away from the conversation. It's obvious he's waiting for an opportunity to flee.

"I suppose this will lead to planning and hosting a party?" My voice breaks the ice, shattering whatever tension lay between us. A breath of fresh air settles in its place and I inhale long and deep.

"Yes, Daughter, that's exactly what I'm implying!" Alaric claps his hands. "To fail at celebrating such a monumental boon from the gods would be insulting to them, would it not?"

Everything inside me screams in protest. *If the gods knew who they were saving, they'd have chosen someone who likes parties and social affairs, not a half-baked warrior princess with no powers!* But instead of saying these blasphemous things, I stiffly nod.

"Excellent! I'm glad we're in agreement. Maverick, won't you stay back and help me devise how we might present this news to our nobles?" My father's glittering eyes turn to me. "Adelaide, you and Finch are dismissed, though not a word of his change or lineage are to be discussed outside this hall, and he is to be followed at all times. Understood?"

"Yes, Father. Would you mind recharging my sword? I'd prefer to have it fresh should Finch step out of line." *And for my own sanity in case his sire is loose.* I won't ever repeat that last line aloud, knowing it would hurt Maverick to be doubted and send our father into a paranoid stupor.

Alaric waves his hand and motions for me to hand him my sword, which I do without protest. Light pours from his hands and into the blazing steel. When he returns it to me, a soft hum erupts from the blade and it clatters into my sheath a bit louder than usual.

My mind must be playing tricks on me.

Turning on my heel, I stride from the room. I don't care what Finch is up to at this point, nor do I want to find out what he thinks about me ensuring that I have a weapon with which to murder him at a moment's notice.

As far as I'm concerned, there's only one place I want to go—the library.

I DON'T KNOW HOW LONG I PORE OVER A MOUNTAIN OF books, but the light streaming through the library's glass ceiling has dimmed and steadily given way to night. I spend countless hours hunched over several tomes, looking for information on the Lasira and Shadow Folk without sires. Unfortunately, I've had little success in either direction and have half a mind to accuse Doctor Richards of lying about the fruit and its godlike origins.

How do I know he didn't lie to me? How do I know he's not the one who poisoned me to begin with? Would the fruit truly have been a death sentence? A way for him to bring me down to the clinic to study? Maybe he specializes in studying failed magical prodigies.

I shut my latest book and try not to let my eyes water too much from the dust that puffs up from it. If it was a book on strategy, Shadow Folk, or even the odd romance, its pages might be more recently loved. By its musty smell, I assume it must have been a long time since anyone read about magical fruits and potions.

My body aches at the thought of how many countless scholars and royals have passed through these ancient halls, their eyes drawn upward to the glass panes and the stars that shine through them, becoming lost as they crane their necks to see the towering shelves lining our library walls.

I've seen larger libraries, but somehow the glass ceiling makes it seem endless. Our royal line might be new, but the castle is not. I don't know its full history—only that it's stood for centuries. Sometimes, when I'm overwhelmed, I come here to ponder what life would have been like if I'd been born in this castle before the age of the Sunfall royals. I imagine what it would be like to open a spell book to do more than just wishful thinking.

I don't have time to stew in this forlorn mood of mine, though, as Finch comes tumbling through the door of the library. His shirt and hair are disheveled, undoubtedly by some maiden in the castle. *Old habits die hard.*

"What are you doing here?" My voice is monotone. I refuse to betray any trepidation about him, though in reality, he terrifies me. I'm not keen about being stuck in a library with one of the Shadow Folk. Then again, it's Finch. My heart and mind play tug of war as the time with him passes.

"I wanted to check in on you—see if you'd started to sprout daisies like they say," he teases.

"You mean pushing up daisies? I think you have to be dead for that, Finch." I roll my eyes.

"And I see you're still as useless as ever at realizing that's the joke I was making."

If I didn't have more respect for these books, I'd throw my most recent one at his head in a foolish attempt to hurt him.

But he doesn't get hurt like me anymore. He won't ever hurt like me. He won't age. He won't die. He'll be here years from now when someone just like me, but not me, is here reading this book whose ink will have faded even more. I'll be nothing more than the dust stuck in its pages.

Darkness clouds my mind and I shudder.

"Listen, I wanted to say thank you... for earlier," he starts.

I hold up my hand. "Finch, you saved my life. If anything, I should be thanking you. I know things are... tense right now, but you're still my brother, undead or not. You've proven that, as far as I'm concerned. I view the guards assigned to you as one more way for my father to fail to find a reason to hold you or try and order your execution."

Finch lowers his eyes. I know he's concealing tears, and I don't comment on them. I yearn to know what's going on behind his eyes—what he's thinking. I wish I could wring the memory from him to find his sire, but I know I won't have any luck. Mind-reading to that level is unheard of, and with my mundane humanity, I'm the last person who would ever be able to wield it.

I lace my fingers together and try to think of something else to say. "Any word on the celebrations my father is putting together?"

Finch shrugs. "I'm just as out of the loop as you are, Princess," he smirks. The tears are gone and his typically mischievous visage is back.

I know his carefree façade is a lie. There's so much darkness loose in his soul, but I'm grateful for his deceit. It hurts to watch him struggle and makes my own fears about being turned that much more real.

Would Maverick and Alaric spare me if this happened to me?

I try not to ponder this question too long. A part of me knows I won't like the answer.

"Think we should go find Maverick?" I let my latest book thump onto the polished mahogany table in front of me and pray I haven't accidentally scuffed the veneer. I'm the only one who cares about the appearance and preservation of the library, but that's okay with me. Of course, my pilfering from the shelves might be seen as contrary to this goal, but if I'm the only one checking them out, who cares if I check the materials back in? It troubles me to know just how many of this library's books might have been lost over the years due to people like me.

"I'm not sure that's the best idea. He'll come find us when Alaric is finished with him. You know how your father is," Finch sneers. "He's... worse than I remember."

I nod. "That's because he *is* worse. He gets deeper into the ale stores every day. We expect to find him dead from all the drinking."

I don't know why I blurt such an admission aloud. I peer out into the hall and realize that Finch is without guards. While this is an alarming security lapse, it comes as a relief. I can't have such a statement getting back to my father. I curse myself for being so careless.

"You can't repeat that," I say. "If you do, I'll have your head."

Finch throws his hands up. "Yes, Your Majesty, I understand. I just... how is Maverick going to take over the kingdom without an heir?"

I blink. "Who told you—"

"I've been back long enough to get caught up on common gossip and politics. How do you think I dodged my guards? I'm rather convincing, you know." Finch's interruption doesn't frighten me, despite the implications.

"Then you've probably heard that... I'm to be betrothed," I say, swallowing the lump that shows up every time I mention it.

"Yeah... He's stupid to do that, you know. A large part of your value is in your skills as a warrior. He loses that if he sacrifices you to child-birth and child rearing," Finch muses. "Not that you shouldn't be able to have those things, but they should be of your own choosing. You're better at planning than him."

"Yeah, Finch, but I don't have their magical light powers." My mood sours. It's so easy to tell him things—another skill of the Shadow Folk. They'll drain you of secrets as much as your blood. But I trust Finch, even though conventional knowledge tells me not to.

"And? You wield the weapons they make even better than they do. Maverick knows this... why do you think he sent you out to look for clues beyond the border? Why do you think he looked like Death when you came back harmed? He would've beheaded me without a second thought had I not been carrying you, and for good reason. You're far more valuable to this kingdom than your father gives you credit for. Even *I* remember that from before..." His voice drops off and, once again, he's lost in a sea of regret.

I place my hand on his shoulder and he tenses. "Finch, you're still my brother. You're still Beatrice's brother and Maverick's. Keep embracing those parts of yourself. Who's to say that anything has changed other than your lifespan and diet? I know everyone is on edge... you're the first kind Shadow Folk we've ever seen. But you were one of *us* before the change and chose to come back. That says a lot to me and anyone else who's really watching. And I appreciate your encouragement but... unfortunately, I have very little control over my future. That's always been in Alaric's hands. As it should be." I'm careful to sound in favor of my father's rule in case anyone is listening. I want to tell Finch more, but it's foolish for several reasons, so I temper my tongue and refuse to say anything else.

It works out, too, because I look up to find Maverick standing in the doorway.

"Plotting in here, you two?" He looks at us with an eyebrow raised. His face is weary and his shoulders sag with the weight of more responsibility than he carried before talking to our father.

I smirk at him. "Only on who can toss your head the farthest," I challenge.

Maverick's eyes sparkle with laughter, but it sounds weak when it leaves his tongue. "I... I suppose you've guessed that Father wants to throw a celebration in honor of your survival. And he wants to use it as an opportunity to tell the kingdom about your impending betrothal."

I sigh. "Of course he does. Will I have to wear a damned dress?"

The way Maverick flicks his gaze away from mine confirms my greatest fear—I *will* have to wear a dress. I slam my fist down on the table, rising fast and swift. "Am I little more than a trophy to him now? Is my survival nothing more than a stunt for him to get more ale and approval from the nobles? A party won't distract from Sunfall's lack of an heir. A party isn't going to distract from the Shadow Folk that still live beyond our borders. Has he gone mad?"

I know the answer and Maverick's defeated shrug does little more than enrage me further.

"This will be the death of us, I know it," I mutter. "That man will ensure that all Sunfall has in the history books is a footnote to caution against foolishness."

A cold draft settles in the library and I shiver, wondering and hoping my words don't hold the same weight that they place upon my shoulders as I dare to consider a life after Sunfall. Of course, my head would be on a platter if such a thing were to happen, so it's hardly a future I'll ever have to worry about.

"When is the party?"

Finch interrupts my angry rambling and I feel foolish, my cheeks growing warm. I've done little more in the last ten minutes than throw a child's tantrum. *Some princess I am.*

"In a week," Maverick grumbles. "He has at least enough sense to realize these things can't be planned in a day."

One week?

"This means he has already chosen suitors... yes?"

Maverick nods and it takes everything in my body not to hurl something at him. I know he's innocent, but my soul is in fight-or-flight mode and I'm not one to let anyone escape unscathed. I take a deep breath.

"Is there anything I should be doing in the meantime? And what about Finch? Are we keeping him a 'dirty little secret', or is he allowed to attend?" I raise an eyebrow, daring Maverick to choose the first option. I don't much like the idea of leaving our Shadow Folk brother-in-law unattended during a royal party. It's a recipe for disaster and betrayal, and I'd rather keep my positive view of Finch. It would be exhausting to believe otherwise.

Maverick appears uncomfortable. "You'll need to be fitted for a proper gown, for starters. Of course he can't attend, Adelaide. People have already heard he's dead. There's already the problem of rumors flying since he came back." Maverick crosses his arms. "You can't expect us to welcome him without the nobles getting flighty or expecting some sort of unwanted negotiations with the vampires."

"Yet, we have him loose in the castle now, which means those rumors will continue to fly regardless, no? We need to get ahead of the rumors and devise a story to explain why he's back so people don't get worried. We can even announce it at the party. Is this Alaric's doing? He's already been revealed," I say. I surprise myself with how calm and cool I sound. Deep down, I'm trembling with the realization that I'm doomed to be married off soon and sent on a fool's errand to conceive an heir.

"That's fair," Maverick remarks. "Father is just concerned about the optics."

"I mean, if anything, I think it could be viewed as a benefit, having me around," Finch interrupts. "I am a servant to the gods that sought to save Adelaide. Even the Shadow Folk have decided to bend the knee in order for her to survive."

Maverick snaps his fingers. "I like it. I'll float this idea to Alaric, but I'm certain he'll buy it. He's on edge knowing you're around the castle, but even the guards saw you bring her here in earnest."

"Exactly," I say, "so there's no need to keep him hidden. I'd argue he needs to be at the celebration so he can explain how I made it back alive. Or else they might accuse *me* of having dark magic. He's a witness to the fruit, along with the rest of our hunting party. They will attest to his loyalty, and we can assure the kingdom that Finch is under close watch. I... do wonder, though. What will Mars think of this? Will he think we're holding one of his Shadow Folk captive?"

I almost hesitate to say the Shadow King's name aloud.

"We haven't heard much from him," Maverick muses. "Ever since he started trying to build a palace toward the south, he hasn't made any major moves. And most Shadow Folk remain focused in the north. We have reason to believe he might not even have control over his kingdom anymore."

My eyebrows shoot up. *Why has no one told me this?*

Finch shakes his head. "I'm not sure I would believe that, Maverick. In the few memories I do have from being turned... everyone knows his presence. Shadow Folk, anyway. I remember being *aware* of his magic and presence. I don't remember seeing him, but... it's like when you wake up... you know who the boss is? It's hard to explain. Clearly, I shook that off and came home, but it's..." Suddenly, Finch's face screws up in sharp pain and he buries his face in his hands.

and I rush over to him, abandoning all thoughts of self-preservation. "Finch? Finch, what's wrong?"

Instead of responding, Finch slumps to the floor and clutches his face in agony.

"Maverick, go get a medic!"

"No!" Finch gasps.

Maverick freezes, unsure what to do next. If I weren't holding Finch, I'd get up and smack him for being indecisive.

"I'm fine," Finch stammers, but the sheen of sweat breaking out along his forehead says otherwise.

"Go get a medic," I say again.

This time, Maverick listens. The look on Finch's face doesn't bode well for having made it in time.

FAMILIAR TERRORS

I PACE OUTSIDE THE INFIRMARY, DESPERATELY HOPING THAT Dr. Richards, Maverick, or *someone* will come out and tell me something about Finch's condition. *Was he poisoned, too? Can Shadow Folk survive poisoning? Would the core from the Lasira heal him, or does he have to eat all the flesh from the fruit as I did?*

Just in case, I clutch the core in my hand, which I tucked into my pockets before running down here. I wanted to get out of this dress hours ago. The stench from our journey lingers all the way down to the stitches, but Finch's health is a priority.

"Come on, Maverick," I mutter. "Get out here and tell me something."

Instead, Rose steps out of the infirmary and fixes me with a curious stare. "You say he did no magic while he was out? Performed no tricks?"

I shake my head. "We all know fledglings don't display magic like that. Not like the elder vampires. They might be capable of a parlor trick or two, but there's no record of them being able to teleport or wield shadows or fire or water or whatever manner of magic they might have." Even as I say these things, I wince. Taking him out there to the border was a gamble based only on evidence we've seen in battle. I make a mental note to slap myself later for such a breach of logic.

"Well, I think we need to update our textbooks, then," Rose tuts. "The boy has been consumed by his shadows. He's... *changed*."

I blink. "What does that mean? I hardly think it's fair to say that when his whole *being* was changed the moment he woke from the dead."

Rose shakes her head. "Doctor Richards would be best suited for this conversation, but let's just say you're lucky he didn't turn on you." Without another word, Rose stalks away.

"Where are *you* off to?" I inquire hotly, as though I have the authority to ask.

Rose turns to look at me, her dark eyes fierce. "I'm leaving. I refuse to provide medical assistance to dragons."

It's Hell inside the infirmary. I look at the hospital bed and try to ignore the blood-red dragon perched atop the crisp white sheets, its legs and wings chained down with Siraltona-infused shackles. I wonder if those same shackles were to blame for his delayed display of magic.

Maverick had him chained the moment the transformation started to take hold, and by the time Rose came out to tell me she was leaving, he was secured.

We think he's secure, anyway.

I wonder if it's the reason he didn't break those chains and bolt, freeing himself of the scrutiny of Sunfall. I wouldn't have blamed him if he did. My heart hammers at the speed of a runaway horse that I worry may never thunder back to the stables again. I wonder if it might careen off a cliff and leave me dead where I stand.

Terrorized and transfixed, I can't help but stare, my heart still pounding. It takes everything in me not to reach out and touch him. I can almost feel the roughness of his scales and the webbing in his wings. The wings look leathery and tough. According to the accounts from all the books I've read, dragons haven't been spotted in centuries. Now I wonder if they were Shadow Folk in disguise. I also wonder if Finch is a signal of worse things to come. Still, the child in me is in awe of the fiery lizard and I swallow a squeak. This changes everything.

I eye Finch with distrust. I have no idea what he might be capable of now. He's not a large dragon by any means—at least, I don't think he is, considering I have no frame of reference and the accounts I read only say they're larger than life. I always wondered if they were sensationalized or representative of what a fully grown dragon might look like, but I guess I'll find out soon. As he is now, Finch is the size of a large dog. The teeth jutting from his jaw are imposing, long enough to dig into his lower lip.

Finch, while distressed, is not doing anything to try and break free. Instead, he looks down at himself with a terror not even his strange dragon eyes can hide.

Shuddering, I look at Maverick, who barks orders at Doctor Richards faster than I can keep up. An explosive might as well have gone off in the infirmary. If my father storms through the door, all of us will suffer. This place would go up in smoke.

"You're telling me there are fucking dragons?" I breathe.

Maverick throws his hands up in exasperation. "You think I knew that, Adelaide? Do you think I'd send my sister to the front, knowing there was a chance these bastards could turn into lizards that *breathe fire?*"

Maverick is shouting now. I hold out my hands to steady him, doing my best not to cast wary glances at Finch who, at the moment, has tears in his great blue eyes and looks more like a lost puppy than a dragon. *A puppy with scales.*

I wonder if he will get larger if left to grow and become a great vampire someday instead of a prisoner of Sunfall. I wonder if one day he might raze kingdoms. I wonder if he might raze ours. A part of me wonders if that might be a good thing. It might be merciful to let them kill us now than let these monsters grow larger and become our downfall once we've gathered something akin to hope.

"And you're sure there was *no* magical signature near where he was turned? Did you taste for it like Father showed you?"

Maverick's voice is laden with worry, but I'm offended nonetheless. It takes me a moment to figure out how to even respond. I know how to trace magic, even if I can't wield it. Still, the fairytale beast in front of us is evidence of a magic stronger than anything I detected beyond our borders. I wonder if it might be worth going out again, but if Finch is any indication of what the Shadow Folk can become, I don't want to risk becoming a snack.

"Just because I don't wield it doesn't mean I don't know it when I see it!" I snap. "There have been fairytales about Shadow Folk with familiars, but we've never *seen* it. Maverick, whoever changed him... they must be powerful. Is it possible they would've erased all traces of his change? Is it possible shadow magic might not leave a trace when raising a fledgling with no sire?" I don't like to even think such a thing, let alone say it out loud. My breathing is shallow. I slump down into the chair adjacent to the same bed I sat in hours ago that Finch now occupies. He lets out a deep rumble. I imagine he's trying to comfort me, but I'm in no mood for it.

If other Shadow Folk can change forms... we're doomed. My mind spirals and I can't breathe. I want to run screaming from the infirmary, but I can't find the strength to do so. And I can't stop staring at the ruby red scales that adorn my brother-in-law. And those *teeth*.

"Familiar," he hisses. *"We have familiars."*

At this, Maverick and I snap our heads in Finch's direction. His voice, now a deep hiss, is still unmistakable. His mouth doesn't move, but the words come out in the same way they would from a human speaking. I stifle a scream. I wonder if, at some point, I fell asleep in the library and this is all a terrible dream.

"I remember my sire saying we have familiars."

"Oh, so you remember your sire now?" Maverick's voice carries an edge. I watch as his fists curl up into tense balls and worry what he might do. I stand, stepping between him and Finch.

"I do not remember their face or name, but I did not rise from nothing. I believe we all have familiars. They have been... repressed until recently. I don't know how we got them back."

"You mean you can all turn into dragons?" I stammer, my vision blurring and my stomach curdling.

"No," Finch answers. *"We change based on what we are."*

So is Finch... something powerful? I make a mental note. I hope his answers mean that other Shadow Folk are more liable to turn into chipmunks than fucking *dragons*.

Before I can get a word in, Maverick curses. "What the fuck does that mean, Finch? I don't have time for riddles. Are you telling me there's a risk that *all* Shadow Folk will be able to access their familiars now?"

"I think so," Finch says. *"The king... he did something. He set them free."* Finch screws up his great scaly face and buries his head, pain etched on his reptilian features.

Doctor Richards stands behind Finch and stares at him as a priest would stand in awe before his god in the flesh. I do a cursory glance and note the dark vials of blood sitting on the table next to Finch.

"Why have you been taking Finch's blood?" I demand, my current concerns cast aside as I realize that Doctor Richards has been taking from Finch without so much as a word to us. Finch can't fight back. Finch can't say no. Finch is on a thin leash and Doctor Richards has swooped in to take advantage while our attention was fixated elsewhere. Without warning, I walk over and smash them to the floor.

Doctor Richards screams. "Foolish girl, what are you doing?"

"Protecting Finch," I say. "Stop taking his blood unless he gives you permission to do so. Do that again, and I'll take your head next!" I mean it, too.

"Stupid girl, do you have any idea what his blood could tell us? We could learn so many secrets about the Shadow Folk—we could trace his sire!"

Maverick claps a hand on my shoulder. "He's right, Adelaide. Let him take what he needs. Don't make Finch's sacrifice count for nothing."

I want to slap my brother and I want to protect Finch. But Maverick is right. Finch is not the same person I knew before he was killed out on the battlefield. Even with him in a totally different body, I stand in denial of the truth. I will never know Finch the same way again. He has become something different and alien to me, and by many leagues, at that. Still, he is my friend.

He is still my brother-in-law, dragon or not.

I wonder what it must've looked like to watch Finch's bones snap apart and rearrange themselves into the creature sitting before us. I wonder how he can feel the pain of needles when his body has completely changed its shape. *Does it hurt them to change?*

Bewildered, I am incapable of breathing as I should. My lungs inhale choppy bits of air and do their best to process them, with little success. If I don't get a handle on my nerves, very soon I might slump to the floor and fall unconscious with terror.

Dragons are real. Shadow Folk have familiar forms. They are their own familiars. The Shadow King has set them free.

I feel like I'm descending into madness. If my father finds out about this, the whole kingdom will be torn apart in a fit of his mad, uncontrolled rage. I look at Maverick, choosing to ignore Doctor Richards as he begins the task of taking more blood. While Finch still seems distraught, he doesn't fight and, if anything, he seems eager to watch his blood being taken. *Maybe he wants the secrets of his origins as much as Doctor Richards does.* I scold myself for being so selfish as to trash the first vials. A more pressing thought replaces this guilt, though. *Father.*

"We can't tell him," I whisper. "If Finch is starting to remember, we can gather the intel needed... but we can't tell Alaric." My eyes plead with Maverick and I hope I've spoken quietly enough so Doctor Richards didn't hear. I can't imagine what he would do if he thinks I'm conspiring against the king. I need to devise a plan to buy his silence, but first, I need to barter with Maverick.

To my surprise, Maverick nods. Sometimes it takes a bit for me to remember that my brother typically sides with me over my father, even though I share so little with him. I don't wield magic. I don't have the weight of the kingdom on my shoulders.

Well, at least I didn't until recently... not like he does.

I turn to Finch. "Are you able to change back? Can you hide what you are?"

Finch rumbles, his great long snout almost quivering, and I wonder how much more shock he can take before going insane. He never wanted this. With each passing moment, he becomes more like the thing he hates most and less like the Finch I knew before he died.

"I'm not sure. I believe I can... but everything feels... off. I'm remembering and not remembering. I am overwhelmed. I promise I am not here to harm anyone, regardless of the remembering," Finch says, his voice garbled by panic and worry.

I pity him, even in this terrifying form. "Okay, let's stay calm and make an attempt."

Watching Doctor Richards scribble notes irritates me. The sound of the quill scratching along paper makes me wonder if tearing my hair out might be preferable. I don't know how we'll ensure his secrecy, or his silence. Something about the way Maverick looks at him tells me I won't have to do much in the way of imagining effective ways to keep him quiet.

"I think it's about pulling on the magic. Hold on... let me see if I can figure this out," Finch says, his voice growing a bit calmer as he focuses on his magic and his current state. Without people shouting or threatening him, he's less likely to be distracted or burdened by his harrowing thoughts.

I wonder if removing his shackles might do any good. Of course, Maverick might skewer me halfway to unlocking them. Letting a dragon loose in the castle probably wouldn't go over well, sister or not.

"Come on, Finch, you can do it." I do my best not to let doubt stain the edges of my tone. It's everywhere inside of me, which makes it hard to keep it from spilling out. I wonder if I might be able to sneak some of my father's ale to my bedchambers later. I'll need a good, stiff drink to help me recover from a day, and now night, like this.

I have more questions than answers as I watch Finch put on the most concentrated face I've ever seen a beastly lizard wear. If I was an artist, I might try to capture it on paper. Admittedly, my attempt would look more like pathetic scribbles and chicken scratch.

My thoughts return to Finch, and I notice he starts to shrink and contort before my very eyes. His face twists in agony and I can't bear to fathom the pain he's in while his body... *rearranges*... itself.

With one last gasp, Finch sits, still in shackles, in his human form on the infirmary bed. To my annoyance, Doctor Richards has the audacity to clap.

"He's not an animal at the carnival!" I snap. "Finch is a person. Stop treating him like he's an experiment for your amusement."

Doctor Richards takes a bow and swiftly places a mask of indifference on his face that I wish I could crack open with one of my swords. My patience is growing thin with him. Maverick reaches out and grabs my hand, sensing the homicidal urges brewing in my twitching fingers.

"Doctor Richards, I will need to speak with you privately while my sister escorts Finch to his guarded chambers. You are to let them leave," Maverick orders. The sharp edge in his tone reveals the magic crackling beneath the surface and I know my brother is about to use some serious magic to force Doctor Richards to stay quiet. I also know that Maverick will need days to recover after performing such a feat. While not expressly forbidden, binding even a portion of someone's will is exhausting to the caster, if not dangerous. Magic takes just as much as it gives, in many respects.

While they've learned to channel those costs by imbuing it into physical things, like my sword, my father and brother have likely shaved years off their life. The graying in Alaric's beard betrays this every time he uses magic for something of grand importance. Balancing the costs of magic is something that takes years to master. I hope for Maverick's sake as well as mine that this secret is worth sacrificing some of his life for.

I reach out and take Finch's hand, not daring to argue with my brother while he's in such a state. While I know he wouldn't kill me, I won't risk my neck with the fallout from whatever spell he's about to set loose in the infirmary. Magic doesn't always strike true at its target, especially when emotions are involved.

Judging by the rage etched on Maverick's face, there's no guarantee I won't get clipped by a blast of light if I don't quickly hustle Finch out of here. I tug him along, ignoring the way his shackles fall from his wrists, now too big to hold him. I don't worry about the fact that he could drain me at any moment or curse me with his awful shadow magic. Right now, I worry about getting my brother-in-law to safety.

We run without looking back when we hear screams coming from the infirmary. It's a cruel form of torture to rob a human of their free will, even if it's for something as small as a secret. Part of the body dies when it is forced in any capacity by magic to do that which is not voluntary. I wish I felt bad for Doctor Richards, but I don't. Those vials of blood weren't taken voluntarily either, even if extracted without magic.

He could have asked Finch first. He could speak.

Rounding the corner, we make it to the wing of the castle where my bedchamber resides, along with Finch's, which is a few doors down. Maverick and Beatrice are farther down in the wing, but still present. I am grateful that my father is in the wing upstairs. The solitude up there might not be good for his mind, but it's good for mine and Maverick's souls. Even more-so, it's good for Finch, who is once again flanked by guards who have sidled up to us. *So much for bribery and deceit.* Finch will have to find a way to get them off his tail again. We've been gone a few hours, which no doubt raised suspicion. I only hope that none of the guards mentioned this to Alaric.

"Finch," I say, as he's escorted to his chamber, "take it easy, okay? I'll be by later with something for you to feed from."

He nods, his eyes dull with exhaustion. I wonder if I'll even be able to wake him. I hope the magic he used to change back into his human form does not tax him the same way the Siraltona taxes Maverick and my father. Still, if it does, that's a reason for hope out there on the battlefield.

But right now, I know in my heart that we're doomed.

HAVE A BALL

THE PAST FEW DAYS ARE A BLUR.

I was right when I assumed Finch wouldn't wake for some time. As it turns out, Maverick recovered from the binding spell long before Finch roused. I half expected that we might need to bury Finch again before we had any luck with getting him to open his eyes. Still, Death did not come to claim him as I feared. Now, he stands in front of Maverick and me, his blond hair tousled and his blue eyes icy. He's no better when first awakened than I am. Robbing me of sleep is a sure way to get someone murdered.

"Adelaide, I'm so sorry." Finch's voice is slurred from the weight of whatever dreams he's just been stolen from.

"Why are you apologizing to me? We thought you were on your way out! You've been asleep for a week," I say, crossing my arms.

If I look like I'm pouting, I'm doing a poor job of appearing to care about it. My mind has been riddled with the terrors of what we might do if Finch were to pass a second time. On the one hand, it would have been useful knowing that we could tax a Shadow Folk to death if we could trick them into shifting into their familiar form. On the other hand, I wasn't too keen on the thought of my brother-in-law being buried or having his body burned, as per the usual precautions. I was prepared to fight my father by providing Finch with proper Sunfall funeral rites instead of the traditional treatment we give Shadow Folk.

"You're going to scold him so soon after we thought he was a goner?" Maverick teases, shooting me a grin.

I glare back at him, refusing to give my brother the satisfaction of seeing me fret any longer. Between us, Maverick is more of an optimist. I can't afford to believe in much when I don't have magic and I'm forced to see the harsh realities of battle without divine light to save me.

"I'm just glad to know he's alright," I say, my arms still crossed. I squeeze myself a little tighter to remind me that I, too, am still alive. These past few days made me question everything. I haven't slept, instead burying myself in the library.

Right now, stacks upon stacks of books sit on those worn tables in the library. Even though there is nothing banned in my kingdom, my father would be enraged if he knew what I was researching. Perhaps it's reckless to leave them out in the open, but I've already woven several convincing stories about why I'm looking through them.

Finch's return alone gives me the cover I need to pore over books on witchcraft, familiars, vampires, and dragons. Admittedly, I've caused a few pages to crumble to dust from reading them over and over again. Luckily, I made sure to transcribe those weaker pages when I noticed them begin to falter, but I'm no bookbinder and our castle is short a librarian or bookkeeper of any sort. A book on bookbinding will soon be in my future if I plan to preserve the castle's collection from my research efforts.

None of the tomes have been very helpful. Of course, the idea of familiars and witchcraft always makes the presumption that the familiar is a divine guide that takes an animal form in the real world and merely binds itself to the wielder of their choice. Nowhere do the books say that the familiar is actually the wielder himself, let alone one of the Shadow Folk.

Part of me wonders why neither Alaric nor Maverick have familiars, since they possess divine magic. How is it that shadows-incarnate are granted powerful, alternate forms, and we are left bereft of any hope save what we find within ourselves? On the one hand, it's refreshing to know we are truly the pilots of our own fates. On the other hand, I am jealous that none of this will ever apply to me, even if it becomes a reality that Maverick and Alaric could have familiars.

I haven't had a pet in years. My last was a small sparrow I tried saving after it was nearly killed in the stables by an eager barn cat. The wretched feline merely glanced its wing, not bothering to deliver the mercy of a killing blow. Seeing it in pain like that hurt me, and I chose to try and heal it. I was unsuccessful, though it proved to be an important week of learning for me. Sometimes, Death is the better option. Death is a mercy. A kindness. Something my sparrow needed, and a gift I was too selfish to give before the damage took a far worse toll. I still know where the little thing is buried.

"I don't think I was supposed to have stayed... *changed*... that long," Finch says.

His sudden voice jolts me back to the present. I have no idea how long I just stood there musing over strange books and a bird that's long been buried by dirt and time.

Am I intent on getting myself killed? *Pay attention, Adelaide!*

"What do you mean?" My voice is notably hoarse. I don't know when sadness decided to choke me, but here it is. I swallow tears while I wait for Finch to answer. It's hard for me to acknowledge, even just a bit, how afraid I am right now.

"I... I think it was supposed to be an initial change. Again, I don't remember my sire's face, but I remember being warned to take my changes slowly. Waking new magic like this is hard... and I'm still new."

Finch blinks, and I notice for the first time the tears in his eyes. I don't feel as alone, though I hate myself for finding comfort in spotting his momentary breach of strength. Crying doesn't make him weak, but it is a sign that he *feels* weak. I shouldn't revel in that. I hate myself for even trying to find comfort in such a thing.

"Does this imply that you'll grow stronger with time? That you'll be able to shift without such a physical tax?" My mind moves faster than my mouth, and I fear the inevitable reality that I might trip over my words should I continue to speak. My questions hang in the air.

"I think so?" Finch's answer is more of a question to himself than anyone else.

For all my reading, I still have nothing to offer Finch in terms of an answer. All these added questions are driving me to the brink of insanity. I fear I might entirely lose my mind if I entertain anything else.

I hold up my hand. "I think that's enough for now. I'll do some more research, but if you recall anything else, be sure to tell us," I say, my voice stern. I can't let anyone think I'm going soft, let alone for the pursuit of knowledge. A creature of fantasy shouldn't be enough to make me lose my resolve. I'm made of tougher stuff than stories of knights, princesses, and dragons in far-off lands. Given the nature of my research, plenty of those stories landed in my pile of reading.

The bone-deep exhaustion of a week of fitful, erratic sleep paired with these fanciful tales, has made me more delusional than ever. I am in dire need of sleep. Letting my focus slip like this is out of character. If my reflexes are slipping this much...

"I'm fine dropping the subject for now." Maverick's voice jolts me to attention once more.

"I think our dear sister needs some rest," Finch pipes up. "All that worrying over me seems to have driven her mute with terror." He winks at me, clearly jibing, but he's closer to the truth than I care to admit.

Not being able to act—to fight something while he lay, as I saw it, dying—was maddening. "How do we keep you from shifting? If your shift was supposed to be a shorter duration... and you clearly didn't have control, then what can we do to keep you from doing it again? Maverick might be able to keep Doctor Richards quiet, but we can't force the entire castle to remain silent if we're in constant fear of a small red dragon popping up!" I quip, though my voice is harsher than I intend. The lack of sleep has sharpened my bladed tongue, and I'm not ready to put it away yet. I need a plan to keep Finch's recent changes a secret. With the royal ball only two nights away, damage control is a necessity.

"I felt it come on and knew I could pull on the tether, for lack of a better explanation," Finch answers. "I didn't know, of course, that the dragon would be the outcome, but I do hope you'll trust me that I know to leave that feeling alone now. At least until I'm older and have a better grasp of my magic."

At this, Maverick chuffs. "Trust you? My sister might, and for good reason, but you saved *her* life, not mine. If anything, I've saved your skin on several occasions now and have no such burdens. You are still under strict surveillance, and for the upcoming royal ball, you will be confined in the dungeons for security. We won't shackle you; I won't burden you with the physical reminders of your imprisonment. But I won't risk the nobles and aristocrats seeing a dragon on the loose in my castle. And to find that it's one of the Shadow Folk as well? That would be grounds for a coup. If you resist, there will be consequences." The edge in Maverick's voice leaves no room for debate.

"When will my actions be enough for you?" Finch's voice shifts to one of hurt and betrayal.

I can't blame him. I'm still reeling from the insinuation that I'm somehow burdened by my trust for Finch. Maybe he's playing the long game, and maybe the sleep deprivation has lowered my guard, but I can't see why Finch would seek to betray us now when he's revealed all this information and given a wealth of information that could help us against our enemies. We know he's a dragon now. We could slay him where he stands and use his body for research. Instead, we let him live and here he is, helping us. We're all indebted to him just as much as he is to us.

"Maverick, while I agree that locking him up for a night might help increase safety, I don't think calling him our prisoner is fair. He's our guest," I argue.

"A guest who can't leave," Finch retorts. "Maverick is right. I *am* a prisoner."

I want to argue, but it's pointless. I know in my heart they're both right, but I wish it weren't so. Instead, I look down at my fingers and clasp them together, noticing how cold they've become. The draft coming in from Finch's open window has settled into my skin and bones. I shiver.

"Listen, Finch, I don't think I'm burdened by my trust in you, nor do I think Maverick is correct in being so suspicious of you at this point. But I understand why he is. A Shadow Folk murdered our mother. For many years, they have been the bane of our kingdom. However, you helped us, even at great risk to yourself. I can't pretend this is an easy thing to grapple with, but I also can't afford to have us arguing. While I trust you have your familiar form under control, we can't risk the chance of being wrong. Are you okay with the arrangements for the ball? And, say, for the next month, are you okay sticking to this wing with me and Maverick?"

Dejected, Finch lowers his gaze, but he nods. He's struggling to come to grips with everything just as much as we are, but I can't grant him any more space than I already am. It would risk the kingdom's safety, and Alaric's expected antics in two days will be enough for me and Maverick to handle as it is.

"I understand," Finch finally grumbles. "On another note, what have you all been up to in my extended absence?"

The sudden change in subject buffets me and my brother with whiplash. I'm taken aback at his ability to shift his face from one bearing sadness to a picture of mirth and mischief. Perhaps Maverick is right to stay as suspicious as he's been. Maybe I do need to re-heighten my guard some. Still, that's something I can grapple with later.

"Maverick here has been getting his beauty rest along with you," I jest. "Strong-arming the medical ward takes some serious string-pulling. I've been reading a mixture of history, science, and mythology books. I figure the truth about you must be scrambled in there somewhere, but so far, I haven't found anything."

I figure there's no point in hiding what I haven't learned. I can't accidentally share a secret if I don't have one, and it's no secret that magic is a drain on the body. Finch would know that even before he changed.

"Beauty sleep for you, too, Mav? I don't know if it worked," Finch teases.

Maverick rolls his eyes. "You're lucky I don't behead people for making jokes like my father does."

Even though he's joking, I wince. Alaric is known for flying off the handle and dishing out serious punishments over nothing. The executions I've witnessed did little to inspire admiration for my father. I wonder how quickly he might have been deposed had he not been gifted with the Siraltona. His gift keeps the Shadow Folk at bay, but that alone is the sum of his worth as a king.

I hope my worth is stored in more than my blades. And, still, a part of me worries that those blades amount to nothing. I am a liability, not a princess.

"You're a better man than Alaric," Finch says. "You always have been.

My father would never have entertained a marriage to Beatrice if you weren't four times the man that Alaric is."

I notice Maverick's cheeks flush, but he doesn't argue with a statement that might get an ordinary citizen killed for treason. My father doesn't take reports of criticism well. In fact, those have landed quite a few people a place on the gallows.

"Do you need any help in the library?" Maverick offers. "Father hasn't summoned me yet. Speaking of... wait... Have you been fitted for a dress yet? You know your suitors will be arriving soon, right?"

I freeze.

"I... I forgot."

Maverick quirks a brow. "Well then, I suggest you get with Beatrice and rectify that immediately."

If I could punch my brother, I would, but I dare not act out against him when he's only recently back to normal after binding Doctor Richards' tongue with magic. I can still see traces of exhaustion beneath his eyes in the dark shadows that have settled there.

"I'll go see the seamstress myself. No need to stress Beatrice with something like that," I say, though I'm always happy to spend time with my sister-in-law. I wonder how much information Maverick has shared with her. I don't want to inadvertently slip up and tell her too much or betray my trust in Finch and give her false hope.

Without waiting for either of them to answer, I leave the room with newfound rage pooling in my gut as I focus on my impending doom. I'm going to be married off, even though it's a futile effort. Right when we've discovered Sunfall is at its weakest with new threats beyond the wall, I'll be expected to become a damned baby factory.

If I could behead my father, I would. But patricide is not the solution to my problems.

I STARE AT THE WRETCHED GARMENT. THE TRIP TO THE seamstress two days ago was a horrid affair. She made me a deplorable silver thing—another dig at the reality that the sun has not roosted in my veins and I am the aftermath of a queen long dead because of my failures.

Tears brew in my eyes. I wipe at them, furious that I'm to be paraded around the castle this evening like a godforsaken peacock. Sleep still evades me; my eyes are droopy and in need of a serious touch-up from my makeup drawer, but I've little reason to try. Let my suitors see me like this, for all I care. Marriage won't stop the Shadow Folk or their newfound powers from storming our doors and eating us all alive.

I suspect that other powerful creatures are looming just outside Sunfall's borders and an even greater suspicion that they'll seek a night like tonight to make us the victims of our own hubris. A party? A party when there could be more dragons or who knows what else out there? A false reason to celebrate my survival... all so I can be doomed to a coffin for the living. A coffin where *died in childbirth* could very much be the outcome, regardless of how good our healers are.

I have not felt such despair in ages, and I fear it might swallow me whole if I don't find something else on which to focus. In a last-ditch effort, I clench my fists, desperate to call for any magic—it doesn't even have to be Siraltona—so I might break my chains and prove I am worth more than just an opportunity to secure dowry. Then I could at least choose my suitor instead of being married off to some pompous warlock for the weight of his bloodline. And what if I'm not a carrier? What if my child possesses magic that's not useful to us in the first place?

I pace in my room like a sad lion whose last days are doomed to the jeers of a crowd at the circus.

The only saving grace about this silver prison is that it's light enough to slip on without assistance. I couldn't bear the thought of calling in my maidservants to help me cinch it. I would lose my mind having people stand around me and chatter in what would certainly be excitement and envy for my role in such a momentous occasion. As far as I'm concerned, I'm about to attend something worse than my own funeral.

I wring my wrists, hoping to free the anxious nerves that have built up in my body, but it's to no avail. Breath leaves me when I realize I am only an hour or two away from being forced to plaster on my bravest face for the sake of the kingdom and ignore the potential threats lurking beyond our walls.

Sweat beads on my forehead and I scramble to my mirror to find a handkerchief to dab at it. I can't afford to show my nerves so readily or allow my people to see how far I am out of my league.

"I will do my best for them. I will be what my father cannot." It is reckless to even whisper such a thing. My exchanges with my father over the past two days have been tense and borderline suspicious. I hid my books in the library, fearing the worst. I wonder if someone saw my selection and reported back to him, and he's saving his accusations for after the ball.

I try not to dwell on such a thought. I can't. Not yet. Right now, I need to focus.

I powder my face and dab rouge on my lips and cheeks. My dark hair frames me in a way that looks more like a gaunt skeleton with stark red strands. The combination of dark hair and a ruddy complexion has never done much for my appearance. My skin is not the fine porcelain of so many princesses in storybooks that you read about. My skin has a more flushed hue. More often than not, my skin is pale but with a pink flush.

"You've got this, Adelaide," I say to myself, twisting my auburn mane into a more respectable twist. The maidservants never made any headway with me; I never let anyone mess with my hair. Never. It is mine and mine alone.

I slip into my dress and grit my teeth. I don't bother looking at my reflection in the mirror before leaving my bed chamber. I can't get back here soon enough.

To my dismay, Maverick and Beatrice are not out in the hall waiting to escort me. I'd rather gouge out my eyes than walk into this ball alone, but that would undoubtedly cause more chaos than it would alleviate. I grab my skirt and hoist it above my ankles, preparing for a long solo march to the ballroom.

Despite the occasion, it's eerily quiet up here. Finch, safely down in the dungeons, is the lucky one tonight. He's not stuck there forever, but if I'm married off soon, I'll be stuck with a total stranger for the rest of my life. All in the name of a fool's errand...

I suck in a breath and descend the stairs. When the sound of chattering voices picks up in the stairway and echoes along the stone walls, I want to turn and flee. I'm not one for crowds, unless it's approaching them in the din of battle. I'd much rather be swinging a sword than preparing my mind for an evening of mindless small talk.

If my father makes a spectacle of me, it will take all my willpower not to tear him to shreds, treason be damned. Still, forcing Maverick to behead his own sister wouldn't be wise, although he'd have to for political reasons. You can't let someone get away with regicide so easily. There must be consequences.

I remind myself of this as I approach the ballroom, which is somehow far greater than the grand hall. My father, in his excessive style, chose to have separate halls for dining and dancing. Why we can't mix the two, I have no idea, but to my father, it mattered.

I realize I'm muttering under my breath and put that behavior under wraps. The last thing I need is for the kingdom to believe their princess has gone mad.

I spot Maverick and Beatrice at once. My brother wears a sharp blue suit and my sister-in-law is adorned in the finest gold I've ever seen on a dress. I look down at my silver dress and note the obvious symbolism that my father has chosen to play up within our complementing wardrobes. I pale in comparison. When I see Beatrice's long, blonde hair styled in an elegant coiffe, I grab at my own knotted style and wonder if I should have let someone help me after all.

"What nonsense are you thinking now, Adelaide?" I whisper to myself. "Since when do you let jealousy compromise your standards?" I cease the self-talk when I notice my father approaching. His pale gray eyes bore into mine from within the mask of joy he wears.

"Daughter," he says, his voice laden with hidden threats.

I know better than to challenge him right now while he's flanked by nobles and courtesans eager to be with him later tonight. I swallow the venom pooling in my mouth and do my best not to strike out at him. If I was the one with fangs instead of Finch, my father would be in grave danger.

"Your dress turned out lovely! I *do* hope you like the color I've chosen for you. It complements your eyes," he croons, his voice like silk.

Offering a small curtsy, I nod. "Yes, Father, it's a lovely selection. I see Maverick and Beatrice are dressed well for the occasion. You've outdone yourself again with the planning."

I don't mean a word of what I say, but I've discovered I can weave lies better than either my father or brother can on select occasions, this being one of them. My father buys my false olive branch and smiles at me. This time, it's more genuine.

"I do hope you will allow us to toast you and your survival," Alaric continues.

I do my best not to let irritation flicker across my face and fight the urge to swear. "Yes, that would be fine," I lie. "I've been told my suitors are here?" I don't wait to ask the most pressing question on my mind. But to my surprise, my father shakes his head.

"Their parties were delayed due to some unusual weather. As a result, they will be here next week, instead. So, consider this a party dedicated solely to you and your feats!"

My father staggers a bit. It's almost unnoticeable, but I know him well. How he's managed to become tipsy this fast is a mystery to me, and I fear our kingdom might run out of alcohol if he continues on this path of reckless consumption. I haven't the slightest clue how we manage to keep him readily supplied. Then again, I'm not much of a drinker and don't fully understand the process of how it's made.

I manage to feign shock and mask my face with what I hope is gratitude. The last thing I need is to set my father off and give him more reason to shout at me in front of the most influential people in the kingdom.

A young noblesse sidles up beside me, a woman with dark hair and eyes. "Did you really taste the fruit of the gods?" Her voice is almost breathless with awe.

I'm not prepared to be asked about my experience so soon and stumble over my words. "Y-yes. I was poisoned... But the gods... saw fit to save me." My voice breaks, betraying my nerves, and I wish I could hurl myself from a balcony window instead of standing here with all the other peacocks vying for royal attention.

A soft touch to my elbow draws my attention; I am relieved to see that Maverick has come to rescue me. He grips my arm.

"I'd like to introduce my sister to some friends of mine. I hope you don't mind me stealing her, Father," Maverick says with a disarming grin.

Alaric laughs. "Not at all! Go! Enjoy the evening. It's just begun!"

If I could bless my brother with all the luck and love in the world, I would. As he ushers me away, I note for the first time the line of worry that's broken out on his face. "Are you okay?" I whisper it low enough that most passersby won't hear unless they are straining to do so, but my brother catches my words.

He moves his head side to side. "No."

My heart drops. It's at this point I realize that Beatrice is gone and there is an edge of darkness in the ballroom.

I pray I am wrong and all is well.

TREACHERY

MY BROTHER AND I ARE STANDING IN THE DUNGEONS.

His hand is tight on my elbow, but my jaw is on the floor. Where Finch once stood is an empty cell, the door blasted from its hinges.

"He betrayed us," I whisper. My heart breaks. How could I have been so naive to trust him? Why did I ever think one of the Shadow Folk could be anything more than deceitful?

Several of our guards lay dead and I shudder, noticing how pale they are. He drained them all on the way out. There is a vampire on the loose in our castle, and it is on a night when we are most vulnerable, just as I feared. I'd foolishly believed our biggest threats were outside and beyond the castle, not in it. I wish my brother-in-law wasn't the one responsible for this destruction, but there is no other explanation for it.

His magic is still new and harder to trace—at least, that's what I believe as I taste the air for it and come up empty-handed. The scent is mingled with fear, blood, and desperation. Some of those are from Finch himself, while the others are mixed with the last moments of the victims who lay lifeless on the dungeon floor. My brother is our only hope. His magic is more suited to tracing someone who doesn't wield as much or with any sort of predictable flare. I am only useful in tracing the absence or presence of magic, not the degrees to which it changes.

Once again, I curse my failings for not being the person this kingdom needs. I wonder when my father will notice our absence... if at all. I hope, for once, that the ale is strong enough to keep him drunk and distracted long enough for me and Maverick to handle this ourselves. The nobles are already wary that we're keeping a Shadow Folk captive for study. If they find that Finch has broken out, we're doomed.

"Which direction do you want me to look?" I whisper. "If you tell me what directions you're tracing, I can go one way and you the other."

His capacity for speech swallowed by terror and rage, Maverick points in the direction he wants me to go. His knuckles are so white I fear they might break through the skin.

I nod and turn to walk deeper into the dungeon. I'm lost in my thoughts while I seek him out, doing what little I can to trace the magic still hovering in Finch's wake. Embarrassingly enough, I don't know how far back our dungeons go, nor if we have any other prisoners who have long been laid to waste by starvation and dehydration. It's been a long time since I heard of any prisoners being taken, and I don't make a habit of visiting this part of the castle.

Why let an enemy live? Tonight is a prime example of why my method is better. Death ensures the safety and silence of everyone involved in a squabble. The opponent, once gone, is truly gone.

Unless they're Shadow Folk, of course...

I pause a moment to take a breath. The panic coursing through my chest robs me of air, and I worry that I'll slump to the floor somewhere, unconscious due to my own stupidity. I can't give my brother or father any more reasons to think I'm weak or stupid.

Over the sound of my thudding heart, I freeze. Deep in the back of the dungeon, I hear weeping. It's soft, but the voice is familiar. *Finch.*

"Maverick?" I call, no longer caring if Finch finds me first. My brother can finish whatever job I start if he attacks me. "He's this way." I wait, my hands bereft of a weapon, and curse my stupidity for leaving my sword in my bed chamber. I only hope I can hold Finch off long enough if he reaches me before Maverick does so my brother can land a killing blow.

To my relief, Maverick reaches me first. As a matter of fact, I don't hear any footsteps that would indicate Finch has moved at all.

"Is he... *weeping?*"

Maverick's voice is clipped with an emotion I can't quite place.

Regret? Fear? Is it still rage? His features have softened so I don't think it's the last option, though I've been wrong before. My brother is an excellent liar with his face.

"I think so," I whisper. "Finch?" I call out his name, hoping he'll respond. To my dismay, I receive nothing. Maverick and I exchange a wary glance and head toward the direction of that awful noise.

We round the corner and are greeted by a gruesome scene. Finch is sprawled out on the dungeon floor with blood pooling around his body.

"I tried to fend them off," he says, his voice hoarse. "I feel my body stitching itself back together." This last statement makes my blood freeze.

"Fight off *whom*?" Maverick demands. "Are you to tell us those guards back there weren't slain by you?"

The edge that's taken roost in Maverick's voice makes me think twice about standing so close to him. I notice the crackle of light in his hands and step back, preparing for the worst of his outbursts. "Maverick, let him talk. If I was wrong, fine, but let's at least hear what he has to say."

The light dims in his hands and my brother takes a breath. I am always amazed at how fast he can center himself. With how volatile I become in battle, it's probably a blessing I don't have power like him. I might've blown up the kingdom a decade ago when I was in the peak years of puberty. Then again, I will never know how I would have handled such power.

I don't dwell on this anymore.

"Finch, who was here?" I do my best to sound comforting and not accusatory.

"A Shadow Folk. I don't know his name, and he wasn't my sire," he gasps.

I watch in rapt fascination as his body repairs the gaping wounds in his flesh and marvel at how it manages to patch new skin as though it was never missing. "That's amazing!" I whisper.

"Focus, Adelaide!" Maverick snaps. "Don't let his parlor trick get in the way of getting to the bottom of this. Do you mean to tell me there's another Shadow Folk loose here in this castle? *Liar.*"

"How do you know that?" I snap, turning to Maverick. "Even if he is lying, we need to act on the information. Too many people are milling around in this castle to risk being wrong. If he's lying, you and I will deal with him if he tries to make a break for it or harm us."

Maverick's nostrils flare, but he nods. He knows I'm right. Cupping his hands, he lets light pool into them to take the shape of a messenger pigeon. He whispers to it, then sets it off in flight to warn the guards to lock down the castle. I pray the message reaches them in time.

I turn to our brother-in-law. "Finch, did you get a good look at the Shadow Folk? We need to give the guards a description."

"No." Maverick holds out his hand. "Don't let him lead us astray with a false image. The magic will be enough to find the Shadow Folk. He can tell us what he remembers, but I won't have our soldiers waste their time looking for the wrong face."

I'm reminded all over again why Maverick is the better ruler. He's always two steps ahead and able to maintain his calm. As much of a planner as I can be, I can never stay this neutral in the face of my own terror. I must act faster lest I lose my footing. But I also don't have magic to buy me that sort of time.

"Dark hair. Dark eyes. That's all I remember." Finch's voice is more even now. He groans and sits up straight as though he wasn't nearly torn apart moments earlier.

I brace myself, waiting for him to lunge at us.

"How did he get in here? How did he break free? And why was he in your cell, Finch?" Maverick's voice is laden with mistrust, and I don't blame him. For once, I share his sentiment and only wish I had been more cautious.

Every part of me wants Finch to be telling the truth, but the evidence and bodies are damning. Without proof of another Shadow Folk, we're left only with his word and the murdered guards in the dungeons. It doesn't look good for my brother-in-law, and I can't afford to give him any more leeway with the blood staining our floors.

I turn my imploring eyes to the wretched figure in front of me. "Finch, this is important. We can't believe what you say unless you tell us what happened. We need evidence. Answers."

"What does it matter?" Finch shouts. "He was here for intelligence and to deal us a blow, and he's long gone now! I saw a crow flee the dungeons; it was probably him. He distracted the guards when they opened the gate to bring me my dinner," Finch hisses.

I pity him... almost.

"Why would a Shadow Folk break in, bust you out, and then promptly leave? What sort of intelligence was he after?" I'm the one asking questions now. I can't believe he thinks I would dance to a song and tune as broken as this. If a Shadow Folk broke in, we would have been alerted immediately.

"How do you expect us to believe he got past the guards?" Maverick demands. "How do you expect me to believe he wouldn't have immediately gone to murder me or my father? And if he came to *you* first, what does that say about your importance to them?"

Finch's cheeks heat with anger. "Because I'm one of them! I can't help that. He thought he was doing me a favor. You stupid bastard, of *course* he didn't go to kill you or your father! He wasn't strong enough. He was just a spy sent here to see how easy it would be to sneak in under disguise. Do you really expect a guard to stop a raven or a crow, or did you forget that we can shift forms now?"

Maverick pales, and I stop breathing. His explanation seems more plausible now. But what was this spy looking for? Why would a spy come tonight, of all nights, and *not* try to murder the royal family? Didn't Finch say he was here to "deal us a blow"?

"Adelaide, everyone upstairs is drinking, yes?"

Finch's gaze burns into my soul and my heart stops. I blink, realizing that my father has been toasting everyone upstairs.

"Are you saying they're waiting until we're distracted?" Maverick asks, his mind not yet connecting the dots.

"No. I'm saying they've already breached us and made us weak. They got past the guards and came in. Who checked your drinks tonight, Maverick? Your food? A party where so many nobles and guards are gathered in one place, and a new power has been awakened? Why didn't you tell your father about familiars?"

Maverick buries his head in his hands, his breath coming in short, panicked bursts. "I... I didn't realize... I didn't realize all of you could change."

At this, I realize all of this is my fault. Maybe if I'd told my father my suspicions, I could have saved us. Didn't Finch tell us this in the infirmary a week ago? Didn't he warn us that they could change forms now? Why didn't we warn the guards?

"We didn't tell him to protect you. To protect the kingdom from realizing that Shadow Folk can become monsters," I say, my voice choking. "And there's no hope, Finch. If Shadow Folk can change forms... Maverick and Alaric aren't enough to hold them at bay."

"I can try." Maverick grits his teeth. "Leave if you want, Finch; I don't care. If I find that you've lied, though..."

Above us, we hear a scream. Without waiting around to ask Finch more questions, Maverick and I sprint from the room. On the way out, I grab a guard's sword, and Maverick wordlessly and seamlessly imbues it with light. A battle is quickly coming our way. When we arrive upstairs, the sight of Beatrice screaming amidst a sea of unconscious nobles and, more importantly, my father confirms this in my mind. I lick my lips, prepared to taste blood all too soon.

The Shadow Folk are coming. And only Maverick can do anything to stop them.

Day

POWERS UNTOLD

The Present

BLINDING LIGHT SEARS MY VISION.

I don't remember where I am or how I got here. I only know that my body is on fire. My feet are distanced apart, my fists clenched and ready for a fight that doesn't come.

My memory floods through me, a torrential hailstorm of terror. I remember me and Maverick realizing how we'd been set up—how the kingdom was drugged and left open for attack by the Shadow Folk and the surge of their newfound powers. I remember hearing the cry of the great black dragon and running from the castle, ready to meet our fate out on the battlefield.

I remember hoping that Maverick would stay behind and flee. I remember arguing with him to try and convince him to stay within the walls and take the fight another day. I wanted Maverick and Beatrice to survive in some other place and buy them time to learn the Shadow Folks' weaknesses.

Mars, their vicious king, is every bit the horrid nightmare I imagined. I blink, the vision of his enormous, draconic form beating against the air with massive wings. I guess I know now how big Finch could get, if given the chance.

What I don't yet understand, though, is how I'm standing. In my last moment of awareness, my mind was a sea of terror at the realization that the kingdom of Sunfall was doomed. We barely had time to absorb that these beasts were more of a threat than their shadowy, familiar forms. So what changed?

I glance down at my hands, confusion ringing in my ears, and tears stream down my face as I realize what happened. A part of me assumed Maverick was consumed by his rage and the Siraltona swallowed him whole.

Instead, the Divine Light of Siralto has come to rest in my hands. And, most importantly, it is still here. I'm crying. My mouth is open in silent sobs and I sink to my knees as the magic courses through my body. It's as though it's always been there, just waiting beneath the surface. I pinch my arm, the searing light blinding between my fingers as I do so, but I do not wake in a cold sweat in my bed chamber.

Above, the shadowy form of Mars and his soldiers are on the retreat, his great wings seared by the light I shot from my body like a bomb when they drew too close—the instant all my hope drained away.

I look over to see Maverick staring at me, his jaw agape.

My body threatens to fall apart in a fit of convulsions, so strong is the power pouring through me. I suck in a startled breath, desperate to hold onto a thin thread of control as I watch the enemy retreat.

What a sight it is, too.

Behind me, I hear footsteps. A hand rests on my shoulder and I turn to see Finch grinning at me like a wild animal. His wounds from earlier are all but gone, with only a few scrapes visible through the tatters of his shirt.

"So you *do* have light!" Finch smirks. "I always knew you were going to find some way to justify that big head of yours."

It's a stupid, juvenile thing, but Finch's joke sets me off with a peal of vibrant laughter. I can't contain my joy.

The Shadow Folk are retreating, and *I'm* the one who took them down. I'm the one who saved our kingdom. Upstairs in the castle, I spot a few nobles who have been sluggishly roused from their slumber staring at me from high above. Though I may be a speck to them, somehow, I know they realize who they're looking at.

This princess can save her people.

I look down again at my hands and more tears fall. Maverick walks over and grabs my shoulders, the light from his hands intertwining with mine.

I notice that his is a lighter shade than mine. While his light is eerie and almost white, mine has a golden hue. I wonder if my light resembles my father's, but I hold out hope that maybe, just maybe, I'm still different enough from him.

"How have you done this?" Maverick whispers.

I stare back at the sky, noting the agitated flick of Mars' tail before he becomes completely obscured from my view, his form lost to the shadowy mountains where the rest of his horde resides.

"Maverick... I... I don't..." I stammer, unsure how to give my brother a proper answer. I hope with all my soul that he doesn't see this as some sort of power move or wonder if I've been holding out to outshine him. Even with this power, I still have no desire to take his place or rule. If anything, the greedy thought of fleeing the kingdom coaxes my mind to consider much more dangerous notions of desertion.

"The Lasira," Finch says. "The gods gave you a fruit. We thought it was to heal you from something, but we didn't know what. Maybe by being near where I was created... maybe it triggered something in you, and the gods knew you would have to be healed to find your power. Or maybe you were cursed at birth, and that curse was undone," Finch rambles on, his eyes alight with the thousands of possibilities tumbling within his mind.

"I believe you're right," Maverick says, his voice still soft.

He looks at me and I crumble, worried he'll have something harsh to say.

Our hands come undone, but my light still does not recede. If anything, it burns brighter with each passing moment, amplifying my nerves.

A shout sounds over the field. I look up and my heart drops. Alaric is rushing towards us, his face stricken with terror.

"Unhand your sister!" Alaric crashes between me and Maverick and shoves Finch to the ground. He whirls on Maverick. "What sort of light trick was that, son? And why turn it on your sister? She was here to help fight, and you come out here and risk your neck for a light show?"

My jaw drops. Is... is my father worried about me? Didn't he see the Shadow Folk fleeing just moments before?

My father's face is creased in fury. "*You* have a kingdom to rule. Your sister can fight; you cannot. You should have given her weapons, not come out here and risked both your lives!" Alaric hisses.

Any thoughts that he might care about my well-being dissipate in a blink. He would rather I went alone on my suicide mission and left Maverick safely inside the castle walls. The Siraltona curled around my palms like a serpent, hissing and crackling, ready to strike at my father.

His back goes rigid and he peers over his shoulder at me, only now noticing that the light he thought Maverick brought to battle came from *me*.

Sweat beads on my forehead. I consider running to fetch my horse. How fast could they catch up, anyway? What risk would there be, now that I am the new nightmare for Shadow Folk to tell their children? I am capable of undoing them all, should I choose. The power whispering through my veins assures me of this.

What's to stop me from cutting my father down where he stands? But I look over at Maverick and am reminded that, once again, this is bigger than me. I am now essential to Sunfall's survival. I also realize that it would not just be my brother coming after me should I take my leave. The whole kingdom would be after me. And that could cause turmoil for the allegiance they place in not only my father, but my brother.

So I plant my feet into the dirt with firm confidence and face my father, but only for the sake of my brother. Only so he can someday have the hope of making this wretched kingdom into something better.

"How long have you known?"

My father's icy tone fails to make me shudder as it once did. The warmth of the Siraltona overwhelms me, lending me strength to hold my chin up and face him. His steely eyes stare like daggers into mine, but I don't waver.

"I didn't know, Father. Finch was just wondering if the Lasira freed me. Perhaps I was cursed this whole time, and the gods decided to set me free."

"What would a Shadow Folk know of the gods' mercies?" Alaric spits. He takes a step toward me.

I don't back away. Instead, I clench my fists.

"I suggest you be careful, Father," Maverick interjects. "Her powers are still new and volatile. One wrong move and we could all be turned to ash."

There is real fear in my brother's voice. I slacken the grip on my power and focus on reeling the light back in, tucking it within my core. To my surprise, it disappears, though I know it still shows itself in other ways. My vision is hazy as the Siralto jolts beneath the surface. I'm alarmed at how easy it would be to allow myself to become a vessel for the light rather than its wielder. Does the magic own me, or do I own the magic? I fear the answer might not be as simple as I always thought it was when I observed Alaric and Maverick using it.

Now I understand their hesitance to use it all the time.

My father's eyes narrow. "Can I trust that you are still an ally to this kingdom, or are you going to cavort about with the shell of your step-brother rather than defend the good people of Sunfall?" Alaric throws his arms wide and I bristle.

"Since when have I *ever* deserted this kingdom?" Inwardly, I wince. I know more than anyone that, given the chance, I would choose *me*—I would choose freedom. But I can't choose me. I've never been able to, nor will I ever be.

"Then will you abide by our laws and customs and use your powers for us? Will you cease to conceal it from us?"

"I did not conceal it, Father! It was suppressed—"

"I'll *not* have you telling the lies of vampires!" he rages. "I care not for the omissions of the past, should you choose to use it for the good of the people moving forward."

If he slapped me, it would sting less. I want to hurl and spew insults at my father. I want to make him feel small and worthless, as he so often likes to do with me and his other subjects. But this tyrant will not live forever, as none ever do. Maybe, if I make myself small, I can lie in wait when he finally falls victim and returns to Tyrladan as we all do in the end. Maybe I can turn this kingdom into something that thrives—something not oppressed by an incompetent asshole.

I grimace and force the emotion from my voice. "Yes, Father. I will use it for our kingdom." I look at my brother, refusing to give my father the satisfaction of watching my face. While a new light courses within me, an older one dies. No magic can save me from this. I'm stuck here.

I'm stuck on behalf of my brother, my father, and a kingdom that would sell me for scraps if it meant their survival. And who could blame them?

I turn to find a sea of people staring at me from within the walls of the kingdom. Some have removed their hats in a show of respect. Others tremble in my presence. A few people squint at me with suspicion while others grip pitchforks and spears, ready to tear me limb from limb if I come after them and their children.

The light crackles to life in my hand and exclamations of awe and terror ripple through the crowd. They gaze at me the same way they often look at my father and brother. A horrid realization begins to settle in my bones; I fear I might become sick.

Ascending to the status of a legend comes at the cost of never being normal again. *Is this why my brother hides in the palace and plays politics with the nobles?*

I hate how everything is beginning to make sense. Our kingdom follows us out of fear. They worship us for our power, not for our kindness or benevolence. We don't have to rule competently if we have the power of literal gods to back us up. My father could drink every hour of every day for the rest of his life, so long as he continues to hold his power.

And I hate myself for it. All the magic in the world can't save me from the crushing realization that magic is a curse. It is an iron sword used to trod upon the weak and eviscerate their hopes and dreams.

For once, I wish to sheath my blade and die at the hands of my enemy. I wish to the gods Mars had torn me limb from limb rather than leaving me to be no better than he is—a monster.

Elements of Matching

I stare out my window at the melting snow, numbly letting the wind whip my face. The biting cold is better than the reality waiting downstairs. I wish to Siralto the snow would come back and the chill would grow colder still so the roads could be blocked off.

I don't want to meet my suitors today.

In the hazed frenzy since my powers were discovered, my father doubled down on getting me betrothed, with strict expectations of producing an heir within the next two years. I half expected him to remove Maverick from the line of succession altogether, but he won't make such a bold move until he knows for sure I'm not as barren as my brother. Reports of his and Beatrice's continued failures have pushed the nobles into a frenzy; they constantly inquire after me.

For once, I'm not invisible. I wish like never before that I could return to the front and find my swift end at the clutches of some vampire daring enough to get close. I wouldn't strike them down now. I'm half tempted to ask Finch to join me in a pact, but it wouldn't be fair to place that sort of pressure on him. He's got enough on his plate.

He's been ordered to give several vials of blood to Doctor Richards and participate in his *studies*. Now that the news of familiars is common knowledge, the nobles are equally concerned that even my newfound powers won't be enough to keep the Shadow Folk at bay.

For once, I'm rooting for the enemy. Any pretense I had about caring for my kingdom was drained of me once I realized magic only makes me slightly more valuable. I'm chattel to be sold for a higher price, now. If Finch, Maverick, and I weren't already conspiring to get Finch out and help Maverick depose our father and ascend to the throne, I would have razed this place to the ground and fled.

I curse myself for being too caring. My skin, now raw, is red with the cold. I fear what my ladies-in-waiting might say when they come to doll me up for today's presentation. Several dresses even gaudier than the silver number I wore at the ball have been laid out as some sort of sick imitation of a choice.

My eyes glaze over as I look at them again. I can't decide what color I want to torture myself with today, and I can't be bothered to fret over it much. Sure enough, servants come rushing through and select a deep violet color that clashes with my dark auburn curls and makes me look paler than usual.

Today, three suitors have arrived and I've been instructed to host them. Never in my life have I ever hosted anyone in such a formal manner. I've hosted my fellow soldiers in dinners over fires as we marched on campaigns, but I don't think those rules will apply here. Today's suitors include Idris of Velyasa, the kingdom named for an instrument of the gods; Alexander of Underland, where Finch and Beatrice are from; and Ivan from Nayeh, the land of death in-between.

Riveting choices, I think to myself. *I wonder what they would say if I cut my hair off and ruined my face...*

Before I can devise any more sabotage, my ladies-in-waiting sweep me into my dress and pull the corseted bodice tight. They style my hair in soft waves and do miracles on my face to hide the tear stains and frost-bitten cheeks.

I wish, for once, they were not so good at their jobs.

Maverick peeks in through the door. "Are you ready?"

I'd normally scold him for checking on me, but the open door doesn't signal much in terms of privacy, and my brother is worried about me. He and Finch have steadily remained in my corner at much risk to themselves, but they can't do too much without alerting my father to a suspicion of patricide. If I wasn't being followed everywhere, I would be in the library with them both, planning Alaric's execution and Maverick's rise to the throne. The future of Sunfall be damned. It's time my brother became king, in my opinion.

But the tired lines beneath Maverick's eyes paint a different story. He needs a break from the spotlight—time to recharge and carefully plan his ascension. Unfortunately, I'm the sacrifice required to buy him that time.

"I guess," I finally answer with a shrug. I don't pretend with my brother. My tired smile isn't enough to garner my father's suspicion, but I don't want to wear it until necessary. I don't want there to be lies between my brother and me.

"I'm sorry, Adelaide." Maverick's voice breaks on my name.

I wave off my servants and wait until they leave before enveloping him in a hug. "It's not your fault, Maverick. This is bigger than both of us. The Shadow Folk forced our hand," I say, echoing my father more than I would like. I don't dare tell my brother how much I've been praying to the gods that Mars would swoop in and kill us all. " Let's just get this over with."

He nods, though it's stiff, and he can't meet my eyes. I know his brim with tears, so I don't pressure him. My brother is no soldier, but he keeps up a pretense of strength like I do. That's a universal truth for anyone who fights battles like we do. I've become so used to wearing masks in the fray that I don't know how to take them back off again.

I take my brother's hand and together, we make our way to the lion's den.

I SIT UPON THE DAIS FOR HOURS AS GIFTS ARE PLACED AT MY feet. My suitors sent their betrothal parties ahead of them. I've met nobles, princes, and kings, all desperate to support me now that they know Sunfall has another weapon capable of mass devastation.

I am a power play and nothing more. My marriage will not be suited for love, and I don't delude myself into thinking such treacherous things. Why would I? My value is in my deadly weapon—the Siraltona I once prayed for has set me up for a lifetime of servitude and misery.

"All rise," Alaric imperiously says.

It takes me a few moments to register, let alone follow his command. His words anger me, but I pay them no mind. He's lucky I'm cooperating at all. As soon as the tides shift, I'll put his head on a stake.

"Introducing Ivan from Yehna!" Alaric's voice booms, clear of the slurring it usually carries by this time of day.

It seems I'm not the only one keeping up appearances.

My eyes fall on a slight figure. Ivan is pale and thin, with dark hair and flashing eyes that pierce through your soul if you stare long enough. With him come cracks of ice in the floor. At once, the secret of his powers is no longer kept.

Perhaps I'd be happy to be swept away in the personification of winter itself. His lips are tilted in a perpetual slight frown, but he is not unpleasant to look at. Still, something unsettling about him gives me pause.

As Ivan approaches the dais, I swallow a violent urge to yawn. This blasted dress sits tightly against my frame and robs me of air, making the world much more sluggish. I fear the day I ever have to battle garbed in a monstrosity such as this.

Ivan ascends the stairs, and after a terse glare from my father, I stand to greet him. His dark eyes simmer, a contrast with the coldness he carries with him, and he places a chaste kiss on the back of my hand.

Despite his sultry glances and handsome features, I can't say I'm drawn to him. Something about him seems... *off*, but I can't let this suspicion break through my mask of polite indifference. I incline my head as a sign of respect, and he stalks away swiftly, like the winter winds that carried him in here.

"Yet another suitor is present!" my father announces.

The crowd is so still I can hear my heart ringing in my ears. It begs to be freed. I wish more than ever that I'd declared myself an enemy or deserter of the state and departed as soon as my powers were discovered. I could have used that frenzy to escape my crushing reality and leave this place with little more than a whisper to Maverick. He could have devised some story, lying to the kingdom that the shadows had devoured me.

Speaking of shadows, I swear the next man who enters must consort with them personally, yet it's fire that he conjures with a mere snap of his fingers. His eyes match the flames he bends with his hands, and I swear he wrenches the very breath from my lungs the moment I let my eyes lock onto his.

I feel a bolt of electricity as the Siraltona comes alive in my veins, and my skin starts to emit a soft glow. If I don't get my emotions under control, the evening sun will set itself alight in my soul right here in the throne room. Maverick gives me an odd look and motions at me, undoubtedly catching my drop of composure. I force myself to swallow a deep breath, fearing the embers casting from this man's aura might lodge themselves in my windpipe if I take in too much air.

"Everyone, it is my greatest pleasure to introduce Idris, who dwells in the kingdom of Velyasa, beyond the realm of the Shadow Folk," Alaric proudly announces.

At this, several gasps are heard throughout the throne room. I notice a few young ladies fanning themselves as Idris passes them, and an unfamiliar sentiment—jealousy—implores me to impale them on the spot.

What has come over me?

Still, my gaze returns to Idris as he ascends the steps.

Alaric continues to boast. "It should be noted that Idris is a king in his own right. Should he claim my daughter, she would be both a princess *and* a queen. Hopefully, our kingdoms could one day be united. Good luck to you, son. My daughter is more to handle than any fire you have ever wielded."

At this, Idris smirks and I falter. I feel a jolt somewhere deep. His teeth are impossibly white and sharp. If I hadn't been assured of his status as a human king, I'd think him an incubus—one of the worst Shadow Folk there are.

Just thinking about it returns the shivers that Ivan's ice brought moments ago.

When Idris leans in to kiss my hand, I fight my desire to tackle him to the ground where he stands.

How dare this man enjoy the effect he has on me! I look up to find that his smirk has grown brighter, and I have no doubt he's aware what he's doing.

His delicate kiss on my hand disappears with little satisfaction. He steps away, bows, and leaves the dais before I can even greet him.

At this point, my mind is a blur. I barely pay attention to Alexander, the ruling noble from Underland. He seems kind, though meek. His soft blond curls are stunning, but I'm hardly interested. I find myself casting covert glances at Idris, who is fully aware and basks in my attention. I hate myself for being so fickle and yet, I'm excited for more chances to see him later. I want to get to know him.

Ivan's piercing, wintry glare lands on me more than once, and I'm overcome with the feeling that he'd rather have my head on a stake than my hand in marriage. Maverick catches on to these odd exchanges and glares at him. A subtle look from my brother tells me I'm not the only one suspicious of the Ice Prince.

I fear that man. I reach for my hip and find it empty of its sword. I swear to myself never to let that happen again, no matter what frilly ensemble I'm forced to wear.

When introductions are complete, my father announces that a dance will be held tomorrow evening and dismisses all who are gathered. I don't have to be told twice before fleeing the room, desperate to find sanctuary in my chambers.

As soon as I enter the room, I shed my gown and change into something more understated. More importantly, I reunite with my blade. Siraltona or no, it is a focal point for me to control my rage. A charged blade would prove effective against any foe, and I don't want to face anyone—prince *or* vampire—without one.

Satisfied now that I am armed, I leave my room to hide in the library, despite the late hour.

I stifle another yawn as I shuffle into what's become a second home within my home these past few weeks. From reading up on Shadow Folk and now to reading up on Lasira and Siraltona, I've spent countless hours ensconced within these walls. Peering down the hallway to ensure the coast is clear, I collect a few of the tomes I've been working through for the past week as I awaited the task of meeting suitors. I try not to think too much about how this might be the last time I can read books from this library before I'm sent away.

How will I help my brother ascend to the throne if I'm miles away, wed to a strange man in a distant castle?

It is lonely sifting through these books without Finch or Maverick here to distract me, but I don't dare try to get past Doctor Richards to see Finch at such a late hour. Rumors would fly, and a premarital affair is hardly a great way to keep my father from naming me a traitor and putting my head on a silver platter.

A strangeness starts to prick at my shoulders, and I look up just in time to find Ivan standing in the doorway to the library, his dark hair gleaming from the candles I set about the room. His countenance is that of a bored man. Despite my earlier feelings, I let my hand fall to my sword and grip it, taking comfort in its cool touch as I address my suitor.

"Ivan, it's rather late! Are you finding the castle's amenities to your liking?" I fake coyness in my tone, but the way his gaze rests on mine tells me he is peeling right past my falsities to see what lies beneath. A little girl. A scared one, at that. One who knows all too well the consequences of being alone with a man she doesn't trust.

"What do you want with me, *witch*?" Ivan sneers. "Your little party tricks earlier with the lights—they're stunning, but they lack control. You're hiding something."

I'm taken aback by his accusation. Usually, when someone accuses me of hiding something, I truly have something to hide. But in this case?

"I'm not sure what you mean." I do my best to keep my smile plastered to my face. Still, a sickness stirs in my gut and light crackles to life in my veins.

"There it is," Ivan purrs. "The little light show. Your emotions seem to draw it from you with ease. Have I frightened you, flower?"

I grit my teeth so hard, I fear I might break them, but I don't give him the satisfaction of an answer. "I'm not sure what you're on about, but I'm no witch and the magic I have is new to me, just as my father likely told you all."

At this, Ivan blinks. "He... did not. He implied it was something you'd had all along."

This last utterance leaves him more like an afterthought. I can see I've become more than a silhouette to him now. For the first time since this morning, he smiles.

"You'll do quite well, then." Ivan grins. "I hope you'll dance with me tomorrow."

Before I can ask any more questions, he exits the room. I realize I'm shivering and I don't have a wrap to shrug about my shoulders. Trying my best to ignore the discomfort, I look back down at my book but find the words blurred by my tears. If I don't swallow my sobs now, they'll echo through the hall and he'll know he broke me.

This time, I don't notice the other person in the room until they place their fur coat around my shoulders and pull me against them.

I jolt and see Idris sitting with me at the table, his arm clasped around my shoulder and his copper hair even redder in the low light from the candles. His flaming eyes sweep over my face with concern, and I hiss as I realize I'm still crying.

"Did he harm you, my fire?"

I blink at him. *Did he just call me his fire?* "No," I manage to say, my voice shaky. "He was just... strange," I confess.

I look down at my book but his hand cups my chin, forcing me to look back up at him. Whatever thoughts I had prior to this go sailing out the window and I want to get lost in him. I want him to take me from this room and sweep me away to his kingdom right now. The pull he has on me is more than magnetic—it's wretched. Evil. And yet, I love it.

"You promise me?" His voice is low, like summer thunder where the heat alone summons it. Soft, yet powerful.

"Yes," I manage to whisper, my breath quick. I wonder when I'll fall down the tunnels of fire in his eyes to be burned alive within his soul. *Maybe I could be safe there.*

I want to pinch myself. We stare at each other and remain silent for several long minutes. Whatever pull he has on me, I seem to have the equal effect on him.

"Who are you to vex me like this?" he asks, betraying his unsureness of the chemistry we seem to have.

"I could ask the same of you," I whisper.

Damn this man. I don't understand what's happening, yet I feel safe. Where Ivan brings feelings of treachery and death, Idris conveys warmth and trust. I know better than to spill my deepest secrets to him, but even as he presses his forehead to mine, the quiet sounds of our breaths lull me into a sense of security.

"What is my fire indulging her mind with this evening?" His voice is even softer, but his eyes manage to pry themselves from mine to focus on the book still sitting in my hands on the table.

"I've been trying to read up on the Siraltona. I... received my powers late," I confess, a blush staining my cheeks.

Idris chuckles. "Is that so? Your father hinted at some things that made me suspect as such, but the strength of your light... I can hardly imagine a child wielding anything like what you have."

It's comforting to hear, and I could almost kiss him for it—almost. But that would be unbecoming and, yet again, would only bring more scandal. I want this man to enjoy the chase as much as I will.

In my heart, I know I won't give even the slightest of my affections to Alexander or Ivan. They might as well leave now, but to turn them away so soon would seem suspicious and invoke wrath between two kingdoms with whom we can't afford to go to war.

Well... technically we could, if it wasn't for the Shadow Folk on the rise. I wonder what Velyasa is like. Do they fear fanged beasts at their door? Do they live their lives in fear as we do?

He must sense my distress; Idris tenderly runs his hand through my hair. His touch is reverent, as though I might shatter like fine porcelain.

"What troubles you? Why do you hide here and read at such a late hour?"

I sigh, knowing that, for whatever reason, my mask is a farce when it comes to him. I want to hate him for it, but I can't. I'm inexplicably drawn to him even more.

"I feel... trapped. I've been kept here all my life to be used as an asset in war. Now I have power I don't understand, and I'm hardly trained to be a proper princess. I know nothing of court etiquette beyond the basics, and I've not been allowed to practice politicking with the nobles. My father wants an heir within two years, and I can't begin to fathom being a mother. I fear admitting these things to you will make me less valuable, but I can't be dishonest. They're... part of who I am and how I think. I'm not a good royal. There are days I can't even stand to be in the same room as my father." The words leave me before I can stop them and I half expect Idris to pull away. Instead, he shocks me and scoops me into his lap.

I can't believe I'm letting him handle me as little more than an expensive courtesan—my father would lose his mind if he saw us! But for some reason, the act doesn't feel sexual. Instead, Idris tucks my head underneath his chin and sighs.

"I hardly believe that of you, Adelaide. You may be behind in some respects, but you have a level head on your shoulders. I've read a lot about you. You've served alongside your soldiers and witnessed the horrors of battle with them. You fought and bled with them as a mortal would, yet you are still kind and look out for your kingdom. So what if you need to learn politicking? That can be learned. What can't be learned is heart, which you have. Even now, as I watch you, you are learning so you can be better. You acknowledge your faults. That's more than most can say. And forget your father's wishes. Your future husband's wishes will matter more. You and he should make decisions regarding heirs and the structure of rule, not your father. And you should not settle for any one of us who would treat you as a footstool and not a partner."

I'm glad Idris cannot see my face, because I'm certain I am several shades of deep red. More crimson than even Finch's dragon scales.

"Thank you," I whisper. "I'm not sure the others would agree, but I can't say I am as interested in them."

There I go, confessing terrible things aloud. I've just met Idris and already know I'm right about what I say. Maybe it's because he offers the least pressure in the most high-stakes choice of my life, but I believe him. I believe his words. I believe he cherishes me. I only wish I knew more about him.

"I can't say I'm displeased with that," Idris purrs. He leans back to look at me and I shyly hide myself in his chest, the soft fabric of his silk shirt sheltering me from his scorching gaze. "Don't hide from me, Adelaide," he commands, though his voice is not harsh. It's imploring and carries with it a hint of worry.

I look up at him and smile. "Will you stay and tell me about Velyasa? Though... it's late. Perhaps it would be better to tell me tomorrow."

Idris chuckles. "I think saving that conversation for another time would be appropriate. Perhaps over breakfast? While I appreciate your concern over *my* rest, I can't help but worry over yours. What say you put the book down and allow me to escort you to your chambers?"

At this suggestion, heat rises in my cheeks again.

He intuits my embarrassment and offers a devastating smile. "I don't mean it suggestively; I just don't trust the icicle prick who had you out of sorts when I walked in here. Trust me when I tell you that anything between you and me will only happen with your insistence. I'm not too sure of *that* man, though."

Idris' face darkens at this last comment and I shudder, praying I will never be the recipient of such a murderous gaze. It takes me a moment longer to register the first part of his sentence. By the time I realize its implications, I've already stood to put my books away and have his hand in mine.

As we stroll through the corridor leading to my chambers, my silent prayers to Siralto are answered when no guards or nobles lie in wait along the way. We reach my door, and I hesitate to let him leave me. Only a chaste kiss on my cheek and a promise that he will retrieve me for breakfast appease my aching heart.

"You'll call for me if there's trouble, won't you?" His last request is spoken with his back to me, as though he almost forgot to voice it before departing for the night.

I tilt my head to the side. "How will I let you know?"

Idris turns to face me, that wicked smile of his firmly in place. He cups his hands together; in his palms rests a small firebird—a phoenix brought to life without a word leaving his lips.

"Sira shall follow you. If she senses distress, she will return to me at once."

The bird flutters from his hands and lands on my nose. Idris chuckles when I smile in delight and raise my hands to retrieve her. I expect to be burned, finding she is warm but not impossible to hold. A small chirp tells me she's happy, and I simmer with something like pride.

"How did you do that?" I whisper.

"I'll show you in the morning. Now, my fire, you need rest. Don't let me find you up and about again unless it's for an emergency... or you're that lonely without me." Idris winks and strides away, leaving me a stammering mess in the hallway.

What just happened?

I can hardly think as I carry Sira into my chambers, waiting as she finds a perch upon my windowsill. I hardly remember changing into pajamas before curling up under my covers. Within seconds, I'm soundly asleep in the embrace of the shadows that are so much like the ones that follow Idris.

CHECKMATE

THE SUN RISES TOO SLOWLY.

I wake long before dawn, my mind itching with questions to ask Idris. Later this evening, a ball will commence, and this time, I'm giddy about dancing with the king of flames.

I'm almost to my door when it swings open. To my surprise, Finch stands in the doorway.

"Finch! How did you manage to get up here? Are you alright?"

A brief once-over fills me with raw concern. He looks tired. All the blood he's been forced to give has left him haggard, and guilt wrenches at me now more than ever.

"I'm... Well, I've been better, but I wanted to check on you. Listen, I don't trust these princes who have come for your hand. There's magic in this castle... I don't know how else to explain it. But at least one of them is not who they seem," Finch says, breathless.

"If you're talking about Ivan, I already know," I say, my voice quiet. "But this stays between us, understood?"

Finch blinks, and rage settles in his eyes before I realize what he must be thinking.

"He hasn't harmed me," I hurry to say. "Ivan tried to set me out of sorts in the library last night, but Idris showed up and safely escorted me here."

At this, Finch blushes.

"He didn't stay!" I stammer, my cheeks hot. "He just noticed that Ivan seemed... unsafe. There is something deeply troublesome with that one."

Finch sighs. "Is he the one who conjured that bird?"

I glance behind me and see Sira perched solemnly on my windowsill. She observes but does not chirp and sing as she did while I slept last night. When I woke, restless, a few times as morning inched closer, I realized that the songs in my dreams were from her.

"He made her so I can call him if there's trouble." I swallow, thinking of the type of man Idris implied Ivan might be.

"And what made you trust Idris?" Finch's tone is harsh and almost accusing, but he's right to pry this way. That doesn't make it any less difficult to stop my heart from twinging.

"I mean, I took a risk, but I was armed. He didn't harm me. If anything, he helped me retain my calm." I shake my head. "It's been hectic with all this talk of betrothal and heirs and political ties. And besides all that, I've only had my power a short while... It was nice to have someone to talk to." I don't like confessing this aloud, as it betrays a weakness.

Finch still finds it in him to be empathetic. Even though he is being treated as a captured laboratory rat, he remains steadfastly loyal to me and my brother. I doubt his loyalty holds true for Alaric, but I can't afford to think of coups and patricide right now, though it's tempting. I shake away these thoughts as Finch approaches.

"Listen, I just want you to be careful. I'm glad you trust Idris, but I don't trust *any* of those pricks. Anyone your father chooses is suspicious to me. I'll be glad if he proves me wrong, but you're my sister through marriage *and* my sister by choice. Remember that. And I will come to your aid—don't forget that, either. Don't ever feel like you don't have anyone else."

My heart drops. "I didn't mean to imply I didn't think I could call you," I say. "I... knew they had you down there. I've failed so far to find a way to set you free, for which I apologize." I hang my head a moment before sheepishly meeting his eyes. "How much blood are they taking from you? Do you need more?" A thought strikes me. "Do you need... magical blood? Maybe like mine?"

Two things happen simultaneously. Finch's jaw drops, and I register a fiery presence before I can say anything else.

Idris.

"What's all this about? Who is this, Adelaide?" Idris's voice is terse, not at all welcoming as it was the night before.

"This is my brother, Finch. Beatrice's brother, more properly, but my brother all the same," I explain.

A look of relief passes over his handsome face and he walks closer. At once, I'm captured by his smoky aura and can't help but smile.

Idris raises an eyebrow. "What was this about an offer of blood?"

I gulp and wonder how much Father told my suitors about Finch.

"I was just about to explain to my sister why she shouldn't make such an offer. Reformed though I may be, at least by your standards, I am still a fledgling and would never risk your life by taking your blood. That can also be seen as an intimate offer, depending on context. Best not to get the castle talking about something that's not true," Finch says, regaining a bit of his teasing charm.

On the other hand, I find this anything but charming and all the more alarming. My face flushes crimson. "I am so sorry! I only meant to repay you for the atrocities my father has ordered upon you."

Finch laughs and even Idris chuckles. "Not to worry, Sister. So... this is the infamous Idris who escorted you to safety last night?"

Idris glances at me, and I nod. My fiery prince comes to my defense. "Nothing inappropriate transpired, I assure you. I simply don't trust Ivan. He seems to make your sister uncomfortable."

At this, Finch nods. "See to it that you protect her, or else I'll be the one stepping between you, him, and anyone else who dares to touch her in a way she doesn't want."

I note the edge in Finch's tone and wish I could find something to say, but he turns away and starts down the hall.

"I'll be in the dungeons, Adelaide, though if they let me loose for lunch, I may come and bother you again," Finch says, though his voice sounds heavy.

I promise to visit him at lunch anyway, king's orders be damned.

"Are you alright?" Idris inquires.

I'm pulled back in by the soft velvet in his voice and let him link his arm with mine. "Yes." I sigh. "I worry for him. I suppose you know what he is, but I don't think we should treat him like an animal."

At this, Idris raises an eyebrow. "Don't you slay them?"

"Yes... but I'm beginning to wonder if that's the right thing to do." I'm shocked when I realize what I just said. I fully expect Idris to haul me off to my father and order me examined for mental incapacitation.

"What makes you say that?" he asks instead, and once again, my assumptions about him prove me wrong. He is even more remarkable for entertaining my strange ideas.

"He saved my life, Idris. There is no doubt in my mind that he is in control of himself. How many of them are, and we just don't know? And there's so much we don't know about Shadow Folk. My father wants to paint them as if they are all terrible. Admittedly, I want to believe him because of what happened to my mother. But... something doesn't add up. Finch has revealed things that make me wonder and question everything I know. I hope you'll forgive the insanity of my words, but I can't help my thoughts and where they tread."

Idris stops walking and pulls me to look at him. "I think you are a far brighter soul than anyone realizes. Never apologize for thinking for yourself instead of foolishly believing the words of others. You are wise beyond your years," he purrs. "It is an honor to see such a powerful beauty up close, let alone hold your attention."

I wonder if I may melt under the weight of his heated gaze where we stand. Instead, I'm interrupted by the awful voice of my father.

"Adelaide! I see you're entertaining the King of Velyasa. Good on you for taking the initiative!" He smirks, though I sense poison in his tone.

What happened to hosting? I thought that's what you wanted. These are questions I think but dare not let slip aloud. I can't afford to make a scene.

"Your Highness," Idris says, though to my surprise, he does not bow. I notice for the first time the contempt that seems to burn within Idris' flaming eyes as he takes in my father. By his glassy eyes, I can tell right away my father has been drinking.

"You're not my first choice," Alaric slurs. "But at this point, I'll let *anyone* take that one off my hands. Though I must say, you'll have to increase your dowry if you want to have my favor explicitly."

At this, my heart jolts. I can hardly look up at Idris as embarrassment floods my veins.

"Not to worry, Alaric, your daughter's hand is priceless in my eyes. Name your price, and I'll pay it. If I was a more reckless man, I'd ask your price to end these courting theatrics and let me have her now, but I want to ensure that she is as comfortable with me as I am with her."

I feel as though someone has slapped me. *There's a bidding war over my head? It's not just a traditional dowry?*

Nausea curls in my stomach and my appetite vanishes. I'm ashamed to stand here with a man as kind as Idris in the face of a man as evil as my father. I hope to Siralto that Idris does not see my father in me.

Idris places a hand on my shoulder to steady me when I start to sway. I can't even look at my father. I hope the intense exchange occurring between Idris and Alaric is enough to keep my father's eyes off me.

"Good deal, Idris. Perhaps you're in better favor with me than I thought," my father says, his voice even more sluggish than before. He will be a mockery for this kingdom before long. Any value I hold as a princess is crumbling swiftly. If it wasn't for mine and Maverick's powers, we'd be as good as conquered.

"That's delightful to hear, Your Highness. I'll be accompanying your daughter to breakfast. She and I wish to regale one another with stories from our respective kingdoms," Idris smoothly says, his voice clipped of any emotion. He's better than me. I would be screaming by now if I had engaged in this conversation.

Idris takes my elbow and leads me down the hall without waiting for my father to answer. For the second time in as many days, he saves me from the scrutiny of a man with ill intent, except this time, the escape is from my own father.

I don't look up as he ushers me through the corridor. If my father says anything else to me, I don't hear it. My attentions have long since been attached to some world distant from ours, though I can't say where. In times like these, I find it easier to just "slip" from my body and come back to reality once I know it's safe to think.

A door closes and I notice we're standing on a private balcony. The winter wind chills me to the bone and I shiver, pulling my fur coat tighter. Idris slides a finger beneath my chin and tilts my head up.

"Does he always speak of you as though you were a common dog?"

I fail to answer, though my lips quiver and tears pool in my eyes. I hate myself in this moment. For all the battles I've encountered and all the Shadow Folk I've slain, I finally got my hands on the Siraltona and it hasn't made a single ounce of difference. I'm still helpless. I'm still replaceable. I'm still worthless. My father will always win, and I will be left on the sidelines of history as nothing more than a mother thrown to the crows when her body has been used up.

I sob. I don't remember when I started, but it registers when Idris pulls me into a crushing embrace. He does not shush me, instead letting me wail at the top of my lungs. I wonder what the other suitors would think if they saw me in such a state. I wonder what Idris is thinking. *What a pitiful creature,* no doubt.

I manage to suck it all in for a moment—long enough to look up at Idris to find a dark frown shadowing his features.

"I am so sorry," I say, my voice shuddering. "He is... something else. He has not been the same since my mother died. He raised me to be a weapon. To fight the thing that took her away from us. I was not raised with magic. The nobles sort of knew, but not to the extent they know now. I was not raised to have children. I was not raised to carry this bloodline. I was not raised to be anything more than a puppet to leave on the battlefield someday when I could no longer fight. I wish Mars had scorched me the other night in the fray. His fire would have been a mercy."

Whatever makeup that once adorned my face is certainly ruined now, as well as any chance I had with Idris. He can't have a lunatic for a wife. *Queen Adelaide the Insane* is hardly a legacy to leave behind.

"Let's have a seat," Idris whispers. "My fire will keep us warm."

"Thank you," I stammer. Until now, I couldn't tell how badly my teeth chattered or how raw my skin had become from the icy grip of the winds curling through the balcony.

I'm not sure where the chairs come from. Maybe they were already here or else he conjured them like he did Sira, who flutters above our heads and watches me with sad eyes. I didn't know phoenixes could show despondency, but Sira makes it clear with the way she lowers her head and hovers close to me.

Idris takes my hands in his and warmth licks through my palms. "Let's get something out of the way, okay? I *do* want to marry you, just as each of the suitors here do. Unfortunately, given your status, you have limited options. If it's not me, your father will marry you off to just about anyone. I want you to have a choice, but I also realize it's not a true choice if you're forced into this situation. In Velyasa, this is not customary. Forgive me, but I was drawn to you and the stories of who you are, which is why I chose to break our customs and come see you."

I blink. "Why would you apologize? I... enjoy spending time with you, Idris. I do. If I could choose now, I would. But my father won't let me. He enjoys the game too much."

I notice he smirks at this, but the concern doesn't leave the bonfires in his eyes and I'm grateful for how genuine he seems. Still, he could be luring me to my doom, for all I know. He could have every intention of carting me away to force me to bear his children, after which I would barely be recognized as a consort—closer to a common whore he could use to carry on his legacy and pleasures.

But it doesn't seem that way when he cups my cheek and offers a sad smile.

"I'm grateful you feel as I do. I have never met someone as intriguing and intoxicating as you. But I want you to understand something: Not all men are like your father. Not all kingdoms are Sunfall. There are places where you would be deemed a ruler just as important as I am or any other king, for that matter. As I have told you before, my fire, you have heart. Your legend stems far and wide. Do you think we want to forge our futures with Sunfall simply because of Alaric?" Idris raises an eyebrow at me.

His words leave me reeling. "Are you telling me you don't want an allyship with Sunfall?"

Idris slowly shakes his head. "No, Adelaide. We want an allyship with *you*. And Maverick. And the Sunfall that *could be.*"

He stares at me so intensely when he says the last statement that I know, from this moment on, I'm doomed. He could tell me to leap from the highest cliff and I would do it without thinking twice. Something tells me that if I told him to do the same thing, he would follow suit without question.

Without thinking, I lean in and kiss him, soft and slow. He grunts in surprise, but his astonishment doesn't last long. His hands find their way to the bodice of my corset and play a sweet, sensuous song along my curves. One eventually finds purchase in my hair, tousling it. Any hope of hiding evidence of our passions is lost when he grips me tighter and hoists me into his lap.

Our breathing is heavy, panting, and loud enough that I fear it might echo into the halls, even with the door shut. Every part of this is dangerous, but I don't care as our tongues plunge against one another. His other hand plays with the lacing of my corset and I know if this continues, they'll find us both undressed and committing the most carnal of acts right here on this balcony. Whatever he wants of me, I'll give him. And I know he's mine for the taking.

He pulls back and peppers my neck with kisses. I tilt my head back to give him better access and moan his name.

His hand slides lower and grips my ass, full and firm. I'm wild with want as I slide my hands along the rippling muscles of his back, realizing with a start that his impressive musculature is hidden by the white, silken fabric of his shirt.

When he pulls away, I want to beg him to keep going, but the look we share says it all.

Not here.

"Once you are mine, I will have you in every part of my castle whenever we please," he says, his voice low.

His promise sends shivers down my spine, and I want to drop all pretenses now and take him back to my chambers. One word from him and I'll risk it all. I don't care. He's the most exquisite elixir for when I'm wounded. "How much longer will you and the other suitors remain here before a decision is made?" I ask, my voice breathless. "My father hasn't told me."

"Another week," Idris says, his voice returning to something like normal.

I ache for him, though I don't know why. My confusion and arousal are mirrored in his eyes. "Then in a week, you can take me home and we can do just that," I say, my eyes lidded.

Idris chuckles. "What a terrible week ahead of us. But... don't you want to know the other suitors first?"

I give a wicked grin. "I don't know... you seemed almost jealous of Finch earlier before you knew who he was. Are you sure you'll even *let* the others take me out and court me?"

Idris laughs, the sound bright and infectious. "You're a keen observer. I must admit, seeing you in the throne room confirmed my desire to make you mine. And I don't *share* what is *mine*," he says, venom dripping from his voice. "But I want you to have a choice. So at least... I don't know... dine with them or something. But don't let them have a taste of you as I have. If you do, I can't promise I won't declare war."

While we both break into laughter, I wonder just how true his words are. Could courting someone else lead to war? My heart flutters.

"We should probably go and actually get breakfast so as not to garner suspicion," I say, disappointed.

"Yes, I suppose, though I think I'm much more satisfied with our little rendezvous than any food you can offer."

Idris slides an arm around me, his hand dancing dangerously low on my waist, but I don't bother to correct him as we step back out into the corridor and head to the dining hall. Then, a haunting realization hits me.

I don't know who this man is. I... don't know who any of them are. And I have to marry one of them in a week.

Velyasa

THE OTHER SUITORS JOIN US AT THE BREAKFAST TABLE AND I couldn't be more irritated. I refuse to sit near Ivan, not that Idris would allow it, anyway. He places himself between me and the icicle prick, as he so aptly named him. Alexander, on the other hand, is kind and more in line with the manners I expect, given my experiences with Beatrice and Finch.

The furtive glances Idris and I share during the meal leave me wanting a hot bath and a scrub to rid myself of all my lascivious thoughts. But when I consider the fact that I'll be wed in a week, my libido is doused with a hiss.

As I eat, I mull over the preposterous fact that I only have a week to pick a suitor, after which I'll be whisked away to a kingdom far from my own. Finch and Maverick will be left behind and I won't be able to help Maverick the way I want to. I won't be able to help him overtake our father or drive away the Shadow Folk. Not until I have an heir.

The plans I've laid for so long crumble beneath the weight of wedding bells I never asked for. I look at Ivan and Alexander and the thought of being either of their wives makes me wish I was dead. But when I look at Idris, despite my reservations and fears, I feel... calm. While not a choice, as he said, he is the only real option I have in the disgusting show into which I've been forced.

I begin hatching a plan. I decide, right now, that it's time to start throwing my weight around. I can't be forced to marry anyone else if there *is* no one else. I can only hope Idris will choose me in a week, despite his claim that he will.

He's seen me in some pretty terrible states so far.

If I fail, there's no doubt I'll be killed or exiled. If I succeed, I might have a sliver of hope in ruling alongside someone who might let me help Maverick and envision what Sunfall *could* be. A coup is easier to stage when you have more soldiers to stand behind it. Maybe kingdom expansion will be enough to convince Idris to help me secure Maverick as the rightful ruler of Sunfall, with *our* heir as the one to inherit it someday.

My mind wanders back to the dull conversations bouncing around me as I grab another tart. Alexander is busy telling me about the courts in Underland and some of the more recent ordinances they've put in place to stop the Shadow Folk from breaching the kingdom walls.

"As of last month, we managed to increase our security by tenfold!" Alexander proudly announces. "We've slain at least ten thousand of the shadow bastards using some of the Siraltona-infused weapons your father sent to us."

I drop my fork. The raspberry tarts aren't that interesting anyway, and I'm about to throw it all back up if what I heard is correct.

"The what?"

Alexander gives a wide smile, thrilled that I'm finally joining the conversation. "Your father had this brilliant idea to outfit us with weapons infused with the Siraltona. I understand this is how you fought the Shadow Folk before you... learned your powers better."

There's a veil of a threat in his statement and I wonder if Alexander knows more than he lets on. *Does he know about Finch? About the struggles I've faced? What has my father told him?*

"I... I believe I made the suggestion to arm our neighbors several times. I'm surprised he took me up on it," I say, refusing to let my father take the credit.

"*You* came up with that? That's just splendid!" Alexander beams, but there's a dismissiveness to his tone that sets me on edge.

Maybe it's my lingering unease, or maybe it's the fact that Underland is too close to home for comfort. Still, knowing that they're thriving because of *my* idea and slaughtering tens of thousands makes me queasy.

I place my hands in my lap and twist my cloth napkin into a tight ball, fighting to control my temper. "When we go on hunts, it's to secure the border. Are you saying you're committing territorial *genocide*?" I launch the accusation without thinking through its implication. "You *do* realize the Shadow Folk have a very powerful king that I've been instructed *not* to hunt down because of the ramifications, don't you? A few skirmishes or battles where we've been provoked first make sense, but hunting them down in such mass numbers? That reeks of political suicide!" I sneer at Alexander, unable to help myself.

I raise my chin. "We know things about the Shadow Folk you wouldn't believe, Alexander, and if you think they're weak right now, you're wrong," I seethe. "Believe me when I say, you don't want to be a target as we are. You don't want to wield divine light as we do. Look how much Sunfall has had to struggle with to overcome her foes!" I say, my voice dripping with distaste. "Your people are not prepared for the onslaughts as we have seen them. I lost my mother to one of the Shadow Folk when they breached the palace walls sixteen years ago."

Silence falls over the table. Ivan watches the argument with sick fascination while Idris regards me with pride, a smile plastered on his face. Alexander, on the other hand, outwardly fumes. His cheeks take on a ruddy hue and his jaw is tightly clenched.

"What do you know, stupid girl, of battle strategy?" he explodes.

I stand so quickly, my chair launches from behind me; my hand already reaches for my sword. "You forget who you speak to, Alexander! My father may have been the powerhouse up until now, but *I* am the one who has fought countless battles to make the Shadow Folk fall back as vengeance for my mother. I lost men on the field and bled alongside them. *As one of them.*" I glare at Ivan. "I have not always been a *witch*, as you all would call me. I am a soldier first, a princess second, and a freak of nature third. The blades you wield were forged on *my* behalf. My brother is too injured to take on the Shadow Folk. Did my father tell you *I'm* the one who drove their latest onslaught back, *alone?*" I haughtily raise my chin. "Now hold your tongue and show some respect!"

I sit back down, stewing in my rage and deciding to ignore anything they have to say in rebuttal.

"My kingdom of Nayeh would not find your tongue appealing, my lady," Ivan hisses. "It is best to let the *men* do the planning and wielding of power. You are a vessel for heirs, yes, but money is what will claim you in the end, and I will clamp your tongue down myself if it means harnessing what you have!"

Without a second thought, I take my plate and hurl it at him. The fine china smashes against his forehead and shatters on impact.

Ivan bolts to his feet, ice crackling in his hands, but my Siraltona is quicker. What I lack in practice, I make up for in raw power. A blast of searing light roars from my hands and sends Ivan hurtling backwards, where his head cracks against a stone pillar. He slumps to the floor, either unconscious or dead, though I don't stick around long enough to find out which one it is.

I can't bear to look at Idris as I turn and flee the room, not caring what my father will say when he learns what happened.

"Cancel the ball!" I call to Maverick as I pass him in the corridor. He fixes me with a look of worry and alarm, but I don't have time to explain my reasons. I storm toward the throne room, where my father and all the nobles are gathered, and pull the doors open so hard, they slam against the wall. "I've made my choice!" I boom. "Cancel the balls. The fanfare. All of it. I choose Idris, if he'll have me after my latest outburst. I'll be out of your hair by the end of the week."

The nobles, all gathered in the throne room with petitions and laws and complaints, gasp in unison. The room goes so deathly quiet, you could hear a pin drop. My father appears to be on the verge of flying into another of his drunken rages.

How he manages to hold court while so imbibed is a mystery I never want to solve.

"Your Highness, I am happy to marry your daughter and speed things along for double the dowry offered," Idris announces behind me.

The blood drains from my face. *I've just cost my future husband a small fortune.*

I turn to face him. "You don't have to do that, Idris! I willingly choose you, and my father will take what was originally offered. I whirl back around to meet the king's glowering face. "Father, as for my other suitors, I believe we will have war with Nayeh, and the simpering noble you chose from Underland seems to have some misunderstanding that the infused weapons were *your* idea." I raise my voice to ring out across the crowded room. "Let me be clear to all those gathered here today that infusing the weapons with Siraltona was *my* idea." Meeting my father's flinty eyes, I continue, "Any hope you had of one of the other suitors choosing me is finished. Let me choose Idris, or there will be dire consequences."

Light pools in my hands again. The room falls into shadow outside the haze of my power. For the first time in my life, fear is reflected in my father's eyes. And I *love* how it feels to see it.

"Very well," my father acquiesces. He knows it's the right choice. Besides that, he's cornered.

"If you attempt to go back on your word, I will turn and stand against you. If you aid me in this endeavor, Sunfall shall have my allyship for life. I was chosen by the gods when I ate from the Lasira. Do not invoke the wrath of the gods who blessed me."

The nobles stare at my father, waiting for a reaction. He fixes me with a dreadful smile so cold it would freeze Ivan.

"So be it, daughter. Perhaps you'll produce better heirs than your mother did. Maybe that will save us all." He waves his hand as if he's bored of our conversation. "Be dismissed; let me finish my business. Have it your way. Idris shall be your husband, *if* he will take you. If he backs out, I will execute you myself."

Try it.

Idris claps a hand on my shoulder. "You've done enough, my fire. Though I *do* wish you'd let me pay more for you instead of betting your life."

I glare up at him. "I can take care of you just as much as you will for me." Turning on my heel, I stride out of the throne room, knowing full well that Idris is following close behind. When we're well out of earshot, I turn back to him. "Will you truly choose me after all you've witnessed?"

He unflinchingly meets my gaze. "In Velyasa, we value our women and their opinions. You held your own in front of high-ranking nobles and allowed no disrespect. That is crucial to being a true Velyasan. Why do you keep asking me?"

"Because I'm pretty sure Velyasa has never seen a woman as foolish as me." I lower my eyes and feel the sudden hot sting of tears.

"Then I think it's time I tell you about Velyasa, as you asked me to do before we got... *sidetracked* this morning."

I wish you'd let us get sidetracked again, I think to myself. But I don't lead him on. Not when we must uphold our image until the marriage is settled at the end of the week. I can hardly believe my plan worked! Even amidst all this dreadful woe, I've managed to secure a silver lining.

"I don't believe you ate enough at breakfast," he notes without a trace of condemnation. "Would it be too much trouble to take you out to the courtyard and ask one of your maidservants to bring us bread? And perhaps some cheese and ale?"

The mention of ale makes my stomach turn. "I would be happy to drink nectar, though you're welcome to the ale. Seeing my father turned by it so often has given me a foul taste of it."

Idris smiles, though it's marked with sadness. "Forgive me, my fire, I did not think of this. Nectar, then."

"Don't be sorry," I whisper, striding up to him. "You have done me more favors in the span of two days than most have done in my life." I reach up and peck him on the lips, not caring who sees. "Thank you."

It's his turn to blush, but I don't wait for him to catch up to me as I make my way to the courtyard, stopping only to ask the maidservants to fetch us chairs and food.

"I hope you won't mind, but after we finish here, I'd like to see Finch and make sure he is being treated well. I worry for him," I confess. The thought of my brother-in-law suffering is still at the forefront of my mind, despite everything.

Idris takes my hand as we sit across from each other in the court-yard. Soon after, the maidservants arrive with bread and cheeses. They eye me warily, probably due to my earlier outburst, but I don't care. Not today.

"I think seeing Finch would be okay, though I hope you won't mind me accompanying you. I know you trust him, but... I wouldn't want your kindness to cost you," Idris says, his voice laden with caution. It is refreshing to have someone care for me in this way.

My stomach growls, ripping me away from my infatuation with my betrothed long enough so I can actually eat. The nausea from earlier is gone, leaving in its wake the reality that I haven't eaten properly in days. The nerves I've tried to tightly rein left me ravenous. I do my best to retain some level of decorum while I eat, but Idris doesn't seem to mind that my manners are more akin to a feral wolf than a lady. If anything, he watches me with a trace of amusement.

"I suppose they don't feed you around here?"

He's teasing, but my face flushes with embarrassment. "I... I haven't eaten much these past few days," I confess. I grab a cloth and dab my face to wipe away the crumbs. Most of my makeup disappeared and my face is splotchy from my earlier breakdown, which I am painfully reminded that he was present for.

"Well, I'm glad I could get you to slow down long enough to take care of yourself," Idris replies with smug satisfaction.

I notice he hasn't eaten much himself, and I wonder if he'll care too much if I pry. Then again, he probably ate more of his breakfast before I lost my cool and lobbed a plate at Ivan's head.

"Do you think Ivan survived?"

"I was wondering when you'd ask!" Idris laughs. "I saw him being carted to the infirmary before I chased after you. He seemed halfway conscious, so he's probably just bruised. He got lucky, though. Had he not been casting when you blasted your power at him, he would've been fatally injured."

His voice is grave and I know he's right. For some reason, this doesn't bother me as I polish off yet another slice of cheese.

"Don't fret, my fire. If he tries to seek revenge, he'll meet more than just *your* light," Idris growls, flames dancing in his palms.

It hasn't occurred to me until now just how dangerous Idris' powers are. If my light is any indication as to what others might be able to do when they wield, then Idris could level entire kingdoms with a snap of his fingers.

I try not to dwell on it too much.

His molten eyes trail up my face. "Tell me... what secret did Finch learn or share with you about the Shadow Folk? Or were you just egging Alexander on?"

I pause mid-bite on a piece of bread. It's an innocent question, but for some reason, it puts me on edge.

"I... I suppose it has to do with their power. I'm not sure about the details, and neither is Finch, as he doesn't remember who his sire is. But something has been awakened. Somehow, the king managed to grant the

Shadow Folk their familiars back." I shudder as I remember the shadowy beasts on the battlefield. "I've no idea what that means, though."

It's not entirely a lie. I really don't understand the magic of familiars or how they came to be, and I have no idea what Mars could have possibly done to invoke that power.

"I suppose Finch might remember someday, or maybe they'll understand the science of familiars more once they get the blood tests they want from him," I ramble. "I don't believe that Doctor Richards is a real scientist as much as he is a kook, but I'm willing to entertain the possibilities. I just wish it could've been voluntary by Finch and he didn't have to give so much."

Idris hums, but he doesn't say more.

I want to know more about my betrothed as the haze of attraction becomes more of a lull. It's there, but now I can focus on more than his impeccable, muscular build and handsome face. It occurs to me just *how* wonderful he looks.

His jaw is chiseled—sharp and angular. Those flaming eyes are framed like the finest artwork in cohesion with coppery locks that sweep in tousled, yet refined poise. His nose is strong, and his white teeth glisten in the light. He gives me a cocky grin, fully aware of me staring at him.

What does he see in me?

It's been a while since I gave myself a true once-over in the mirror, but I'm far from stunning to look at. Maybe it's the years of being hardened by battle, or maybe it's the lack of care placed in my appearance overall, but I'm no beauty. Striking, perhaps. But not beautiful. At least I don't think so.

"What are you thinking?" Idris levels me with a gaze that tells me he's onto me.

"Just that there's still so much I want to know about you and don't. You've heard so much about me, but I know so little of you. I've heard a few things about Velyasa but... not enough to understand its customs. If I'm to be your queen, I should hope you would give me some indication as to where I will live." I tap my fingers on the table, feeling more bashful than brave.

"Fret not, my fire. I will tell you everything you want to know. I suppose I should start by explaining what I meant when I said we value our women. While we are a male-dominated culture, similar to many others, we do not pride ourselves in owning our women or treating them as nothing more than vessels for childbirth. We see them as our counterparts—our confidants, if you will. When we take a wife, we gain another part of ourselves—the other half of our soul. She is ours to protect, honor, and cherish. While she may not formally rule the house, they are the unspoken rulers in our society. In your case, I would make it no secret that you are my equal. My partner. The one I trust above all others," Idris explains.

My heart races and I fear it might explode. "How can you already feel this way about me? How can you pledge to take me as a wife when we've only just met?"

Idris chuckles. "Our society is founded on the notion of finding... I'm not sure there's a term for it that makes sense in your language... but it's essentially the same concept the gods devised—the idea of a soul-mate. When you find someone who is made of the stuff you are made of, or perhaps even the polar opposite, you are drawn to them. Who are we to question their logic?" His face creases into a blinding smile that takes my breath away.

"Instead, we make it a point to dedicate our lives to that person and learn and grow with them. Love is not easy. It is a choice. So why fight the easiest part of that choice? When I saw you, I knew. End of story. Now we begin anew. I will take you home in a week, and then we'll begin the most important adventure: *the rest of our lives.*"

Everything he says makes me want to drown in him. I want to know when the fantasy ends and reality begins, but I'm afraid to reach that point. Instead, I smile and swallow the urge to let him sweep me into his chambers. While I've never made love, I'm certain that with him it will be the best experience. I could trust him and truly indulge my whims.

As if sensing the salacious direction of my thoughts, he winks.

"Will you accompany me into the dungeons to see Finch?" I ask, willing myself to change the subject and ignore the heat creeping between my legs.

"I suppose," he sighs. "I can't have my future wife eaten alive by one of the Shadow Folk right beneath my nose."

I roll my eyes, then stand and hold my hand out to him. He takes it, but he does not pull on me to help him to his feet. Despite his massive stature, he is nimble. The bulk of his frame is a deception. All his muscle is lethal—pulled taut and ready to spring at a moment's notice. These things should frighten me, but they don't. Instead, I laugh and pull him towards the dungeon, where my brother-in-law is being held captive.

I notice too late the shadows forming in the distant horizon. By evening, they'll have changed everything.

THE DUNGEONS

I CALL FINCH'S NAME, BUT HE DOESN'T ANSWER.

Panic wells up in my throat, but it subsides when I hear his soft voice answering from deeper within the dungeon.

I run to him, eager to make sure he hasn't been damaged beyond repair. Part of me senses that my light can heal, and I won't hesitate to test it out to ensure Finch's long-term health and success, despite what my father or Doctor Richards wants.

"How are you feeling?" I ask as I stride into the main wing of the dungeon. It's been modified into a mock infirmary so Doctor Richards has easy access to his needles, vials, and potions. Several potions are boiling in beakers, steam emitting from a few of them. The impulsive part of me wants to hurl them at the walls and watch them shatter, but I know better than to start drama where it's not necessary. I flinch as I recall the plate this morning. *Desperate times*, I assure myself.

"I'm feeling peachy," Finch says, his voice sour.

I try not to let his words hurt me, but it stings. I wish I had more than a week to wrench him free of this awful place. The putrid smell of stale water and vomit reaches my nose and my eyes water. Idris looks paler than usual. I worry he might keel over if I don't keep gripping his hand, but he does not waver despite his obvious discomfort.

Idris peers around the dungeon as we walk over to Finch. I examine his arms and am horrified to see lines of needle marks worming up his flesh. A few have begun to heal, but even the rapid healing powers Finch possesses aren't enough to replenish himself at the rate that Doctor Richards keeps pulling from him. I bite back a shriek and, without pause, summon a few drops of Siraltona to my fingers. It's strange seeing the light in such a viscous state. When I dropper it to his skin, it hisses upon impact but does just what I hope it will.

In seconds, his wounds disappear. He and Idris stare with their jaws agape as I smooth my fingers over the last of Finch's wounds, watching as they close. The siren song of my powers dulls, and I'm returned to a state of normalcy as the light recedes from my veins.

"How... how did you do that?" Idris asks, his voice full of wonder.

"The power just knows. I'm not sure how everyone else wields theirs, but mine comes to me when I need it. It's strange," I confess. "It's not how I've heard magic being described."

Finch whistles. "That fruit really was a blessing. Granted, you looked practically dead when I found you with it, so it stands to reason it must've been a miracle."

Idris winces. "You mean to tell me she was truly near death?"

Finch nods. "Poor thing was a sack of potatoes. I ran her back inside the walls of Sunfall with hardly any time to spare, but the fruit had already begun to work its magic. Then she went out into battle not long after and became a walking sun in the flesh. Who knew?"

Finch shrugs after his horrid attempt at humor, which I reward with a tired laugh. His humor is the most resilient part of him, and I don't want that piece to die as his mortal being did.

Idris bows. "I am grateful to you for saving her."

I make note of this. He wouldn't bow to my father. *His respect really does have to be earned.*

Finch raises an eyebrow but offers a genuine smile. "Any time. How is the courting going?"

I lower my gaze from Finch and try to find the right words to explain my actions. But Idris beats me to it.

"Well, my future brother, she threw a plate at Ivan and insulted Alexander so gravely that I fear his ego may never recover!" Idris chuckles. "She also blasted Ivan with a wall of pure sunlight. Did you see him down here at any point?"

Finch laughs. "I did. They patched him up, but he's in pretty bad shape. I won't be surprised if his kingdom declares war."

"Pity," Idris laughs. "In any case, your sister chose *me*."

Finch glances at me, but there is none of the reservation I saw in his gaze earlier. "I had a feeling the other two suitors were a problem. Their signatures were... *off*. The magic I sensed with them was just wrong, you know?" He shakes his head ruefully. "For starters, Ivan reminded me of the vampire who freed and then incapacitated me before he poisoned the court the night of the ball. Ivan shared the same energy as the Shadow Folk who breached our walls."

I blink, suddenly feeling foolish for not digging deeper. "Did... did we ever find the Shadow Folk who poisoned our court in the first place?"

Finch hums. "No."

Silence descends and dread creeps up in my gut. I know deep in my soul that our complacency has cost us everything this time.

How did we not think to investigate further? Why didn't we go looking for the bastard that set us up for Mars to try and infiltrate us?

I pace the dungeon corridor, consumed with worry.

"You're thinking what I'm thinking, aren't you, Adelaide?" Finch levels a gaze at me that threatens to send me to my knees in desperate prayer to Siralto.

"Finch... Ivan isn't... Ivan isn't the Shadow Folk who broke in, right? We wouldn't have invited a vampire into our castle, right?"

Before I can say anything else, Idris runs behind us both and bars the door to the dungeons. Above us, we hear them. Screams and clattering swords.

The castle is under siege.

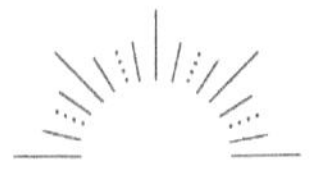

I PACE FOR WHAT FEELS LIKE HOURS, THOUGH I KNOW IT'S only been minutes. I can't believe how foolish I've been—how naive. Idris and Finch shout directions and grab weapons while I try to remember where I lost my way over the last few days.

Ivan made me uncomfortable from the second I met him, yet I overlooked my discomfort and assumed I disliked him because he was trying to court me. I was so swept up in romance that I ignored my instincts. I know when and how to spot a predator in our midst, yet I let this one slip right past us.

My father meant to marry me off to him, too.

I don't understand how Ivan managed to parade among us without being discovered until now. Is this the result of the powers Finch warned us about? Is this what Mars awakened among his hell spawn?

I look to Idris and Finch for guidance.

Idris' eyes lock on mine and he walks over to me. "You better not blame yourself for this," he whispers. "*I* am to blame. I have guarded you from him and never once listened to the warnings going off in my own mind. I should have known why he made you feel such dread in his presence. The Shadow Folk can't stand to be in the presence of one imbued with Light. I've no idea how he managed to stay standing when you struck him."

I shudder, realizing what he means. *How did he survive? Does this mean they are growing immune to the Light? Are we even more lost than we thought?*

My mind won't stop racing as I try to piece together how Ivan escaped me without being sent straight to Kohlu, where he belongs. I grip the hilt of my sword, solemnly promising not to let him escape Hell's grasp again.

I shake my head in horrified bewilderment. "How did one of the Shadow Folk make it past our gates, and how did we not know the prince of a neighboring kingdom was afflicted?" I can't focus on next steps until there's a reasonable explanation in my mind. I want to know how much trouble we're in.

Finch shrugs. "I guess your father really *would* let just about anyone with royal status through the gates."

I glare at Finch, but something tells me he's right. *Did my father screen any of these so-called suitors, or was he so eager to be rid of me that he simply looked at the loot and hoped for the best?*

Part of me wants to use the chaos upstairs as a cloak so I can plunge a dagger into my father's throat. The less savage part tries to focus on the task at hand. "How did I not kill him?" I whisper aloud. "How did he manage to survive when I struck him?"

Idris shrugs. "I don't think you meant to kill him, Adelaide. You just healed Finch with your powers. Unlike your father, you don't seem to resort to using your powers only to kill. Would your little phoenix Sira kill you with her fire? I wager the answer is no. My fire can be destructive as much as it can be creative. I presume your power is the same."

I flinch at his suggestion. It implies I wanted to show Ivan mercy, even as uncomfortable as he made me—even as he plotted my demise. But does that mean Shadow Folk are immune to kill strikes?

"We need to get up there and help," I say. "We can't hide down here and wait. I hear screaming, and we know he's breached our walls. He failed to secure my hand and must move to Plan B. Who knows what he's up there doing?"

I unsheathe my sword and barge ahead, hoping Idris and Finch won't try and stop me. To my relief, they follow suit. Idris carries a blade with him I didn't even know he had on him. The sword is massive; he could cleave a man in two with little more than a single swing.

Finch, on the other hand, begins to sprout red scales. Under ordinary circumstances, I'd ask him not to change forms here in this castle. Walls will crumble if he grows much larger, and then people will know exactly how dangerous he is.

Maybe that's not such a bad thing.

By the time we reach the top of the stairs, he's a full-size dragon and we charge ahead to meet our foes. Idris shouts and Maverick slides in beside us, his blade at the ready and his veins alight with Siraltona.

I doubt mine will answer, but she swiftly awakens for me and assuages any uncertainties I still carry. My Light is still deadly. She drove back Mars' hordes. *But how did I manage to draw her the way I did?*

Above me, Sira flutters and calls out as she flies ahead, leading us into the fray. My mind is scattered, and I can admit for the first time today that I'm terrified of the Shadow Folk and the threat they pose. They've breached our walls twice now and this time, they almost carted me away as a bought prisoner with my father's blessing. Sunfall's king would have been none the wiser and I would have paid the price.

I fume when I think of how foolish my father has been these past few years. I hatch a fresh, new plot to dethrone him as we hook a corner and find Ivan and several of his soldiers clashing in battle with a few daring nobles. Alexander and his soldiers are present as well, fighting for Sunfall, their weapons the only thing keeping the vampires at bay.

I watch fangs plunge into the necks of many high-ranking nobles and officials, and my blood hits a boiling rage so hot I fear I might catch in flames. If I did, I wonder if Idris could ever put me back together again.

I don't wait to find out.

"Ivan!" I shout. "Show yourself."

I center myself with my sword and light travels down the blade, arcing and spitting sparks all around. Two faceless soldiers run toward me, but I am quicker. I easily cut through them without a second thought, leaving their mangled bodies on the palace floor before making my way through the fray. Then my steps falter.

There are hundreds of them.

Somewhere in the din, I hear Idris shouting. Overhead, Finch swoops down and breathes fire on a cluster of Shadow Folk. He's small enough to sweep around the ceiling and deliver strategically brutal hits, but I can't stop to admire his killing swipes and fierceness. I will thank him later by ordering my father to pardon him—*after* I expose the king's folly to the nobles.

Speaking of whom, my father is nowhere to be found. I wrench my sword through vampire after vampire, but I fear our efforts won't be enough. By inviting Ivan's party inside our palace walls, Sunfall's king doomed us. I call upon the Siraltona, hoping she will charge forth as she did when I faced Mars, but it's only a fraction of what I had before. *Why doesn't it work?*

My eyes slide to Idris, who has locked his blade against three Shadow Folk. Several others inch closer to him and I blast them, my light growing brighter and hotter by the minute. I realize now why my Light is growing in its ferocity.

You had nothing to lose out there, I remind myself. *Now you could lose your only ticket out of here. Or... you could use this diversion as an opportunity to escape.*

I pause, tempted by my own musings, and this is where I mess up. I hear Ivan approach a millisecond too late. I turn just in time to see him swoop down on me, fangs bared and his dark eyes all-consuming. I freeze in panic, colder than the ice that crackles through his aura, and am rendered motionless.

In this moment, I accept death. I will not make it out alive.

Right before impact, a flaming blade cuts through Ivan's neck. The vampire's face widens in shock and a single, bloody tear travels down his face as he is separated from his body. A few moments pass, and the life in his eyes fades.

Astonished, I look up to see Idris staring down at me. I expect him to yell at me, asking how I could have been so foolish. Why did I freeze?

Instead, he reaches for me and pulls me into a kiss. "Never stop burning, my fire," he hisses.

My heart jolts as he turns away and continues to fight off the hordes of enemies headed for us. I don't have time to stop and swoon. Instead, I pick up my sword and continue to fight until my hands ache and my arms threaten to give out from exhaustion.

How can I carry on like this?

Pulling deeply from my last reserves, a fountain of light comes to my aid and I manage to kill many more Shadow Folk. Finch picks them off one by one from his lofty perch, still circling above. Maverick holds his own, but his bad leg threatens to give out with each parry and lunge. Just as the Siraltona surges to life, the soldiers begin to fall back.

I don't care that they know they're losing. This is personal. These fools trod upon *my* soil under *my* banner and tried to steal *my* hand. Ivan may be dead, but their audacious behavior will be met with punishment, down to his last remaining soldier.

I'm crazed as I cut through them. The light scatters from my body in all directions, winged blades cutting and slicing through every Shadow Folk within reach. I am destruction incarnate. Gone are my fears. Gone is my quiet acceptance of the end. In its stead, I find the rage I need to clean this floor of the shadows still staining it.

I don't know how much time passes or how I manage it, but heaps of Shadow Folk are dead before they finally retreat.

My breathing is heavy. Sweat pours from my skin and drenches my once-beautiful dress, along with the blood of several hundred Shadow Folk. If it wasn't for my Siraltona, this would not have been possible.

"Adelaide!" Finch calls out.

His tone is urgent, but I don't register his words right away. He shouts so loud that my head pounds from the insistence of his words, but I still don't understand.

Only when I turn my head do I know why his voice carries a hysterical twinge.

Shifted back into his human body, Finch is slumped over the body of the one person I'd begun to care about.

Idris is dead, a blade jutting from his chest.

I scream.

MOURNING

I FLING MYSELF OVER IDRIS' LIMP BODY AS RAGGED SCREAMS bellow from my chest.

For a man I've only known a few days, I feel like I lost my one chance at a lifetime and a love that could have been mine. Instead of Queen of Velyasa, I am widowed before I am even married.

Tears flow freely down my cheeks and drip down my chin. I fight Finch's desperate attempts to pull me away, despite his insistence. Maverick has long since left, presumably to find my father and inform him that the betrothal is off and two of his chosen royals have been murdered.

My father will have my head. It doesn't matter how hard I fought. It won't matter that my actions saved the Kingdom of Sunfall from the damnation of the shadows. He will only care that the betrothal fell through and only the gifts Idris brought remain. All my father wants is my dowry. If he can't secure it, he'll eliminate me. I'm nothing more than a liability now.

"Finch, I... I'm doomed!" I wheeze. "I loved him. I didn't know him, but I loved him," I cry brokenly.

Finch cradles me to his chest and I let myself go as all my hopes of love and freedom die with Idris. My betrothed's flaming eyes are now glazed over, the secrets of death carried with him beyond and into Tyrladan.

"Who will inform Velyasa? We just lost them their king! They'll want vengeance," I choke. "My father allowed Shadow Folk inside our walls and look at how we have suffered!"

My devastation is quickly replaced by pure, raw, white-hot rage. I look at Finch and darkness settles over his face. Right now, he's not a Shadow Folk; he's my brother. And he, too, sees the reality of my father's sins.

I grab the hilt of my sword, ready to rush to the throne room and do the world a favor when Finch catches me by the shoulder.

"Adelaide... don't do that! Don't give your father such an easy excuse to kill you. Please!" Finch beseeches. "We can still save your life. Don't let Idris' death be in vain. He loved you, Adelaide. He was willing to die for you. Don't squander that."

I can't see my brother for the tears clogging my eyes. I brokenly sob, but I don't let him hold me this time. My body trembles and I lurch to my feet. It takes every bit of the rage and loss coiled in my bones to keep me upright. Everything feels wrong. I want to curl up with Idris' body and weep while I await my father's axe to behead me.

Maybe it's fitting that Finch keeps his head while I lose mine.

It's not rational to feel this way. Idris was a stranger to me. For all I know, he could have been just as brutal and cruel as the other suitors. But for the past two days, he gave me hope that something could change, and I dared myself to usher in feelings I'd worked so hard not to allow.

For the sixteen years since my mother's passing, I've lived with the knowledge that I would be killed by the hands of shadows, either real or imagined. I had no future, save by my skill with a blade. Now, any chance I had at a different life was wrenched away by the same creatures that killed my mother.

Rage gnaws at me. I'm not sure how long I've been standing, transfixed by the body of the man I'd started to love. He's beautiful—dangerously so—even in death. I kneel beside him one more time and pepper a feather-light kiss on his forehead.

"Take my love to the grave with you. It is better served with you," I whisper.

I vow to never love another. I don't care if my father kills me or marries me off to a rancid prince in a far-flung kingdom. No one will ever have my heart again.

When I meet Finch's gaze, his face is plastered with fear. He has never seen a rage like this in me. Now, it's amplified by the raw powers of a sun that lives beyond the veil of the living. The goddess Siralto chose me to bear her power. She healed me of my shortcomings. She gifted me with her weapon.

Above me, the tiny phoenix Sira still burns brightly. I wonder how powerful a man Idris must have been to keep magic alive even when he is dead.

She flutters down to me and perches on my hand. I don't hide my tears, nor do I offer a single word to my brother-in-law. I take a mournful vow of silence. I will not speak again until the next day. I'm resolute in my decision as I stalk from the room.

As I leave Idris behind, I wonder what they'll do with his body. Will they send it home? Will they bury it with proper rites here in Sunfall?

A few hours later, while I'm up in my bedchambers, the maidservants return to find his body gone.

I have not left my room for days.

My vigil has gone from a day of silence to almost a week. Finch and Maverick have tried several times to speak to me. They've pounded at my door, offering food, drinks, and merriment. A few times, they came to just sit, slumped against the door in the hallway so I wasn't alone in my grief.

I've been informed that Alexander of Underland, with his golden curls and acid tongue will be the man I marry, whether I like it or not. The threat of a traitor's death was sent by my father, who is the only one who has *not* come to see me. The wedding, to my relief, has been pushed out for at least a week. They're giving me time to mourn my first choice of a fiancé, a mercy I didn't expect from my father.

I sit and pick at my cuticles and try to ignore the grumbling ache in my stomach. I wish I could fling myself from the castle's highest balcony and meet my end far, far below, but really, I want to wrench my hands around the neck of the Shadow King himself. I want to kill him for destroying my chances at freedom.

All this time, I've been sitting—plotting.

Idris, though I did not know him well, has become a beacon for my heart, mind, and soul that pushes me into a frenzy where only murder will satiate my desire for vengeance. Either my father's head or the vampire king's head will do, but these days, I favor the latter.

My father invited them to walk inside our walls, but without the Shadow King's influence, this never would have been an issue in the first place.

Is that really the case?

My self-doubt lingers. Sira chirps from above and flies down to me, her flaming eyes etched with concern. I wish I could raise Idris from the dead so I could kiss him once more, just for the gift of her. The diminutive phoenix has been my only companion during dark days and anguished nights.

My head spins from a lack of food and water. I fear if I stay in here much longer, I'll never get up again; starvation will lay claim to me from within the most privileged place in the kingdom.

Another knock at the door.

"Adelaide?"

It's Finch again. He's come to visit more than anyone else. I was relieved to hear he was pardoned and is free to live as a royal within the castle, so long as he doesn't step out of line. He sounds brighter. I'm happy for him. I'm glad he's proven his loyalty and earned the respect he deserves. He's the only Shadow Folk I'll ever love, even if it's only as a brother.

"What?" I finally answer, my voice hoarse.

"Please open the door. I brought fruit and water. You know... things you need to survive?"

I roll my eyes and bite back a number of insults I'd like to hurl at him, then sigh. He doesn't deserve my ire, as much as I want to find reasons to lob them in his direction.

My legs shake and I do my best to stand. My battle-worn clothes are filthy from lying in them for days, saturated with the stiff, dried blood of vampires still over the fabric. I haven't had the strength to stand, let alone bathe. I fear that Finch's supernatural sense of smell might cause him to keel over if he gets a whiff.

"Pass the food through the door. I'll be out before long," I say. "I need to bathe."

"I was about to say," Finch sneers. The door clicks open and he slides a plate inside.

I grab a simple, cotton dress and head for my bathing chamber, then take my time freshening up. The water takes a few minutes to warm and fill the tub. As it does, I sit and ponder my life and how I reached this point. Glinting light glows within my palms and I'm tempted once again to do the kingdom a favor by ridding it of Alaric and his tyrannical rule.

Surely there's already a movement against him somewhere within the kingdom.

Unearthing such a plot would be impossible to complete in a week, though.

I'm desperate for freedom now. I was so close! Even so, I can't fall short of it now, Idris or not. I was a fool to rely on him to save me, anyway. Beautiful as he may have been, he was mortal, just as I am. And life is far too short to sit around and wait for some prince or king to change it. And since when have I ever sat around and waited for that, anyway?

By the time I wring the water from my hair and dry my skin, I know my future is not here in Sunfall. My future is out there, where the shadows creep. Whether they lead to death or life, I don't care. I always knew where I would end up. A betrothal never should have stopped me from seeing that.

"Finch?" I call out. When I step back out into my bedchambers, he is sitting in a chair by the fireplace, waiting with a knowing smile.

He winks. "I'll ready the horses. I knew you'd come around eventually. Let's get you out of here, Adelaide. This is no place for people like you and me."

I nod, grateful that he reached the same conclusion.

I will never marry any suitor picked by my father.

I will not rule Sunfall. Its future lies with Maverick.

Me? My future lies with the Shadow King—either with my life ended in his sharp maw, or his head on my spike as I lead my people into a new dawn.

ABANDONMENT

CHALLENGER WAITS IN THE COURTYARD FOR ME, ALREADY saddled. The kingdom is as quiet as the Reaper himself, the night sky ablaze with a multitude of stars. I stop and drink them in, uncertain whether this night will be the last I see them or if I'll have decades more. Frankly, I could die right now if my father orders arrows to rain down from the castle walls to slaughter his traitor princess.

A smirk pulls at my lips just thinking of such a title. After everything I've done for my kingdom, I know my fate will end up the same. Traitor. Failure. It doesn't matter what I do. There is no winning until there's nothing left. With Idris gone to Tyrladan and Alexander as my only remaining option, I much prefer the chains of death that would let me die and leave this dreaded place. Even if I fail, at least I tasted freedom.

I think once more of Idris and how much I wish I knew of his home, Velyasa. He told me in earnest that the women there were loved for their fiery spirits. Perhaps I could go there and offer myself as a servant to atone for the crime of losing their king. Maybe I could explain to them that I was his missing piece and he died protecting the other half of his soul, as he seemed to believe I was.

My eyes are misty as I swing my leg into the saddle and settle in for the most difficult and exciting trip of my life. Finch rides beside me on Shadow. To my surprise, Ronald comes running out of the stables, though he doesn't seem to be on any mission to stop us. Instead, he comes up beside Challenger and reaches for my hand. I give it to him, and he plants a firm, gruff kiss to it.

"I'm proud of you, little princess," he whispers. "Your father never saw you as we do. I've told the men to hold his guards at bay while you escape. Not all will follow my order, but it will buy you some time."

My lip quivers before I can stop it. "Thank you, Ronald," I say, almost breathless. "It has been an honor serving with you."

Ronald salutes me before rushing back off into the stables. I will never hear about his wife Brenda or his children, Rose and Sean. I will never get to toast in merriment with them after hard fought battles, whether won or lost.

Hell, how do you know who wins or loses, anyway? The only way out is death.

My chest is heavy with grief as Finch and I ride away, our pace still urgent despite our bought time. Not all the soldiers listen to Ronald, Devon, and Jack. Not all of them are comrades in arms. Loyalty can be bought, and I'm no stranger to treachery.

I cast one last glance at the castle over my shoulder before easing Challenger into a swift gallop. Without all the equipment to weigh us down, I set a brutal pace that my steed is all too eager to match.

The strides between home and the land north of us feel like they take several lifetimes to reach. I keep waiting for a hail of arrows or the shouts of angry men, but they never come. By the time I glance over at Finch, I realize the grandest truth—we made it.

We left Sunfall.

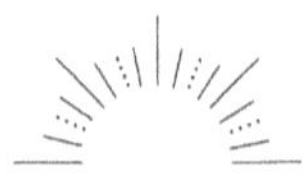

Finch and I don't stop until the sun starts to rise. Only the panting of our horses clues us in that it's time to stop. We find a place beside the river to let them get a drink. Patches of snow along the bank have just started to melt. I am grateful that spring is delayed. The cover of winter will make it harder for us to be tracked. By now, I know that at least Maverick will have noticed I'm gone.

"Did you tell Maverick?"

Finch shakes his head. "I didn't want to burden him with that kind of traitorous information. We need his head to stay *on*. He's the only hope that kingdom has."

I nod, once again grateful to Finch for his wisdom.

"To think—a couple months ago, you never would've been caught out here with me. Yet here we are, the only two people in the world in the land beyond the border. Unless you count the other shadow suckers," he laughs.

"Finch... you *are* a shadow sucker," I tease.

"Yes, but I am the *best* shadow sucker there is," he counters with a gleam in his eye.

"You know, I find it funny that you're using insults about what you are to describe yourself. I haven't heard that one in years," I chuckle.

"Meh." He shrugs. "Figured I'd bring it back. Helps me cope."

A beat or two of silence. "How long do you think we have before they start following us?" Finch looks at me and I groan, knowing what he's about to say.

He shakes his head. "Not long. We have a couple hours to rest, tops, before we need to start moving again. The less rest we get, the more space we can put between them and... wherever we're going. Did you have a particular place in mind?"

"The Shadow King's palace," I reply without hesitation.

Silence descends between us before Finch lets out a low whistle. "You know, maybe vengeance against the most powerful vampire king the world has ever seen for a man you dated for two days isn't the best choice."

I wince. "Maybe, but it's inevitable. They'll never stop coming after me. I'm what they hate most, Finch. And I'm even more powerful than my father or brother. Why do you think they jumped to try and marry me off, for Siralto's sake?"

At this, Finch merely hums in understanding.

"Besides, it's only fitting that I meet my fate in battle," I say. "It's the only place I can be *me* without some dumb political requirement attached."

"Is that true, though?" Finch presses. "You seemed pretty happy with Idris, even if it was only for a short while. What if there's more to your life than ending it with a foe's blade?"

I laugh. "If that was true, I would've been born to a father and mother in a kingdom where vampires weren't knocking down our doors to kill us because of who we are."

"Has it ever occurred to you that they might think the same of you and *your* lineage?"

I huff. "All the time, Finch. You're a huge smack in the face of everything I once believed."

He grins. "You're welcome."

"You know what I mean." I roll my eyes at him, but a smile tugs at my face. Even with the weight of a mountain of grief on my chest, I feel better. Even without Idris, I've found a silver lining—a way out. A golden thread to lead me somewhere better is all I ever wanted, even if it means the end.

"You don't have to follow me, you know," I say. "You could be whoever you want now. You could go assimilate with your people and have a wife... kids. A future." My voice drops off with wishful thinking. I almost miss the aghast look on Finch's face.

"And leave you? Oh, no. That's not happening, Sunshine," Finch argues. "I figure I can call you that now, since royal pretenses are out the window and you have your little light power."

"Yes, a little light power that can level kingdoms and reduce you to ash," I sneer.

"Details," Finch scoffs. "Listen, I'm going with you, end of discussion. Even if it's on a stupid suicide mission to kill the Shadow King. But... why not try and go to Velyasa first? Maybe you could rally them to your cause. I mean, the Shadow Folk *did* kill their king."

I consider this. "But... aren't we just as responsible for his death? He came to court me and left a corpse. My father failed to screen the potential suitors he invited and got my betrothed killed in the process."

I still don't know how to process my grief. It's like living with an anvil chained around my heart and neck, and I never know when it's going to drop. I've been jostled on such a wild ride between numbness and sorrow that I wonder if I'll ever find "normal" again. I would give so much just to see Idris and apologize to him—to let him know how sorry I am that he lost his life because of me. All I did was mope and cry, and he still found it in him to die for me.

And why? He didn't know me, either. He only knew about me from stories.

If Finch wasn't here, I might tuck my knees under my chin and wait for either a vampire or one of my father's soldiers to slay me on the spot. But self-loathing never helped. It didn't pick me up when I needed to keep pushing, even in all my years where freedom was *never* a thought I had. It was always the next battle.

"So, you'll go with me?" I hate how small my voice is as I betray myself once again for how vulnerable I've become. All my walls have been shattered. There's no sense in hiding any longer. If Finch was going to use it against me, he would have by now.

"Yes, Sunshine, I'll go with you. Now, why don't you let me hunt while you gather some non-divine fruits or berries to eat, and then we can carry on, okay? It would be the height of foolishness to get this far only to get hauled back to those dungeons again." Finch shudders. "They're not as comfortable as they look."

I lift one brow. "Who said they were meant to be comfortable?"

"Exactly." Finch claps and motions for me to follow him. "Stay here and gather stuff. I'll make the hunting part easy. You don't need the blood from my kills anyway."

When Finch licks his lips, I wonder if he would be offended if I vomited right about now. Something tells me he would, so I hold back on the gurgle brewing in my stomach and turn my attention to the tree line for any signs of things that might bear fruit in the winter instead.

I have a bit of luck with some berries I recognize are harmless and gather enough for a few mouthfuls. It's more than I've eaten in days, aside from what Finch brought me. I'm grateful for it.

"How far north is the castle?" I ask aloud, even though Finch isn't back yet. Sira, silent as ever, hovers beside me. I look to her, hoping maybe she can still track things as she did when Idris was alive.

To my relief, she rises against the horizon and points due north. Part of me knows I should go to Idris' homeland. Sunfall's soldiers would never expect me to do that—or at least they wouldn't suspect it as much as they might suspect vengeance against the people who slaughtered Idris.

My father knows how much he meant to me. I was foolish enough to reveal my hand in the throne room by demanding he cut out the rest of the participants and let me choose Idris for myself, even with the threat of death. But I know that most will be frightened enough not to follow through with chasing me down, even if they know the truth. The farther north we travel, the better chance Finch and I have of reaching the point of no return. None but the most stalwart will follow us once we arrive at the base of the mountain where the castle sits, perched at the very top. I've seen illustrations of it.

When did I become so sentimental? So... reckless?

When my mind wanders and I start to really ponder these things, Finch returns with a freshly killed rabbit. I don't comment on how limp it is. Instead, I gratefully take it from him and let him start a fire while I skin and clean it. He doesn't say much while I eat the roasted beast, instead watching the sun rise higher in the sky, midday fast approaching.

"When do we set off?" I finally ask.

"That depends," he answers. "How long can Challenger and Shadow ride after such a short break?"

I laugh. "Challenger has carried me into many battles, and Shadow went with us when we tried to find where you died. Neither are strangers to long journeys like this."

"Then we carry on now," Finch says, his tone final and sharp. He's on edge, despite his humor. He has more to lose than I do if he's captured again. They'll use him up before they kill him. My use is long since spent and death will be the first thing they give me, which, as I think about it, is more of a gift than a curse.

I won't go down without a fight, so there's still that part. It won't be as swift a death as I want.

I'm my own worst enemy, I decide, as I resaddle Challenger and climb onto his back. Sira hovers above my shoulder. I call to her. "Show us the way."

Her wings flutter a few times before she sets off, just within the edges of my sight so I know where to run. Challenger opens up at speeds we've never reached before. If I fall off, my neck will snap on the way down. I pray no gopher holes or ditches are hiding beneath the snow.

Siralto blesses us, giving us a clean stretch of land upon which to run.

By the time night falls, we're far, far away from the kingdom of Sunfall and inching closer to the Shadow King and his forces.

That much closer to the end.

Wilderness

Finch and I stay silent for most of the trip.

After three days, we still haven't encountered a single sign of a living or unliving being, other than a few birds and the few hares Finch has managed to hunt. We suspect the landscape has been picked clean of large game and the hunting bands have moved farther south, leaving the north emptier than usual.

My bet that Sunfall wouldn't follow us far seems to be holding out. Finch and I decided to wager on it, though we're betting with acorn caps rather than real currency. But it's as good as any out here in a market of two, especially since we share no similarities in diet, clothing, or hobbies. Except riding, of course, but swapping horses would make little sense at this point, and I know for a fact Challenger would launch Finch into the sun if he tried to ride him.

I'm conscious and breathing. Challenger doesn't need anyone else. My horse is stubborn and selective; even Finch has caught on to this, giving my chestnut steed a wide, wary berth whenever we aren't mounted and riding.

We decide to dismount and stretch our legs, allowing our horses to rest. I finally break the silence. "How does it feel to be out of the dungeons for good?"

"Hold on now, Sunshine, let's not reverse our luck," he cautions.

I click my tongue. "It was just a question."

He cocks a brow. "I'm teasing, Adelaide."

I glare at him.

"Mostly."

Before Finch can say anything more, I sneeze. Over the past few days, the snow betrayed us and left in its stead new spring grass. A few trees are already burdened with blossoming buds in this warmer pocket of the north and have begun to pollenate. My eyes water and sting worse than they usually do. We don't typically see trees like this around Sunfall.

I wonder just how far we've traveled as I sit and munch on a handful of berries. I wish I'd brought a kettle with us. I could make tea with some of the flowers up here. They're a standard mix of non-poisonous wildflowers and they make a nice, airy tea that helps soothe the soul.

More than ever, I need something like that. Every night I've awakened to tears streaming down my cheeks with dreams of Idris, the palace, and my mother haunting me. My mind is finally free to process all these horrors and more. Finch hasn't said a word about them, instead letting me wallow in the memories alone.

I don't know whether to thank him or smack him. I favor the former, but the latter is tempting more often than not as our trip progresses. Any shred of sanity I had prior to Idris' death is gone. I didn't know I had any left to lose, but grieving a man I knew for two days like he was the love of my life seems to solidify this for me.

Granted, he kind of was the love of my life. And who am I to decide how long is enough time to love someone?

I try not to stew on this for too long. I look back at Finch and prod him for an answer. "Well? Are you going to at least give me a hint about what you think about all this?"

Finch casts me a look that would make a lesser woman cower, but I'm not a lesser woman and this vampire does not scare me.

"I think you've lost it," he says. "This is as reckless as it is foolish, but even so, I'm proud of you. This is the first time you're doing something for *you*. You're going to stick it to the man, even if it's not the one you ought to be sticking it to."

I freeze. "What?"

My brother-in-law fixes me with an impenetrable stare. "You and I both know who you should *really* be going after," he presses. "He locked me in a dungeon, mocks your brother for being unable to produce heirs after he lost said ability to horrible injuries in battle, and was willing to sell you to the highest bidder, to the point of letting rabid vampires into the castle. What more proof do you need? Besides that, he's a horrible king. You *do* know he overtaxes the people, don't you?"

I nod, my neck stiff. I can't bear to look at him because I know he's right. "The Shadow King had my mother killed," I say woodenly.

"Do you think she'd want this from you, though?"

I whirl on him, light crackling to life in my hands. "What do you know of my mother?"

"That she was kind," Finch answers, unmoved by my outburst. "That your father didn't deserve her, and he's wrong for holding her death over your head like it's your fault."

I flinch, but a snappy comeback doesn't come to mind. Slumping my shoulders in defeat, I pick up the pace and move away from him. "I'm going to slay the Shadow King. I've got the Siraltona. I finally have what I need to accomplish everything I ever hoped for. If I do this, I can return to Sunfall a champion or use it as leverage to help my brother overtake the throne."

Finch was incredulous. "Don't you want to rule? Why don't you become queen?"

I give a bitter laugh. "No."

I don't turn to look back at him, or else he'll see by my face the truth I've been hiding. Of *course* I'm jealous of Maverick. Who wouldn't be? He's had power, presence, and influence afforded him from birth that naturally incline him to the throne, while I'm the annoying princess who happens to be good with a sword. I'm the one who let my mother down. She was with *me* when she died, after all. I couldn't protect her like Maverick or Alaric could've.

"Well, you keep telling yourself that, Sunshine. In the meantime, why don't we come up with an actual plan for this rather than charging in with bells tied to our toes to let them know dinner is served?" Finch says.

I can practically hear his eyes roll and feel the unmistakable urge to slap him for it. What's worse is I have the audacity to chuckle at his stupid jokes.

"Fine," I say, conceding to him. "I would like to be taken seriously as a ruler. I don't crave power... just... respect. And if power came with that, why not have some of it? Why do my sacrifices count for nothing? I know Maverick has earned his place, but what about me? Haven't I gained a place, too?"

Finch smiles. "There's the truth, Sunshine. I'm glad to see it. That still doesn't get us any closer to a plan, but I think putting your cards on the table is an excellent first step to understanding what sort of hand we have. First of all—have you figured out why your powers didn't kill Ivan?"

I freeze for a moment, doing my best to catch up to Finch's jumps from topic to topic. I can tell he's nervous. When he won't land on one thing to talk about, it's his way of subtly letting someone know he can't afford to linger. He wants to move. It's a tell of his that I've figured out over the years and my hackles rise as I realize what kind of predicament we're in if he's nervous.

How do you even kill the Shadow King, anyway? What if he's immune to my powers? What if the battle the other day was a fluke?

I brush these thoughts aside to grapple with later. "Idris presumed the reason was because I didn't really want to kill him," I answer with a shrug.

"Did you?"

While I think on this, Finch pulls out a knife and starts to whittle a twig. Most would find this infuriating, but I recognize it for what it is. He's staying busy. He's plotting just as much as I am. Whether he agrees with my rash decision or not, he will help me on my reckless errand.

Even though he's right. My father is the one who should pay for Idris' death with his blood.

I wish more than ever that Idris was here to weigh in on things. I don't know why I firmly believe things would have been better with him, but everything about him represented the life I wanted and almost had. I could've been a queen. More importantly, I could have been his equal. I could have been loved.

"I guess... kind of. I was already planning my escape," I admit. "I knew that if I didn't pick one of the suitors, I would be left to the mercy of whatever choice my father made. So, I decided to create a scene and stack the deck in my favor. I'm a force my father doesn't understand.

I'm too valuable to get rid of outright, but acting openly treasonous would have lost me my head. I knew Idris would accept my outbursts and I could dissuade the others from choosing me if I did what I did that morning at breakfast. Originally, I was just going to throw my bowl at Ivan, but then he made me angry and I just... lost it. I don't believe I thought about murdering him at all. I wasn't... *thinking* at all."

Finch points his knife at me. "That's your problem. You know magic requires focus. When you don't focus, the outcomes are varied—wild. You didn't concentrate it enough on him. You didn't will it to do what you wanted."

"Will it?"

Finch hums and holds out his hands. Between his fingers, tendrils of shadow snake their way up his fingers, hugging his skin as closely and delicately as fine, silken fabric. It weaves around him, a living being that is both part of him and separate. Before I can react, the smoky shadows find their way across the melting snow, up my legs, and coil around my arms. My Siraltona starts to glow, ready to rise to the challenge, but I sense it's not a threat and I don't summon it forth. Instead, I allow the shadows to hum along my skin and relish in feeling power different from mine.

"These shadows, when used properly, can be fatal," Finch explains. "I'm willing them not to kill. I'm not even thinking of killing. I'm thinking of showing you something—of teaching. I'm demonstrating a point. Therefore, they touch you but they do not harm you. How do you think you're able to hold Sira without burning yourself?"

At the mention of my phoenix, I look up and find her perched in the branches of a tree not far from us. Lately, she's been more solitary. She flies ahead as usual, but she's been taking space for herself. I wonder if I've done something to offend her or if the grief of losing her creator has finally caught up to her.

"Then how is it that the Siraltona kills every Shadow Folk that encounters Maverick or my father?" I challenge. "How do we know I'm not just weaker or my magic isn't as consistent as theirs?"

My veins hum almost angrily at my challenge and Finch chuckles. His shadows retreat before my light can try to swallow them whole.

"Adelaide, all they think about when it comes to creatures like me is killing us. The Shadow Folk are a threat to their sovereignty. They imbue weapons with their light, which significantly diminishes any chances that the magic won't work right. You're working with the divine blessings in the raw. That means you have to work harder to control it and bend it to your will, or else you need to find a vessel—like your sword. You didn't struggle cutting them down in the castle, did you?"

"I hate when you're right," I pout. I wouldn't let myself be childish with anyone else, but my brother-in-law has seen me in worse states.

"I know." He grins and runs his fingers through his hair like a true show off. I roll my eyes at him. "So, going on with me being right... don't you realize how reckless it is to go into the Shadow King's realm without a plan? You're marching in to slay this bastard, and you haven't even gotten your magic under control! You're allowing your grief to get the better of you. Why not try to find people who can support you as you learn your magic?"

My nostrils flare and I open my mouth to interrupt, but Finch presses on.

"I'm not suggesting we go back to Sunfall, but Velyasa lies north somewhere, right? Why not change course and find the way there? Would Sira be able to lead us?"

I look up at where the tiny phoenix is perched and she raises her head to look at me. I know I don't imagine some of the sparkle returning to her eyes. She seems... *brighter*... at the mention of her home. "Sira, I believe I'm done moping. Would it be alright if we change course and you lead us home—to *your* home?"

She lets out a cry; it's the first time I've heard her make a noise. The sound is clear and piercing like a wooden flute.

"I think she agrees," Finch says.

We rush to our horses, eager to carry on with my phoenix as she directs us in a more logical direction.

"What will I say to his people?" I nervously ask.

Finch answers without hesitation. "That he was your first and only choice and you abandoned your people over your father's reckless choices that led to his death. Adelaide, your honesty will buy you more friends and allies than you realize. You've chosen to stand for something."

I notice Finch is not nearly as breathless as I am as we swing up into our respective saddles. "I hope you're right," I mutter, just loud enough for my ears.

"I know I am!" he shouts, his voice smug.

Damn Shadow Folk hearing.

We race ahead in roughly the same direction as the Shadow King's castle, and I start to wonder where Velyasa lies.

Is it beyond the land of the Shadow Folk? Surely, we don't have to go through it...

The thought of running across hordes of vampires and being spotted by the Shadow King weighs heavily the more I ponder Finch's guidance. I chastise myself for being so reckless. I have no idea what I'm up against in my quest to take that horrid monster down to Kohlu, but blindly charging in is undoubtedly a fool's errand. Worse yet, if they were desperate enough to breach our castle walls to get to me... how much more of a target am I out here in the open?

As the wind whips my hair, I try not to think about the prospect of being hunted and watched. Surely Finch would know by now if we were being followed and he would have us change course.

Up ahead, Sira flies steadily along the horizon. I only hope she knows to lead us *around* the kingdom of the Shadow Folk and not through it. I swallow, realizing I have no idea if this is even possible.

What have I done?

BOUNTY

AFTER COUNTLESS DAYS OF CONSTANT RIDING, MY LEGS ARE chafed and throb with a bone-deep ache. Finch is more sour than usual. I suspect it's to do with the lack of blood in his system. We've stopped a few times, but our horses are ragged and, true to my fears, we're now on the outskirts of where the outermost vampire peasants reside.

Their towns resemble the peasant squares within Sunfall, but they somehow seem more magical. Where magic is a luxury to mortals, it's a common commodity among vampires. A few nights, Finch nearly snapped my head off for watching too closely from the bushes, watching them hustle and bustle to trade their wares and earn their keep.

I wonder if vampires grow crops or if they only rely on hunting. They consume things with a life force, with blood being their favored drink. But do they ever crave bread? Cheese? Ale? Wine? All these questions spin in my head as I wrack my memory for any hints that might be left from the books I used to read. A pang of regret passes as I think of the massive library waiting for me at Sunfall if I'd only chosen to stay back. Then again, my father would have married me off to Alexander by now and I would already be holed up in Underland, prepping to bear an heir for a man I loathe.

"The books can wait," I whisper to myself.

"The what?"

I look up, belatedly realizing Finch is listening as we trot along a strange, weaving path that leads toward a mystery. The theme of this journey is obscurity, and I've grown weary of it. I want to embrace something familiar, but I know that is not my path. This makes mourning my losses so much more intense. I curse my father again for thrusting me into this situation. I've pondered Finch's words over and over and realize that my folly was in not slaying my father first.

Too late to go back now.

I half expect Alaric or Maverick to pop up between the trees somewhere and order me to return home to the castle or behead me on the spot. As much as I trust Maverick and our shared hate for our father, by now, he undoubtedly considers me a deserter. A *traitor*. But I can't sacrifice my life and freedom for the sake of a *chance* at something better. This is especially true as a woman, because marriage would permanently prevent me from being tied to Sunfall without the strings of a husband attached. The political complexity is too far above my head to ponder on an empty stomach.

"Finch," I whine, "we need to stop. You're one day away from draining me to feed, and I'm starting to see stars. Challenger and Shadow need rest, too."

My horse snorts, his strides slower with each passing day. We've taken small breaks along the way to afford the animals some rest, but the long travel has worn on them. Finch, at one point, suggested trading them in a town we were passing through and quickly realized that would be a deadly decision on his part. My decision probably seems unnecessary to most, but Challenger is all I have left of the world I once knew and loved.

He shakes his head. "Not yet. We should put a few more lengths between us and that last village you so foolishly decided to snoop in," Finch snapped, then groaned in frustration. "You smell like a delicate meal, Adelaide. When will you realize you can't get that close without garnering attention?"

I glare at him but wisely don't respond because he's right. My curiosity *has* been getting the better of me lately; my rational side has all but flown away in the breeze. Maybe it's the fresh smell of spring which has finally arrived in earnest. It's early in the season and the whipping winds still sting, but early flowers perfume the air with heady scents and more green is visible. The sight makes me positively giddy and perhaps a little more reckless than usual. I've always suspected that I thrive better in the sun, but adjusting to it after the long winter always comes with more questionable choices on my part.

"Okay, what if we get through that clearing up ahead and on to the next copse of woods beyond it—would that be far enough away for us to rest? You need to feed, Finch, and I'll be damned if I'm going to be your lunch," I sneer. "The last time I offered, you told me it wasn't an appropriate option and I agreed. I'm not about to let you stoop so low as to attack me because you're ravenous with hunger."

It's more of a barb than a joke, but it sets him off laughing anyway, returning signs of mirth and joy to the paleness in his cheeks. His pallor has faded, and I know he's in need of something to return more color to his skin. He looks like a walking corpse.

I know from reading that newer vampires must feed more often. It's why they're known for having such ravenous appetites. Their body has to adjust to the change of being resurrected from the dead. Although Finch is technically a few months old now, that's not long enough to garner the control and poise of an experienced vampire.

I wonder how often the Shadow King feeds.

Shuddering, I note that Finch hasn't answered me, so I take that as a sign that he agrees with me. I'd press Challenger to speed up, but neither of us has the energy and the next copse of woods seems *so* far away. I fear I'll keel over before we reach it.

Instead, I change the subject. "What will you do when we get to Velyasa?"

Finch turns to me, a mix of exhaustion and irritation passing over his face. "Why ask me that now, Adelaide? It's not going to distract me from the knocking pain in my stomach."

Before I can retort, we hear a rustle in the bushes ahead and Finch veers his horse in front of mine, ready to block and protect. I grip the hilt of my sword and allow my powers to leak into the steel. I still don't trust that I can get a decent hit in with my raw power—not until I learn why I failed to slay Ivan on the first go.

The rustles get louder and ice travels down my spine until I fear I'll be sick. Hunger-filled nausea curls in my stomach. I don't have any lunch to lose, but bile still burns when it comes back up.

"Adelaide, be prepared to run," Finch whispers.

Beneath me, Challenger tenses. Despite being exhausted, my horse always seems to find a second wind. I envy his strength and am grateful for him in moments like this.

From the bushes below, I notice a flash of red. I bite back a scream as a small child walks out onto the wooded path in front of us. I presume he is around four or five years old, but I know nothing of how vampire children are reared. I didn't even realize they could procreate in that fashion. I assumed all of them were turned in death.

"A child?" I whisper.

Finch looks at me, his eyes wide with alarm.

The child has blazing red skin and yellow, lamplight eyes framed by sleek black hair. He looks like the cartoonish devils and demons I saw in the fairytales I read back home in my library. But this is no fairytale.

The child looks up at us and smiles, showcasing pointed teeth.

"Who are you, little one?" I ask, suddenly brave enough to find my voice.

Finch wheels back to look at me, his eyes full of icy terror. "Do you want to summon every villager this way? Adelaide, you need to *go*. Now. Ride ahead. I'll see what I can learn from this child, but you need to leave before someone else comes to look for them and sees you!"

I hesitate, still eager to learn more, but he's right. Without another word, I urge Challenger into a canter and take off, hoping Finch knows how to catch up with me. I figure my scent should be enough. Sira is up ahead, perched in the branches of the trees where I wanted to rest. I know now that the promised resting spot still isn't far enough away. There's no way I can rest here when Shadow Folk are so close.

A part of me wonders if it's wrong to leave Finch behind. Won't the child be curious about where he came from? I don't know how often new Shadow Folk are created. But Finch is right. If I stick around, my aura—my shimmer—will continue to attract them and the Shadow King will know exactly who and where I am.

I hear Sira crooning in the trees, but she has disappeared. I assume she's circling up ahead, searching for plump mice or squirrels. Those creatures seem to be her favorites to prey on. Normally, she doesn't make noise unless she spots something worth swooping on. Her little cry of joy always tugs a small smile across my lips as I consider how happy she is when she has a full belly. It's odd that living fire would have to eat at all, but it's fascinating all the same.

Even more odd is that she is still burning strong when, back in Sunfall, Idris has undoubtedly been given proper burial rites or sent back to Velyasa to his people. I can only hope they will accept me. I still can't grasp why or how I became so attached to him in such a short span of time, but everything about my interactions with Idris was intoxicating—ethereal. Perhaps he was a metaphor for something I'd lost in myself. He was the dream I let go of when I felt I would never have magic.

Does that mean I merely loved the idea of him?

Still not satisfied with the answers in my head and heart, I slow Challenger to a walk and search the branches for where Sira might have lighted to feast on whatever poor woodland creature she'd caught. Finch remains absent, and I try not to let my heart stammer through my chest on a panicked retreat.

I still can't believe I was almost foolish enough to hunt down the Shadow King. Perhaps it was desperation, or possibly a lack of self-preservation when I knew my chances at a life outside of restrictive oppression were dashed.

My stomach curdles at the thought of being wed to Alexander. He's a far cry from the kindness that Beatrice always showed me. The Duke of Underland is a foul man whom I have no desire to marry. In the few minutes it took me to know that Idris was my fire, I knew at once that Alexander was my end, just as Ivan was.

I'm peering through the branches, unable to find Sira, when I hear Shadow's thundering hooves. Turning, I spot Finch galloping at me and waving, his eyes and movements frantic. *No rest today*, I think to myself. I don't wait to hear what he has to say, already sensing the coiling darkness beneath the very ground where Challenger and I have stopped.

I don't see Sira, but the little phoenix will catch up when she's finished filling her belly. Urging Challenger into a fast gallop through the trees, I pray we don't land in a gopher hole or trip over an unseen branch or rock. My hair streams in the air behind me and whips my cheeks. I duck as much as I can to dodge the tree limbs swaying overhead, the very earth trembling as I drown out the sounds of Finch's screams and the undeniable sound of thundering hooves not far behind him.

They know I'm here.

I want to know *who* among them knows. The villagers? Nobles? The King himself? How fast does word travel in the kingdom of shadows? I half expect to see a giant, black dragon overhead just as I did the night I saved Sunfall from its own folly. I wonder if I should have done it. I'm convinced I only staved off their inevitable destruction.

"Finch!" I call, realizing he's no longer beside me. My peripheral vision is blurred by the haze of my terror as I continue to press on, Challenger unwilling to yield to any of the barriers between me and freedom.

Finch remains missing and I struggle to breathe as panic claws up my throat. Sira cries out overhead and I finally see a flash of flame against the horizon; she's still pointing us onward.

I don't have time to stop and look for Finch. If I turn back now, we'll both be swallowed whole. I can only hope he makes it out.

But he saved me when I needed him most.

I crane my head around and realize I've been galloping for quite some time. Challenger has put ample space between me and what I fear is an angry mob of vampires behind me, but my heart drops as I realize Finch is still nowhere to be seen.

Now, I am alone in the woods of shadow. By dawn, everyone will know I'm here.

WANDERER

Challenger's energy wanes and I can't keep pushing him as I have. We've scarcely stopped for two days. I've dared to call out for Finch several times, hoping he'll pop up and declare this all a horrible joke. I can't imagine how he went from speaking to a small, innocent child to being swept away by his own kind.

Guilt eats me alive for leaving him behind. *I should have gone back.*

I alone have the power to stop the hordes of Shadow Folk. I could have driven them off for him. *Wasn't that the same mad plan that Finch told you not to go on, though? Are you really enough of an expert to hold them at bay when you don't even know how you get your powers to work?*

I wish for the life of me that I had asked Idris to train me rather than sucking face with him during the short time we knew each other. I was so excited at the prospect of learning more that I put it off, thinking I'd have a lifetime in Velyasa to learn those things with my betrothed.

Now, I am lost in the woods following an echo of my betrothed's magic, praying the little winged creature is leading me to where he once ruled. Throughout our harried escape, Sira's light has grown dim. Sensing my distress, she pushes ahead without stopping. Sira is a beacon of light, but even she needs rest.

If I rest now, they will find me.

I haven't seen a village, let alone an outpost, for days. Signs of life are all but gone. Other than a few short stops to get water and let Challenger nibble on the last bits of grain I have, we have not stopped.

My horse is tired. I am tired. My bones are tired. Perhaps they yearn for the comforting earth beneath. Maybe it is my time, and it would only be fitting that I should die in a way similar to my mother.

Would my mother be proud of me now as I race against the ends of time in an unfamiliar land? Would she approve of me abandoning my role in a feeble attempt to find help against my father and the Shadow King?

Tears blur my vision and I decide to let Challenger pull back. He groans with exhaustion, his pace cutting down to a slow walk. I halt him and slide to the ground, opting to lead him by his reins for as long as my legs will allow me. Sweat shines along his red coat and I chide myself for not cooling him down better. This is the longest I've ever pushed him. Without his unyielding energy, we would not have made it this far.

I lift my head and scent the air—water can't be far. I hear it on the silent breeze that rustles my hair and sends chills down my spine. Although dread settles in my core at the thought of stopping, my horse needs water. *I* need water. Sira needs a break from flying ahead, a constant speck of sunlight no matter the weather or hour of day.

When we finally reach the small river, I dive into it. Challenger buries his head deep in the water and I barely stand back up in time to remove his tack before he joins me in the water. I don't watch to see where his tack lands when I hurl it. Above, the sun beats down on my skin, but the cool stream sings a song of relief.

Challenger seems brighter simply being immersed in the water. Above, Sira perches in a tree branch and sings a happy song, a squirrel dangling in her fiery talons.

The thought of food makes my stomach grumble. Finch was always so good at hunting. I'm not a bad shot—if anything, I'm excellent. The problem is finding something to kill in the first place. I consider asking Sira to help me find animals and try to ignore my growling stomach.

Before I can formulate such a request, a twig snaps and I'm on alert. Challenger jolts to attention and I can't blame him if he decides to bolt. It's not customary for a horse to stick around when there's danger—it's not in their nature. Still, a part of me hopes wistfully that he might wait so we can bolt together.

Light hums to life in my palms and I try to soothe my frayed nerves, reminding myself that I *do* have power. I *can* protect myself. Idris' words about control and emotions haunt me even as I let the light grow brighter and the power whispers secrets to me in the darkest parts of my mind. I don't understand its words and I wish I had paid more attention to what Maverick shared regarding magic. I wish I'd read more about it, even as the sensation of someone *watching* kicks my heart rate into a fervent sprint.

I must leave.

I turn to find that Challenger is still watching, his fur soaked. I wince, wondering how long I can stay on with his fur so slick. I don't want his tack to rub him raw, either, so if we run, I'll have to abandon it. Without his saddle, I can see how thin he is. *Can he really keep running like this?*

My foolhardy escape plan is in tatters. I was foolish to take off as I did on a suicide mission with no knowledge of where Velyasa lies. Why didn't I just plunge my sword into my horrid father's throat? If I'd murdered the king, what's the worst that would have happened? Imprisonment? Death? I was sure to feel its sting, regardless. Better to die doing something worthwhile rather than how I'm about to go now.

I realize I'm not breathing and attempt to take a shaky breath, my eyes darting every which way to spot the source of the snapped twig.

Relief floods my eyes with tears as I see him—*Finch*.

He comes running and I don't wait. I scramble from the water and rush him, tackling him with a forceful hug. Caution be damned, my brother-in-law is alive and well.

"Sister," he whispers, "you're okay."

I look up at him and hardly see his face through the curtain of tears blurring my vision. "Where did you go?"

"I had to get them off your trail," he answers, a nervous laugh escaping him. "They can see your light, Adelaide. They know what you are. The Shadow King likely knows you're outside the bounds of his territory by now."

Dread coils within me. The serpent of fear fills me to the brim, even within my veins. "Does that mean we have to keep running?"

Finch nods. "Not right away, but we do need to get moving soon. If we stagger our efforts and vary our travel patterns, it might help throw them off. And, as always, I'll protect you where I can."

"I'm just glad you're alive!" I sob. "I'm so tired and hungry, but at least you're here and breathing and not being tortured by your own kind."

Laughing, Finch sets me down. "I'm glad you're alive, too, Adelaide. I was beginning to worry that maybe that bastard Shadow King had sent his men to catch you already. I have no idea how fast they can send information back to him. I'm probably the worst Shadow Folk to know in that regard." Blushing fiercely, Finch rubs his hand along the back of his neck.

"No, you're the *best* one to know." My return smile is weak but genuine. The light has subsided from my hands but lurks just beneath the surface—warm and content. Idly, I wonder if I can weave fire as Idris did back in the palace.

I still can't fathom why my attraction to him was so fierce and ... resolute. At what point did I lose my mind enough to seek vengeance for a man I hardly knew? I've never been reckless. Ever. I rue the day I ever act that way again. I can't give in to such impulses if I want to survive the Shadow King's efforts to come and claim me.

What has become of me? I'm out here risking mine and Finch's life to avoid marriage and to avenge a man whose kingdom I haven't even seen!

A horrid thought occurs to me and I glance longwise at Finch, who seems to catch on to the feeling of dread creeping between us. "Should we even go to Velyasa?" I ask. "Is it fair to bring this creature to their doorsteps? Perhaps we should turn back. Maybe we should rally Maverick to overtake my father instead."

Finch hums and strokes his chin. "That *is* a predicament. Do we bring enemies to the doorstep of the man who died fighting for you? Are they equipped to fight off shadowy vampires far less dashing and handsome than myself?"

I shake my head. "We can't do this, Finch. Innocents will die. This fight rests with Sunfall. I've been a fool coming out here, reckless and ignorant."

"Yet, if you go back, you will be married off and sent to Underland before you can help Maverick. Your father will clap you in irons and send you on your way. And as much as they tout a strong defense, I hardly doubt Underland can fend off the Shadow King's entire army."

My skin goes pale. "So, wherever I go, I damn them to the realities of the Shadow King's hordes and there's no way to rectify this?"

Finch doesn't answer and I lower my head. *Should I end myself and rid the world of this predicament?*

"If you're thinking what I think you are, then *no*. That is *not* the answer." Finch's handsome face is grim. "I think, instead, that we should be upfront with our intentions when we reach Velyasa. There is a *reason* the Shadow King wants you, and it's not just because you're a pretty girl, Adelaide. You have *power* and you need to learn how to use it. Once you do, you are the Shadow King's worst nightmare. Don't you realize it? Going back would be a suicide I can't allow."

He shakes his head, his stance resolute. "No, we go onward and present you to the Velyasans as a weapon, because that's what you are. Do you really think you'd be well served as a wife in a place where they despise magic? Magic is the only thing that can save mortal lives from immortal terrors, Adelaide! And mortals deserve to have the choice on whether they want to become fanged beasts of the night, don't you think?" Finch jerks a finger at himself. "Don't you think *I* deserved a choice?"

I flinch, realizing just how personal this has become to my brother-in-law. He willingly came along to protect me, but it also seems he came so he could give others a chance to escape the fate he endured.

"Don't forget, you are hope incarnate, Adelaide. You went from knight to goddess overnight and saved Sunfall from utter destruction against an ancient *dragon* vampire with no formal training. Give yourself a damn break and stop doubting yourself so much! Just take your shit and quit moping," Finch sneers. "It's not a good look for you."

He might as well have slapped me, but his words strike home and settle deep in my gut. He's right. I've been wallowing in fear and worry and sadness that aren't mine to carry. The only thing I *should* be mourning is the loss of my kingdom and betrothed.

I am not powerless.

Straightening my shoulders, I fix Finch with a hard stare. "You're right," I admit. "I don't know what came over me. First, I became obsessed with a man I barely know, and now I'm out here wallowing in self-pity. Forgive me, brother; I have no idea why I've been like this."

Finch waves a hand at me. "Don't sweat it, Adelaide. It's not every day that young princesses abandon their kingdoms and set off to avenge their almost fiancés on a suicide mission—against vampires, no less. Nor is it every day that they commit treason, but here we are."

Chuckling, Finch looks over at Challenger. I'm relieved that my horse has not bolted. Instead, he seems relaxed again as he drinks from the placid waters.

"I think it's best we give ourselves a bit of a break before we push on," he offers. "This area is farther from their encampments. You made good distance. I think we can afford to let Challenger rest."

For the first time, I realize Shadow is missing. "Um, Finch? Where's your horse?"

Finch frowns. "Bastard broke his leg a while back. I had no choice but to let him go on to Tyrladan. Alti'le."

My eyes widen and I gasp. "How will you keep up?"

Finch shrugs. "I really only rode the horse for appearances' sake. I can move a lot faster than he could anyway, and we've no need to hide what I am in this part of the world."

I eye my horse with disbelief. "You can outrun Challenger?"

"You *do* remember I can take the form of a dragon, right?" He rolls his eyes. "And, yes, even in this form, I can. I am an apex predator, Adelaide. I've been taking down prey with my bare hands this whole trip... Haven't you been paying attention?"

I glare at Finch and curse my foolishness yet again. I can't believe how unaware of everything I've been. In retrospect, this entire trip feels more like a bad dream than anything else. "Fine. I'm sorry we lost Shadow, though. Poor horse."

Shaking his head, Finch turns to peer at Sira, who sits preening herself in the trees. "That dumb bird couldn't have brought you food this whole time?"

I listlessly shrug one shoulder. "I don't know. I was just about to ask her when you got here," I admit. "I was so focused on escaping that I didn't really stop to process just how tired and hungry I am."

He scrutinizes my face. "Fair. I'm glad you focused on getting out of there. It bought us the time we need to plan the rest of our trip to Velyasa. I'll scout ahead after I bring you some food. I need to get an idea of the course we're taking and what threats might be waiting for us along the way."

I swallow. "You're going to leave again?"

"I have to. You're our region's biggest asset in a war that's just gotten bigger than anything Sunfall could've imagined." He casts a shadowy glare at me. "Riding in blind is never wise."

Before I can devise a defensive remark, he vanishes. I hate how I've ignored all his new abilities until now. I swear he seems stronger than ever, and more wise. More mature. It's a wonder what he'll be like in a few centuries when I'm long gone and he's still living.

Will he even remember me?

I'm mulling over my mortality when Finch returns with a few drained rabbits strung over his shoulders. He shoots me a toothy grin and I blanch at the sight of his pink-tinged fangs.

Noticing my discomfort, he rolls his eyes. "Come on, Princess, I thought we were past that by now."

I don't respond as he places them on a spit over a fire I don't remember him starting. I suppose as a dragon he can summon flame, but the idea makes the hairs on my neck stand up anyway.

The Siraltona doesn't seem as put off by his actions. Over the last few days, I've noticed it warms when I am afraid, but it is quiet. I still don't understand how to channel it as I did that night against Mars. Once again, I find myself wishing Idris was here for more than just his chiseled body and dashing face. He could have undoubtedly taught me so much.

I'm lost in thought as I watch the rabbits roast and barely notice when Finch slips away to make good on his promise to scout ahead. For once, I'm not afraid for him. Instead, I look up into the branches to search for Sira, who always checks on me when I'm most morose. She's nowhere to be found.

Did she set off with Finch to help him triangulate?

It's a foolish thought. The creature is tied to me. I'm through my second rabbit when her continued absence starts to gnaw at me. I don't know which instincts to trust anymore. Finch's words have poked and prodded at me ever since he returned. A few hours of self-reflection have me doubting everything about myself save the fact that I occasionally bear light.

When he returns, he confirms the coast is clear and we can rest. Sira returns with him, nestling within a perch of branches just above. I find comfort in their presence.

"Thanks for looking out for me." I look at Finch with the same fondness I hold for Maverick, even though I haven't known Finch as long. He really is like a brother to me. We might as well have been raised in the same house.

"Always," Finch says. "Now get some rest, Princess. The coast won't always be clear."

I look over at Challenger and see that, while standing, he is dozing. I'm glad he's getting rest and has had time to stop and fill his belly, though I regret we don't have more grain. I wonder if Finch could sneak into a town and swipe some along with some hay. Anything to help my boy stay well-muscled is what I'm after, and I'm not too shy to ask for it.

I realize that, for right now, we're safe. I can sleep. I can rest. Finch looks just as exhausted as I do and I know that even he, in his immortal state, will need sleep.

I do my best to get comfortable next to the fire, bundling up in a few of our smaller blankets. The Siraltona tinges my skin with a warmth that braces against the chilly spring breeze and I sigh, hoping I'll get something in the way of true sleep.

Despite these comforts, I wake every hour on the hour throughout the night, my legs restless and twitching. By the time morning comes, I'm more exhausted than ever. It seems I won't find relief for quite some time.

FINCH SETS OUT EARLY IN THE MORNING WITH SIRA TO SEE IF we're still in the clear. While he's gone, I do my best to focus on cooking the rabbits Finch brought back before he left. I haven't finished the ones from yesterday, but he insists I work harder at keeping full. I know he's right. Before long, we'll be on the road again and food won't be as abundant, especially if he separates from me.

My mind races when I think about how far I've come and how many more miles we still need to travel. I somehow have to convince an entire kingdom of my power with nothing but the divine powers flooding my veins to make my case. Not to mention the blood of their king on my hands, even if I was not the one who murdered him.

This is the first morning where I'm not consumed with thoughts of Idris. The haze of my fervent adoration for him seems to be clearing, leaving me of sound mind again. It's both refreshing and horrifying. The reality that I was so easily swayed feels like a bad dream. Then again, the poisonous threat of marriage would turn anyone sour and desperate, especially when it wasn't what they were trained or raised for. At least, that's what I've been telling myself. I'm trying to give myself permission for my foolishness, even if only once. So long as I return to my customary state of planning and resolute strength, I'll be alright.

I can redeem myself yet. I can stand for something or nothing, but I've got to try.

The sound of Sira's screaming calls ring out against the sky and I freeze. I've never heard her make a sound of distress before, but I'm certain that's what I just heard.

I put out the fire as fast as I can, deciding to leave the two remaining rabbits to whatever scavengers might find a roasted meal more appealing than a raw one. I pray to Siralto that Sira is okay—that the fire bird Idris left me hasn't been injured or worse as I rush toward the sound of her cries.

I can't ask Challenger for anything more. I make my chase on foot, craning my neck in the hopes of hearing my phoenix somewhere among the branches of the trees that swallow me deeper and deeper into darkness the farther I tread into the wood line where she once perched.

The clearing is far behind before I realize it, and the light of day is extinguished by the oppressive night, which still comes far too early in early spring.

"Sira!" I call, my voice quavering, not caring if I reveal my position. If there are Shadow Folk lying in wait, the quickened beat of my heart would undoubtedly give me away. I need my bird to hear my voice so she can find her way back to me. "Sira!"

I wish Finch had stayed close by. Perhaps whatever creatures crouched beyond the wood line were just waiting for him to leave me again. They were wise to do it if this is their plan, as my fear keeps me walled off from my magic. I call again and again to the Siraltona in my veins to no avail. It knocks against the inner walls of my soul, but it won't burst free as it has before, even in poor form.

What's happening?

"Adelaide!" Finch calls from deeper within the forest. The panic in his voice drops the temperature of my veins into the cold abyss of Kohlu.

It feels fitting that Hell should be full of ice rather than fire. It certainly feels as though I've been dropped into eternal torment.

"Finch!"

"Adelaide!"

He calls out again and I pick up the pace. I sprint toward his voice, praying I make it in time. I scream his name, tears pouring from my eyes as I call again and again to the light in my veins that refuses to breach the surface of the weight holding it back.

I race towards a clearing up ahead, my breath coming in ragged gasps as I tear through the trees into the broad nighttime...though I don't need light to see the horror before me.

Finch is being held by his arms, flanked by two Shadow Folk soldiers whose eyes gleam with violent thirst as they survey him. He fights against them, but his thrashing is weak. "Adelaide," he groans, "run."

"No!" I draw the sword from the scabbard at my left hip and pray there might still be some Siraltona charged within the blade. The dull metal doesn't shine against the night sky as it would if it still held power, but my feeble hopes remain pointed in its sharp end. If nothing else, I can drive it through my chest and release myself from the agonies of whatever end might otherwise befall me.

Better to die by my own blade than by their fangs.

"Halt!" one of them says as I rush forward, sword swinging.

An invisible force stops me in my tracks. I look up and see Sira has been locked away in a cage of shadows. It hovers, held by seemingly nothing, above our heads. I fight against the invisible tethers holding me back with little success. The Siraltona is a feeble whisper within my mind; still present, but suffering just as I do as I watch them hoist Finch to his feet.

"Let him go," I choke. "Take me. Let him go. He's innocent!"

The larger of the two vampires laughs, his vibrant blue eyes glowing. His hair is masked by a dark helm covering his face. "He's out committing treason like the rest of us. Taking up arms with the little light-bearer," he coos.

"Who are you?" I demand.

"Call me Jupiter," he sneers. "I'm here to take you and your *friend* back to my lair before my brother gets his hands on you."

I stiffen. *Jupiter? Who's his brother?*

"You might know him as the Shadow King." The soldier laughs, as if reading my thoughts aloud.

He has a brother?

If Finch reacts to this news, I can't see it, though his face is twisted in agony as they pull harder on each arm.

"Let him go!" I demand again. "If you do, I will go with you without a fight and help you against your brother."

Jupiter laughs again, his enjoyment evident in watching us suffer. I continue to strain and struggle against the dark powers holding me back, to no avail.

"I have your father's alliance for that. You're nothing more than a tiny pawn in this game, darling. And Fitch... or whatever his name is... is an unfortunate casualty in this war."

Before I can ponder the veracity of his startling words, he and the other vampire flanking Finch do the unthinkable. I can't look away as they both wrench on either side of him and tear Finch straight down the middle. His dark, black blood pours like shadows into the dirt beneath him and his innards spill. Some of the splatter lands in my mouth as it opens in a breathless scream.

Time stands still. A surge of light finally comes crashing to the surface and I break my unseen chains and charge forward, rage coursing through the fixed point of my blade as I rush at Jupiter, revenge the only clear thought on my mind. Above me, the bars of Sira's cage dissolve and she joins me in the fray, setting fire to the other vampire whose name I don't care to know. My only foe here is Jupiter.

I swing down at him, ready to cleave him in two and dance in his remains, but my feet slip in the slick gore left where Finch once stood. Crashing forward, I manage to nick the tip of Jupiter's armor before he dissolves into the shadows. I collapse into the puddled remains of Finch's shadowy blood and can't find it in myself to stand again. The power that surges through me all but consumes me whole.

Behind me, I hear Jupiter re-emerge and feel a heavy boot stomp on my head. He slings a fist into my back and I flip around, ready to fight to the last of my breath here in the remains of the one friend I had left in this world.

Jupiter's fellow soldier goes up in Sira's flames and I watch helplessly as Jupiter slings a blade straight at the stalwart little phoenix. It strikes true and she plummets to the ground, the light and fire in her veins gone faster than a candle in the nighttime.

Rage consumes me as Jupiter reaches back to punch me again. I don't stop it.

I imagine I must look like a star when it explodes—frozen in the process of dying for all but myself to see, as I'm blinded by the light of my raw power.

I don't know if Jupiter is still present, or if Sira managed to kill his lackey, or if both will live on like the embers scattering from her feathery corpse. I don't know how I managed to fall this far. I hope Challenger is galloping off to some distant kingdom where a stronger knight than I can ride him into the fray.

In the meantime, I accept defeat. I'm ready to meet Death right here in this clearing, somewhere just outside the Shadow King's realm without a single drop of vengeance on my tongue.

My light flares out and I'm lost to darkness.

DUSK

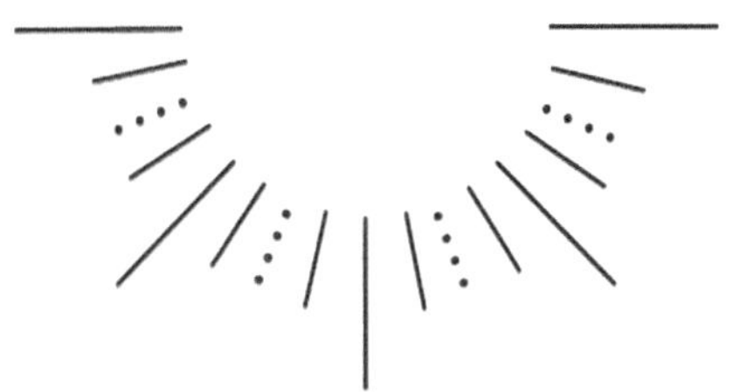

PRISONER

I WAKE TO FIND THAT I AM YET AGAIN IN CHAINS.

They use chains in Kohlu?

All around the dark, blackened metal are runes etched in a language I don't recognize. I assume it might be the language of the gods, or perhaps that of the shadows, but I'm too dizzy to properly make them out. My body aches and burns, which I know is my penance. Agony courses through my veins.

I try to get a sense of the time of day, if there is such a thing in Kohlu. When I find no windows to offer a frame of reference, I accept my fate. My muscles ache from the fight I try hard not to remember. The flashing images of Finch being torn apart play over and over again in my head. I'm lucky my stomach is empty, the rabbits long gone when I shed my mortal body.

But then I look down and realize that I'm still within said mortal body and I am *not* in Kohlu. The fires of damnation do not lick at my skin as foretold in so many of our religious tomes. Instead, the blood and mud from that clearing cakes my flesh and Finch's blackened blood still stains my armor and fingers.

"Hello?" I croak. My voice echoes against stone walls and my throat squeezes, parching thirst constricting it. I sound more like an old crone than a kidnapped princess.

Am I in Jupiter's keeping? Am I trapped by that bastard vampire who killed my brother?

I hear the clink of chain mail and brace myself, preparing for the worst. If I'm here with Jupiter, then perhaps I have a chance at scoring vengeance for Finch. Despite my brother-in-law's earlier words, I know a suicide mission may be my only option and I'm willing to take it. I won't be a bargaining chip for Jupiter to use against my father or the Shadow King. I refuse to be a pawn on anyone else's chessboard but my own.

I call to the Siraltona in my veins but find it cut off by the dark powers of the runes etched in my cuffs. I'm powerless to whomever is coming to check on me. I am a circus animal on display for the entertainment of others.

"Adelaide," says a voice, and I freeze.

I can't turn around. I can't look at him. I can't bring myself to face the voice of the dead.

I hear a hand slip between the bars, but I don't pull away in time. Repulsion simmers in my core as I'm forced to turn around and see *him*.

"Idris!" I breathe. "You... How...?"

He closes his hand around my throat and pulls me flush against the bars. I'm limp, my body so weak and tired. My eyes struggle to stay open enough to focus on him.

His flaming eyes rove over my body, bruised and blackened. I have no idea how I became so injured. I imagine Jupiter's soldier or even he might have harmed me more than I realized. The journey was harrowing. Everything from the night Finch died is a blur.

"Who harmed you?" Idris demands, his tongue flicking over his bottom lip.

I notice it's stained dark with blood and my heart hammers. Answers try to rise in my throat but they are lost—plagued by exhaustion and the heavy weight of betrayal.

He's one of them. Idris is a vampire.

Tears start to fall and I can't stop them from spilling over my cheeks. I'm held motionless—weak—before the enemy who, not long ago, I was willing to avenge at all costs. Was he changed there in the castle by Ivan, or was he a vampire the whole time he courted me? The intense feelings

I had around him suddenly make more sense. I must have been in his *thrall*. He was manipulating me. I can no longer see him through my tears.

"Who harmed you?" he demands again.

His voice is roughened with rage so deep, I whimper at the sound of it and hate myself for being so fragile.

He drops me and I crumple to the floor. I weakly try to break my restraints to no avail. I notice the blood that has pooled around my feet and know if I'm not patched up soon, I will die here in this infernal dungeon.

The bars swing open and Idris steps inside.

"Please," I whisper, "kill me. End it now. Don't leave me here for the Shadow King to find like this."

He kneels over me. His hand is soft this time as it grabs the back of my neck. He hoists me up so I can look at him. I notice dark tears in his eyes.

"*I* am the Shadow King, Adelaide," he utters, his voice hushed. "But I need to know: *who hurt you*?"

My blood pounds so loudly in my ears, I almost don't hear his question. I go rigid as fear locks my body into a state of irreversible paralysis. "Kill me," I beg.

"No," he answers, his tone resolute. "Tell me who harmed you."

Any resolve I have is gone. I begin to sob before I can stop myself, just as I did in front of him back at the castle. My mind is a raging tsunami of pain and disgust. What's worse is the relief I find when he cradles me in his arms. No longer do I feel drawn to him by a false flame. Instead, I feel protected. Safe. Soft.

"J-Jupi-Jupiter," I gasp, my head nestled into his shoulder. "Your brother."

His grip on me tightens as he lifts me from the floor. "You're coming with me," he insists.

I'm a limp doll in his arms as he cradles me, carrying me from the prison cell and out into the dark halls of his dungeons. "Was-was I- was I just a *game* to you?" My lips tremble as I look up at his devastatingly handsome face.

His flaming eyes bore into my soul as he looks down at me. "You were never a game. You are a formidable opponent. You are my worst nightmare. You will be the death of me before anyone. I should kill you now as you have begged me to do."

I swallow, awaiting a swift snap of my neck or the feeling of fangs plunging into my flesh, but neither sensation comes. As we ascend a lengthy set of stone steps, he speaks again.

"I should kill you, but I won't. I should break you, but I won't. Your punishment will suit your crimes against my people; I will deliver it personally. But I will not end you. I will not do as I should. I can't, my fire," he hisses. "I can't do those things to you even if I wanted to. I want you to know I hate you for that, too. And yet, I love you all the same."

I can't fight the weight of exhaustion anymore. I fall limp in his arms.

WHEN I WAKE, I FIND THAT WHILE MY SHACKLES ARE STILL on, I am cleaner and bandaged. One of my chains is linked to an iron bed frame. The faded sheets and a jumble of medicine jars on the other side of the room clue me in to my location. *An infirmary.*

The dazed memory of Idris—*Mars*—carrying me from my prison cell and confessing his hate for me... and his *love*... come blazing to the surface and I gasp. Alertness returns to me with blissful relief.

"Where am I?" I demand. My voice no longer shakes and tears no longer clog my vision. Instead, anger settles in my veins. *He deceived me.*

"Ma'am, please stay calm," a voice says.

I look up and find a strange woman looking down at me. She wears a gray gown over a starched white dress, a nurse's cap settled on her head. Her hair is fine, white silk and her skin is dark violet. Her glowing, golden eyes survey me with a mixture of fear and pity. "You are in His Highness' medical quarters. He's instructed us to help you recover from an attack you suffered. Tell me, how were you harmed?"

I snort. "You think I'll just tell you?" My pitch rises. "You think I'll tell you anything about me? You think I'll make it easy for you to break me? You might as well kill me now. I've nothing to offer you. I'm powerless, but not stupid. I'll never be deceived again!" I go to cross my arms and belatedly realize I'm still shackled. Instead, I allow all the righteous indignation I can muster to shine through my narrowed eyes.

The woman's eyes harden. "Your Highness, don't be ridiculous. If you won't tell us, His Majesty will pry the answers out of you himself. And besides, you're only harming yourself if you don't explain what happened to you. Don't you realize? If you don't tell us, we can't help you; if we can't help you, you remain injured longer. Something happened to you when Jupiter attacked you. You seem... spent."

"Spent?" I say, my voice incredulous. "I was starving to death running from *your* people in an attempt to find what I *thought* was Velyasa, to avenge a man named Idris who, I've learned, *never* existed! Pardon me if I'm *worn out*. Rage consumed me... until I had nothing left to give." A trickle of fear ebbs down my spine. "Why? Is my power gone?"

She shakes her head. "I don't think so. I think... I think it wasn't quite done *merging* with you until then. Have you looked at yourself since the attack?"

I shake my head. "Lady, do you think your dungeons come equipped with mirrors?"

At this, the nurse laughs. "My name is Sherry. I'm His Highness' personal medic. I'd prefer you use my name."

It strikes me as inappropriate to argue with Sherry about this, so I keep my mouth shut. "Okay, Sherry, do you have a mirror I can borrow?" I feel asinine even entertaining this conversation. I have half a mind to try and wrench these chains off and go on a killing spree. I'll save Mars and his lying ass for last.

She strides over and hands me a small, handheld mirror and I gasp. My hair, once a dark, dull auburn, now has strands of glowing light woven all throughout it. My skin has taken on an even ghostlier pallor and my eyes glow bright and *gold*. I slap a hand over my mouth.

"How does this look *spent*?" I finally ask when I drop my hand.

"I think in usual circumstances, you would glow brighter," Sherry answers. "You seem... worn. The light doesn't glow as brightly as we anticipated it might."

"Anticipated? And who is we?" I demand. I look around, finding only three beds in this room; mine is the only occupied one. The rest of the room is institutional and dreary. The walls are free of the decor we have in our infirmaries. Granted, I always felt they were stupid and unnecessary, so I can't critique Mars too much for not having a more elegant medical wing. But still.

"Adelaide, every kingdom within a thousand miles probably saw your little explosion!" Sherry laughs. "It's not every day that the sun crashes to earth. My understanding is that several of my *people*, as you call them, are now blind, thanks to that little stunt. Did you ever pause to think what your power might be capable of doing when left unchecked?"

"Did you stop to think that maybe I wasn't in control of it?" I retort. "I was busy fighting your king's psychotic brother after he slaughtered one of *your* kind. Finch. He was my brother-in-law, and I loved him as though he was my blood. He was a *dragon*, too. Powerful. He could have been someone important, and now he's gone."

My voice buzzes with an unfamiliar power and I clap my mouth shut, fearful of the consequences if I keep talking. I feel the Siraltona rumbling and roaring in my veins and wonder if I might be on the verge of another star-like explosion. Despite our argument, I kind of like Sherry and I'm not keen on the thought of blinding her.

"No, but that is important for us to document," Sherry says, scribbling something in a gilded notebook I notice for the first time.

"Are all of your medical records kept in such a fanciful manner?" I sneer. "And again, who is *we*?"

"That would be me," Mars smoothly answers, his voice collected but soft. He is as much the picture of control and resolve as he was when he found me in the dungeons. "Understanding your medical plight is paramount. I need to know what I have on my hands."

"What you have on your hands?" I ask, my anger rising. "I am not your pet!"

"No, Adelaide, you are not my pet," Mars chuckles. "You are so much worse than that."

I swear his eyes sparkle despite them being walls of solid flame. I want to vault out of this bed and attack him, but my chain draws taut and I am stuck. Despite his earlier declarations of love, I don't believe him. He would kill me in an instant. Fear creeps into my veins. Worse yet, I feel excitement in my core. He's *strong. Powerful.* And some demented part of me likes that about him.

My father would have me drawn and quartered for such thoughts. Still, his punishment would be far less than anything I would do to him. My father, should he ever see me again, has a fate worse than death waiting for him.

I fix Mars with a heated glare. "Oh? And what is worse than being someone's pet?"

"I don't think you want to know the answer to that, but you are worse for *me*, Adelaide. Let me clarify my earlier statement," Mars purrs. "You look to be in much better shape. Tired, but healing. I can live with this outcome." Mars turns to Sherry and nods. "You may leave us for now. You have done well. You can keep your head today."

"Keep her head?" I ask.

"He threatened to kill me if I couldn't fix you." Sherry grins. Her fangs sparkle in the low light from the infirmary's candles and I shiver. "I'm grateful I was able to fix my king's newest... fixation."

Mars turns to her, looking positively feral, but she retreats from the room faster than I can blink. He sighs, which sounds more like a low growl. I wonder if he'll take this opportunity to kill me himself, when my guard is at its lowest. It's not like I can stop him, either.

"How are you feeling?" His question is innocent, yet laden with many unspoken thoughts.

"What a stupid question!" I snap. "How do I *feel*? You *tricked* me! You've chained me in this infirmary, and I just learned you are the king of my enemy kingdom! And you have the gall to claim I *wasn't* a game to you?"

Mars nods. "I meant that. You were no game. But coming to court you as I truly am didn't seem like a viable option."

My cheeks heat up and I want to disappear from the room. "You lied so you could *court* me?"

"Marry you, actually, but yes. That was the goal. Ivan's arrival was unexpected and it put a wedge in my plans. Had I let my powers truly show themselves in that room... everything would have come crashing down. He knew who I was in that moment—my thralling charms had fallen apart, thanks to a certain someone." He chuckles. "It's been a long time since I've been so entranced by a woman. I never let my magic falter and yet, seeing you in the heat of battle... What can I say? I was distracted."

Bile rises in my throat. "You pretended to die because you were aroused and couldn't control your magic?"

Mars shrugs. "When you put it that way it seems simple, but there was much more at stake. For one, I had to fend off thoughts of draining you when I arrived. You looked so innocent and delectable alone in that library. You would have made a quick and easy snack, just as Ivan had planned to make of you before I got there. But then I realized there was *something* about you I couldn't quite shake. The more I am around you, the worse it gets."

"So you're keeping me alive because you think I'm interesting?" I spit.

"I'm keeping you alive because I knew, from the moment I saw you, that you were *mine*. Even if you deny it until the day Tryta and Siralto level the world as we know it, I know you belong to *me*."

"So I *am* your pet," I hiss.

"So much worse," Mars answers.

He looms over me, his grin white and feral. His fangs are much more terrifying up close. They look almost like a human's teeth, but they end in wickedly sharp points that could end my life with a single snap of his jaw. But he doesn't lunge after me.

"What are you planning?" I demand. "Why am I here?"

He hovers over me, his nose almost touching mine, and my cheeks go scarlet when I feel arousal pool between my legs. *What the hell is wrong with me?*

"Did you not hear me? You're *mine*. I don't care in what capacity, but I'll not have you under your father's thumb or in my brother's keeping. I brought you here. I knew you felt strongly enough about me to seek out vengeance in my name, and I knew Sira would lead you here, Tryta rest her soul."

My heart pangs for my phoenix, even knowing now who she was and that the devil himself made her. She couldn't help how she was programmed, but she died fighting for me. I know she cared for me.

His thumb sweeps up to brush away a tear that falls on my cheek. Without thinking, I lean up and kiss him.

He acts before I can respond, launching over the side of my bed and resting on top of me, kissing me back with desperate passion. Our tongues dance and his hands travel along my body, eager to learn each of my curves as I lie helpless beneath him.

"I missed you, Adelaide," he breathes. "I hate you and yet I missed you. Why did I miss you?" His demand is weak as he caves and begins to kiss me again.

"Your Majesty?"

Mars doesn't get off me, but he does turn to look at the vampire standing in the doorway of the infirmary. A young scribe with pale skin and blond hair stands uncertainly, his voice trembling along with the quill and scroll in his hands.

"The council is requesting your presence, Your Highness. They... want to know what you plan to do with our newly acquired—ah —prisoner?"

Mars laughs. "I'll do with her as I please. I'll come tell the council how I plan to punish her, but for now, you'll leave me to continue pleasuring her, are we understood?"

"Sh-shall I tell the council those exact words?" the young scribe squeaks.

"Tell them I'm familiarizing myself with her territory." Mars chuckles darkly. "I'll be up when I'm certain I have a fair idea, though I'll need much more time to explore over the next few decades..."

Decades?

I'm certain I'm redder than his copper locks, but I don't struggle when he leans back down and continues to ravage my mouth with his tongue. I'm locked in heated bliss, content to die right now should he end me. I'm conflicted, but I can't deny how *right* it feels with him.

If another man were to speak about me like that, he would lose his favored member to the end of a sharp blade. For Mars? If anything, it makes the heat between my legs worse.

"If you hate me so much, I fear what it would look like if you actually liked me," I say, egging him on.

He slides a hand beneath my tattered top—still blood-stained from battle—and cups my breast. "As I told you, I love you as much as I hate you. If you truly fear that, Adelaide, know now that you should be quaking."

He presses his thumbs into my peaked mounds and presses hot kisses down my neck before settling into the crook and sucking—hard. I know he'll leave a mark, but I find his ministrations more exciting than terrifying. My legs fall open beneath him.

"Look at you, so willing. So right for me. So much worse than any pet," he hisses. "I would take you right now, but I can't."

"Why?" I blurt.

Mars laughs, then peppers me with tender kisses. "Not until I have your hand in marriage, as is the proper rite. I'm prepared to wait as long as you need, but the proper mating rites must be observed. In the meantime, I'll have to resort to pleasuring you in other ways. But know this— once I have your hand, not a soul will ever doubt you are mine and mine alone. You will reek of my scent forever, and not an inch of your skin will go untouched by me."

I lean up to kiss him again, but he's out of the bed and standing beside where I'm still shackled before I can purchase more pleasure from his awful mouth.

I want to kill him. Yet, at the same time, I want to scream his name while he does unspeakable things to me in this infirmary bed.

What is wrong with me?

"I'm just as conflicted as you are, my fire. I suppose we have plenty of time to decide what we need from each other—what our bond means. But in the meantime, I must go speak to the council about your punishment. I have just the thing in mind."

He leaves the room, leaving me breathless, afraid, and hopelessly obsessed with him.

"I hate you, Mars," I whisper. "Come back when you can."

PUNISHMENT

I DON'T REMEMBER FALLING ASLEEP AGAIN, BUT WHEN I wake, I feel even more rested. I find the hand mirror by my bed and find that, sure enough, my neck is bruised with the signs of just how far I let the Shadow King get with me the night before—at least, I assume it was night. My sense of time is skewed beyond repair and, until I see the sun again, I doubt I'll ever know how long I've been trapped here in Mars' damned castle.

Sherry is back in the room, and she smiles when she notices me sitting up. "I see the king treated you to a real show," she says, her tone suggestive. "I've never seen him this riled up over a prisoner before. Tell me... how far did he get with you?"

I sit up straight, appalled at her question. "Excuse me? What makes you think I'll share anything with you?"

Sherry blinks in surprise. "Is it not customary for friends to talk about escapades with their lovers?"

"Friends?"

"Aren't we?" Sherry asks, a tinge of hurt in her voice.

"I mean, you were angry with me when you left, and Mars threatened to kill you over my injuries. I assumed you hated me."

Sherry waves her hand. "That bastard threatens to kill me at *least* once a month. And you know, we should stick together. Women with rare powers are few and far between. You didn't know you were going to blind so many people. I spent more time with your files. You're a real mess, you know that?"

My jaw drops. "Uhm, thanks? I guess?"

"Wasn't a compliment, darling. You need some serious rehabilitation. Speaking of... Mars has decided your punishment."

I swallow. "He said he wouldn't kill me."

Sherry nods. "He's not going to kill you. He made that explicitly clear with the council. A lot of them are angry about it, too. They'd love to see your head mounted in his throne room."

I grimace. "That's... reassuring. Thank you, Sherry."

She laughs. I notice for the first time just how long her silky hair falls and I'm inexplicably jealous of how effortlessly beautiful her violet skin is and her soft jawline. She looks more like a fae than a vampire—something ethereal.

Sherry winces. "I'm not supposed to give you details, only to assure you that death is not your final sentence. Instead, I'm supposed to get you ready to come to the throne room."

My eyes widen. "The throne room? Am... am I to be judged in front of a crowd?"

The beautiful vampire nods. "Don't tell them I told you, though. I'm doing you a solid. Before you go, though, let's get you cleaned up. Mars wants you looking fresh for the occasion."

"Should we cover his mark?" I say, gesturing to my neck. "We don't want his people thinking he's a sell-out for... well..."

Sherry rolls her eyes. "You want to protect his reputation when he's about to punish you?"

"I mean... when you put it *that* way..." I shrug.

She unclips my chains from the bed and points a finger just under my nose. "No funny business when you're unclasped. I have permission to render you useless by any means necessary. I know more poisons than you have brain cells in that smart little head of yours, so don't think I won't incapacitate you if you so much as *breathe* funny," Sherry snarls.

I fall back onto the bed, shocked by her vehemence. "What happened to girls watching out for girls?"

"You always have to watch out for yourself first, Adelaide. That's rule number one. You can't give to people what you don't have. My life and safety aren't up for debate."

I nod. "Message received." I move slowly as I get out of bed, careful not to startle my nurse and make her think I'm up to no good. My mind is a blur as she helps me out of my torn trousers and blouse and into something much more regal than I expected.

I stay still as she cinches me into the gown, the corset lighter than the ones I'm used to at home. It sits snugly along my frame and nothing more—it's truly just there to hold it to my body, not trap me in it. I could weep. I'm grateful she would think of my comfort, even as I'm off to be punished for tormenting her kingdom for more than half my life.

If our situations were reversed, we would not show them even an ounce of the same kindness. The bruise on my neck reminds me that, most of the time, they probably would not be so gentle. The dungeons I first woke in seem more in line with the treatment regular mortals would receive. Not everyone has the fancy of the vampire king in their back pocket as a defense. At least, I tell myself this. I have no idea what the standard treatment for prisoners is here, but I know for sure mine is not normal.

"Alright. Let's get you up there!" Sherry trills. The excitement in her eyes makes me wonder if maybe she is, on some level, happy to see me suffer.

I look down and notice I'm wearing a plain, white dress. There is no pattern or stitching that renders it unique. The only feminine aspect to it is the corset I was grateful for moments ago. My feet are clad in soft sandals that don't bite and bruise my skin as my boots normally do, but I wouldn't call them pretty.

"Wait!" A thought dawns on me. "Did they find my horse when they found me?"

Sherry looks at me for a moment. "No one saw a horse when we reached you, Adelaide. He must have run off."

As sad as this makes me, I'm also relieved. My riding boots retired with him. Challenger is free somewhere. I refuse to consider any alternatives. Even death would be freedom for him now.

Only I am left to suffer for the crimes committed by the nobility of Sunfall. I plan to meet my fate with dignity and poise. Whatever Mars has planned will not shake me.

"I'm ready," I say, lifting my chin. We walk from the infirmary arm in arm. As we do, I try to convince myself that I'm as ready as I pretend I am. When we step into the throne room, I'm no longer so sure.

All around, hundreds of Shadow Folk have gathered. Some look human; others look like stunning fae or gods or naiads, all draped in fine clothing and jewels that clue me in to who they are.

The nobles have gathered.

At the front of the throne room, Mars sits, waiting between several guards posted at either side of him. I chuckle, thinking for the first time of how fearful they all must be of me. I know I have a fearsome reputation among them. I have slain many Shadow Folk in my lifetime to avenge my mother and protect my kingdom. The fact that I am unchained and loose in their castle with a bruise from their king on my neck must be the scandal of the century.

Which is like a decade for them, if the stories are true.

I keep my head held high and let the light in my veins shine a little brighter. I trust myself not to let it run amok with such a simple move. Bearing light is as easy as breathing. Controlling it or shaping it is another story.

As I proceed up the aisle towards Mars' throne, some of the nobles jeer and some cry, but most don't show any emotion as they witness the feared *Shadow Slayer* who slaughtered so many of them walk to be judged by their king. A few throw mourning flowers in front of me, my feet brushing along their soft petals. It's a jarring sensation in the midst of such a harsh scene.

I wonder how Shadow Folk execute people?

The method of their execution remains hidden, as Mars offered little information upon my capture. Just a sentence of punishment. A part of me grows nervous as I realize this could mean *anything* and there are many things far worse than death. I find I'm not quite as eager to solve the method of merciful punishment he's promised.

Several royal guards stand in the center of the throne room. Mars stands up between the few closest to him. His flaming eyes sparkle at the sight of me, making my stomach flip. I wish I could stamp my feelings out in the wood beneath my feet, but I'm unable. His betrayal still stings, now that I know who he is. How he used me—deceived me.

Holding my head up high, I offer a radiant smile, showing him I am no unwilling victim. *He'll not get the satisfaction from me!* Still, his eyes rove over me with something akin to the hunger he had for me before he revealed his true nature, and even from the night before.

A damned Shadow Folk you'll always be.

The guards release me from Sherry's grasp and lead me up to him. I note the clouds of an autumn storm rolling in through the open windows; the petrichor in the air has the flavor of a dying Earth. Mars' deep laughter reaches my ears, and, to my surprise, I manage to laugh with him.

"Adelaide," he starts. "I see you're in good spirits. It's honorable that you should greet your punishment in such a way. I expect nothing less from the Shadow Slayer. The courts never could have taught you such bravery."

I say nothing, instead choosing to greet his fiery gaze with a stern one of my own. *You don't frighten me, vampire.* The fire in my core says several other things about how he makes me feel, and I hate myself for even considering them.

He grins wider, his bright, white fangs on display for all to see. I know how terrifying they are once they're magnified by the great black dragon coiled within him, always ready to strike. His copper hair gleams in the dying light as it's eaten by the storm clouds that roll in, casting shadows through the open windows.

"The gods must find it fitting to weep for you. How poetic," Mars purrs. "Perhaps if you'd used those gifts for things other than senseless murder, they could be tears of joy."

I thought he wasn't going to kill me? I realize that maybe, just maybe, he is toying with me and this is my end. Even so, I refuse to be swayed by his words and vow to stay calm and collected. I'm proud of myself for holding on to my last shred of sanity, even in a moment like this.

"Look around you. Each and every one of the nobles gathered here has been impacted by you in some way. They have lost brothers, friends, daughters, sons... all in the name of Sunfall—the kingdom your wretched father sends to ruin even as we speak."

His words hit home. I bow my head, hiding the sting that settles in my eyes. The guilt of each of the Shadow Folk I've murdered becomes more real as I take in the faces of those gathered to witness what might be my execution. I refuse to admit my feelings aloud.

It seems I am doomed to be taken advantage of. Perhaps a dance with Death is exactly what is best for my soul.

When I look back up at Mars, I'm not ashamed of the tears that stream down my cheeks. I'm not worried about the strange glances I receive from all those gathered. The only thing I yearn for is understanding. Why was I doomed to be a pawn on a chessboard so much more terrible and intricate than I could ever understand? Why would my powers come just in time for my end?

Why didn't Mars just take the kingdom sooner?

Leaning down to me, Mars whispers in my ear. "I sense all your questions, even if you don't say them aloud. You'll understand in due time, little flame." He brushes a kiss against my cheek, leaving it burning, and my heart almost bursts from my chest.

A sob almost breaks free, but I silence it. His eyes and face stay blank, but I swear for a moment that his lip twitches. The spark in his eyes goes dim.

"Adelaide, you are hereby sentenced to death. You are sentenced as such on account of your crimes against the Shadow Folk whose innocent blood you have spilled in the name of our enemy kingdom, Sunfall. Have you any last words before you are given your punishment?"

Blinking, I take a moment before I speak. I've never been in such a position, let alone been allowed to speak to the Shadow Folk so candidly.

I raised my voice to be heard throughout the hall. "I want you all to know I was used just as I used you. It does not excuse my actions. I did mean to murder, steal, and pillage. I was raised to understand you all to be monsters. I lost my mother to your people, and my father turned my talents into a weapon of vengeance. He used my suffering to turn me into a trained killer. I have murdered so many of you, stopping just short of children. As much as I was brainwashed and tormented, I had every opportunity to stop and chose not to. I am deeply sorry for letting my demons make you into my targets. I accept my punishment and hope that, in the spilling of my blood, some of you might choose to forgive me wherever I go in the next life."

My admission brings stunned silence. A few moments pass. In the distance, a broken sob breaks free. Sherry runs to me and clutches at my arms. "You were so young!" she shudders. "They used you. I cannot speak for all, but I forgive you."

A few guards shuffle forward to drag Sherry away, but I scold them. "She is my friend and is no bother. Let her go."

Mars chuckles. "Ordering my guards even as you're on your way to the end? I admire your spirit, Adelaide. I only wish I could have encountered it under different circumstances." Then, his face clears of all emotion. "Bring her forward," he commands.

The guards lead me up between their circle, grasping my wrists as they settle me at the Shadow King's feet. Mars raises a hand.

"Adelaide Sunfall, on this first day of autumn, I condemn you to the darkness."

Closing my eyes, I await the end.

For a moment, I wonder when I will feel the cold kiss of a blade so similar to those I've used on so many innocent Shadow Folk.

Instead, I gasp when I feel teeth sink into my neck. Stifling a cry, I hold still, refusing to fight. *I won't give him a show.* The blood leaves my body at an alarming speed, rushing from my neck and into the mouth of whichever creature has been ordered to drain me. I won't open my eyes. Not yet. Instead, I focus on the horrid feeling of my life flooding away from me and into the maw of some wretched creature.

At first, the bite hurts. But within a few moments, the pain subsides. My memories slide through my mind like the rain that spills outside the window. The drops fall sideways, drowning the land around them.

May the spring rain bring my people a bountiful harvest this autumn. May the crops be full and sustain them in the name of my sacrifice.

It's a nonsensical thought that overcomes me as I weaken. I hope in my soul that Mars will give my people more mercy than I gave the Shadow Folk. I hope he will kill Alaric and avenge me.

I hope the Siraltona dies with me... that the shadows will fall and the kingdom of Sunfall will see light no more.

The curse echoes within my mind, a binding thing that swirls and leaves my body even as my veins run cold. With my last bit of magic woven in the threads of the universe, I collapse, letting the darkness drink me down to the very last drop.

A New Dawn

I open my eyes, expecting the shadows of Kohlu to consume me. But instead, beneath my back, I'm shocked to find the cool embrace of... *bedding?*

Groaning, my eyes try to adjust to the light, only to find none. Somehow, I can still see through the stifling pitch black in this strange... *bedroom? Is the Afterlife an eternal slumber?* I hold my hands before my face, finding all five fingers intact and wiggling beneath my command.

As I fuss about, hoping to figure out where I've been taken, I hear a dark chuckle.

Sitting up, I find myself staring straight into a pair of flaming eyes. *Mars.* He gets up and stalks to my bedside like a prowling lion. His fangs are on display, and his expression is... *hungry.* I know, somehow, that he's the one who drained me.

Was that a dream?

Reaching up, I feel at my neck, confirming my fears that the fresh bite marks are still weeping with the congealed remains of my lifeblood.

"How am I still here?" I whisper in the dark, hoping to Siralto that he won't answer me with the truth I already know, my heart hammering in my chest.

He reaches down over me, a seductive rumble audible within his chest, and pulls me into a deep kiss. His tongue dances with mine for several long minutes. I hate myself as I moan into his touch, even after he did the unthinkable.

When he pulls away, he laughs, the cruel sound breaking any resolve I have left.

"Welcome to a life in the shadows, Adelaide," he hisses. "It's more than you could have ever bargained for."

Acknowledgments

I would like to thank my parents, my brother, my sister Gabs, my cousins Julia and Camii, and my soul sisters Rachel and Journey, and my bestie Hannah, for standing with me as I wrote this. This was a book that came from a place of finding my love of writing again. That's not to say I don't love my others, but this truly was a passion project and the love and support I got were invaluable.

Thank you to all of you for reading my snippets, listening to me ramble, and putting up with Mars. You are amazing.

And lastly, thank you to my readers.
Hopefully you will enjoy staying for a bite—or two!

Author's Note

Thank you again for taking the time to read *Magic Bites*.

If you liked what you read, I do hope you'll check out my social media accounts, my website, and maybe even sign up for my mailing list!

Also, if you don't mind and have the time, if you could leave me a review to let me know how I did and what you thought of my little world, I would love to hear your thoughts. Whether that review go on Amazon, Goodreads, your preferred social media platform, etc., I want to hear it. Be as honest as you like. My goal as an author is to provide you with stories that matter and that inspire. If I've done that, I'm happy. If not, I want to know how to improve. Without you, dear reader, this book would be for naught.

www.erismarriottauthor.com
facebook.com/ErisMarriottAuthor
instagram.com/erismarriott